SPY YOUR HEART OUT

IVORY TOWER SPIES BOOK THREE

EMILY KAZMIERSKI

Ivory Tower Spies Series

For Your Ears Only
The Walk-in Agent (a short story)
The Eyes of Spies
Spy Your Heart Out

Also by Emily Kazmierski

Malignant
Life Among the Ashes
All-American Liars

For Adam,

the only person I want to be with the next time I get chased by security guards in a foreign country.

Chapter 1

Confusion crackles around the airplane hangar.

"What plane?" Royal asks, catching my arm before I can bolt out of the building.

I shake off his hand. "My private plane. How else do you think I got here? All of the commercial airlines were booked for the Olympics."

He cocks his head at me. "How did you pay for a private plane?"

"About that. I may have compromised one of the entrances to our hideout. And Summer knows I'm not an ordinary teenager."

"Summer," Royal says, his face settling into a stern expression.

"Summer, as in your boss at the concierge desk?" Lotus asks.

When I raise my eyebrows to indicate that he's correct, his hand flies up to cup his mouth.

"Oh, you're in it now."

Beside Lotus, Julep's eyes are wide as she watches the exchange.

I shrug quickly. I was already in enough trouble, and I

haven't had time to think about how mad Royal will be once he hears the next bit. I eye him, and he gestures with one hand for me to continue.

"She saw me coming out of the waterfall." I shake my head, pushing away that line of thought and rushing on. "That's not important. All that matters is that we get Clarity back. Beppe Arnoni took her and I bet they're going straight to his lair in Palermo, wherever it is."

Royal's jaw clenches. "I agree. We'll talk about Summer later. Right now, we need to confirm that Clarity isn't in the area." He lifts his watch and pushes several of its buttons with his free hand. "I've pinged her watch. It looks like it's near the entrance to the airport. Julep can you…"

But I'm off at a run before he can finish his statement. My legs pump with all their might as I careen down the taxiway toward the entrance gate. Several airport employees wave at me, yelling in Russian, but I ignore them. One of them, a tall, lanky guy with a shaved head and a goatee, gives chase, but I outstrip him easily. Being twenty years younger and in excellent shape gives me the advantage.

Running at a full-out sprint, I pass the terminal on my left. I'm only a few hundred yards from the airport entrance now, and begin to slow. "Send me the location of Clarity's watch," I huff into my earbud between long, controlled breaths.

"I'm sending it now," Royal says with consternation in his voice.

My watch pings and I look down at its screen. According to this map, Clarity is only about fifty yards ahead of me. I scan the area, but all I can see is the road into and out of the airport, lined by empty, brown fields on both sides. I slip past the gate and stop. The map on my watch screen shows that I'm right on top of Clarity, but she's not here. There isn't anyone in sight as

I scan the area.

Across the road and several hundred yards away over the field, there's a large building complex that looks like a shopping center. "How accurate are the locators on our watches?" I ask.

"Down to the foot," Royal responds.

I curse under my breath. "She's not here." I pivot slowly in a full circle. "She's not here."

"Look around. See if you can find her watch."

Even though I know he can't see me right now, I bob my head. My eyes study the ground around me as I spin in another circle, my steps careful and measured. A shrub by the road catches my attention. I cross the pavement toward it and kneel down. The dry, brittle branches scratch at my arms as I push them aside to peer at the dirt below the plant. Clarity's watch is there. Its face is cracked, but it's still working. "I found it. He must have tossed it out his car window."

Tears come unbidden to the backs of my eyes, and I lean into a low squat, swiping at them with my empty left hand. The cold face of Clarity's watch digs into my palm as I squeeze my fingers shut around it. A sniff escapes me.

"Loveday, are you all right?" Starling asks through my earbud. It's the first thing he's said in several minutes.

"Yes," I grind out, my voice rough. I push to a stand and walk toward the airplane hangar at the far side of the airport. This time, the airport personnel on the ground don't pay any attention to me. They're busy flagging a plane down the runway. At the sight of it, I freeze. It's a mid-sized passenger plane with the logo of a top European airline emblazoned on the side. "Dad!" I yell. "We have to ground the planes. Clarity could be on one of them."

He sighs. "I don't have that kind of power."

"We don't have time to argue." I'm running again, but this

9

time I'm heading straight for the passenger plane. If I can beat it to the runway, they'll have to stop. My leg muscles push hard, harder than ever before, but still the plane is going to get there first.

"Help me!" I yell.

"Loveday, stop," Royal responds. "You're not faster than a commercial airplane."

Without looking, I can feel his presence in the prickle on my skin. He's standing outside the hangar, watching me.

"I have to try." But my legs are already slowing. Royal is right; I'm no match for a jet's engines. It barrels ahead of me down the runway, picking up speed as it advances.

Clarity might be on that plane, but there's nothing I can do in this moment to stop it from taking off.

The plane's frontal landing gear leaves the ground. Its nose tips upward. The rear landing gear follows, and the plane is as good as gone.

I stand, transfixed, watching as the vessel disappears into the white sky.

My heart contracts within my chest as if it's been pinched by an unseen hand. If Clarity is on that plane, she's just flown out of my reach.

Chapter 2

"Hey."

That one little word makes me jump. But it's not Clarity standing there when I turn to look.

It's Starling.

His face is trained on me, and his eyes rove across my features, gauging my expression.

My face falls in a frown. "I lost her." Sadness rises in me until I'm sure it will slosh out if I move even an inch.

Starling gives a slight shake of his head and closes the gap between us. His voice is soft when he speaks. "You didn't lose her. She was stolen from you. None of this is your fault."

"That's not what it feels like," I say, and again the tears threaten to spill over. I don't let them. My teeth bite down on my tongue, and the unwanted waterworks recede.

"Let's go back," the tall boy standing before me says, gesturing toward the hangar with his thumb.

I take a deep breath, and nod.

Starling slings one arm over my shoulder, and pats my upper arm with tentative fingers.

It's a surprise even to me that I don't want to shove him off and get as far away as possible. Instead, Starling's touch has a steadying effect on me as we walk to the hangar side by side. I fall into step with him, taking two steps for every one of his, since he's so much taller than I am.

When I don't push him away, Starling's shoulders relax, and he smiles. "You run amazingly fast in heels."

My lips curve in a faint smile, but I don't look directly at him. I'm too busy watching Royal stare at us from across the apron. "I've had lots of practice."

He tilts his head down toward mine, much too close. "It shows."

If I wasn't trained to hide my emotions, I might have blushed at that comment.

Once we reach the hangar, Royal steps aside for Starling to go inside, but when I move to follow, he blocks my path.

Our eyes meet.

There's frustration etched in the lines of my dad's face

My own expression falters. I'm in trouble. Again.

He steps around the corner of the building and I follow. I'm barely there before his lecture starts.

"You can't run off like that again. It's not safe."

"I had to see if Clarity was still here—"

"No. You wait for orders, or I'll send you straight home and go on to Sicily without you."

I glare at him. "You wouldn't."

His chin lifts. "Try me. This is exactly why I took you off the team in the first place." He doesn't flinch at my scowl, so we're locked in a staring contest for several seconds. The silence around us deepens, but still neither of us moves to break the stalemate.

A groan sounds from the field that spans behind Royal's back out toward the ocean.

It's the security guard The Chin hired, waking up from

being tranqed.

Royal pulls his tranquilizer gun from his belt, twists at the waist, and fires another dart into the barely conscious man's thigh. The guard's head falls back into the long grass, and a snore rattles in his nose. He's out again.

When Royal looks at me, I open my mouth and push out the words. "I won't run off."

"Promise me."

Fighting an eye roll, I say, "I promise."

"Good. Now let's get back inside."

We step into the hangar, and Royal locks the door behind us. "The first step," he calls to our teammates, who are huddled around the table where his laptop sits, "is to confirm that it was Beppe Arnoni who took Clarity." He strides across the hangar and sits in the chair recently vacated by Lotus. "Hopefully we've got a satellite in the area that I can access. See if we can find images of Clarity outside in the last half hour."

My eyebrows rise at this. It's going to take forever to do that, when we already know exactly what happened. Knowing I'm on thin ice, I speak in a slow, controlled tone. "Don't you think that will take too long?" When he doesn't respond, I try a different tactic. "Clarity must be scared, wondering if we've noticed she's missing."

This time Royal looks up at me. "Stop pushing," he says, voice even, as he types on his keyboard. "I know you're positive he took Clarity, but we have to make sure first. It won't do us any good to fly to Sicily only to discover that Mr. Arnoni isn't there." Casting a cold look at my aunt, he sets to work typing.

Megan huffs and glares at the floor.

"This is going to take forever," I mutter, sinking into the nearest folding chair. All of the exertion I've expelled in the last few minutes, coupled with lack of sleep, is taking its toll. I fold my arms, placing my hands behind my head, and lean back in the chair. Yet, my mind won't slow down. My thoughts spiral further into the black unknown. What if, by the time we make a move, Clarity's trail is gone without a trace? What will I do then?

A shudder rolls down my spine, and I push the thought away. I refuse to think about that. It's not even a possibility. Is it?

Chapter 3

Julep crosses the room and stands, looking down at me. "We'll get her back," she whispers.

My gaze rises to her face, and she takes my hand, giving it a squeeze.

I return the gesture. "Thanks."

"Starling," Royal says, looking at us over the top of his laptop.

"Yes, sir?" he asks from where he's leaning against the wall a few feet from my chair.

"Go into the airport terminal, and see if Arnoni and Clarity are inside. There's a possibility that he's attempting to take a flight from here."

"I will." He stands upright and makes for the door.

"And Starling?"

The boy pauses, turning to meet Royal's gaze.

"While you're there, get everyone some food. I'm sure we all could use it."

"I will." Starling's eyes meet mine for a second before he turns to go. Without saying anything, he's asking me if I'm okay.

My eyes scream back: No. No. No!

He bites the inside of his lip for a second, but then he leaves. He has orders, after all.

I bolt out of my chair, but Royal stops me with a slow shake of his head. "You stay here."

I frown, but sit back down. My arms cross tightly over my chest, and my eyes fall to my matte black heels. They're sturdy leather with tiny bows over the toes. Even though they're more overtly feminine than the clothes and shoes I usually wear, I like them. Maybe I should wear them more often.

"There it is!" Royal says with enthusiasm in his voice.

My interest perks at this, pushing me upward in my chair.

"Lotus," Royal calls. "Come look through this footage for any traces of Arnoni returning to the parking lot outside, or of Clarity leaving."

"Will do."

Royal stands, and Lotus takes his seat at the laptop.

"It's too bad we didn't have eyes on our camera footage," Lotus says without lifting his eyes from the laptop screen. "We would have seen what happened."

"We'll have to make a change for future missions," Royal says, pulling his phone out of his pocket and making a call. "Haru?" He is silent as Haru talks on the other end of the line, his mouth forming an amused smile.

It almost makes me laugh. She's probably prattling on about something she's excited about, not realizing that there's a reason for his call other than to check in on her.

"That's great," Royal says, "but let me stop you there. We've got a problem here, and I need your help. Use the security codes I gave you to access the airport's departure schedule. Find all of the flights leaving here today and tomorrow that land in Italy, France, Austria, Switzerland, Slovenia, or Croatia. Scan their passenger lists for Beppe

Arnoni and Antonia Arnoni." He falls silent again. "I understand. Get back to me when you can." He hangs up and deposits the phone in the pocket of his slacks. Then, he makes for the door. "I'll be right back."

"Where are you going?" I ask, jumping out of my chair.

"To call my contact at the CIA. They'll have to send someone to pick up our friend, over there." He nods toward where The Chin is sulking in the corner, handcuffed to a table leg.

"But who knows how long that will take. We have to be ready to go the minute we've confirmed Arnoni kidnapped Clarity."

Royal drags a hand down his face and walks over to where I'm standing. Lowering his voice, he speaks. "I'm in a hurry to get her back too, but we were hired to do a job, and we are required to finish it. We must deliver The Chin into the custody of a U.S. government official before we can leave St. Petersburg."

My shoulders slump. He's right. We have to finish our job. It will put Arnoni a few hours ahead of us, but I don't think he'll hurt Clarity. She's his granddaughter, a member of his family, biologically, at least. And from the way he spoke about his grandson when I encountered him in Palermo, family means something to him. Something important.

"What are we going to do with the traitor?"

Royal's eyebrows rise in question.

"My so-called aunt?"

"The embassy agent will take her into custody as well."

I purse my lips.

"What?"

"I was hoping we'd leave her here to rot in a Russian prison. I bet the conditions aren't as nice here as in our prisons

17

back home."

He narrows his eyes at me. "We aren't leaving her here to rot. We'll have her taken back to the U.S. to be charged and tried. It's the just thing to do."

"What's with you and upholding the letter of the law?"

My dad smirks. It's a look I haven't seen on his face in, maybe, ever. "I wasn't always such an upstanding citizen."

I nudge him with my elbow. "Are you sure about that? You seem pretty squeaky clean to me." I flash a smile.

"I will have you know, Charles and I broke lots of rules, back in our day."

"What, like jaywalking?"

Royal chuckles. "I'll be right back."

I watch him go. At least now I know where I get the penchant for rule-breaking. I always guessed my mom had been the wild one, but maybe I was wrong.

"I'm finishing up in the terminal," Starling says in a low tone. "Our flight is already gone."

"Roger that," Lotus says, still hunched over the laptop.

"Come on back, then," I say, lips pursed. I could have told him Clarity and Arnoni wouldn't be there. I drum my fingers on my thigh, impatient.

Next to our prisoner, the auctioneer begins to stir. A low groan escapes him as he pushes himself off the floor with both hands, rising to a seated position. His eyes widen at the sight of The Chin handcuffed next to him. "What's going on?" he says, his voice higher than it was during the auction, laced with a note of panic. He tries to scramble to his feet, but I react before he can take a step.

"You're going to have to stay here with us for a few minutes," I say as I walk over to that corner, not moving my eyes from him.

"Why?" He glances over my shoulder. "Oh." His eyes widen and he takes several steps into the corner of the hangar, hands raised.

Julep comes up beside me, brandishing her tranquilizer gun. "Do as she says."

He nods vigorously. "I will."

I handcuff him to the table leg on the opposite end from The Chin and leave him there, trembling and grumbling under his breath.

The door squeaks as it swings open, and Royal and Starling enter. "Any luck yet?" Royal calls to Lotus, who merely shakes his head, his gaze fixed on the computer screen.

The older man nods, his expression grim.

Starling strides across the room and joins Lotus, setting the bag of food down on the table and focusing his dark eyes on the laptop.

Royal walks up beside me. "The embassy is sending someone to extradite The Chin, and your aunt, back to the U.S., and we're to wait here until the agent arrives."

My lips flatten into a tight line, but I say nothing. Even though I understand why we're waiting around, it still feels like we're twiddling our thumbs, when everyone in this building knows Arnoni's taken Clarity to Sicily. But I don't belabor the point. Instead, I cross the hangar, flip a chair around, and plop down onto it backward so that I'm a few feet in front of my aunt.

She's handcuffed to the chair now, but there's an easy expression on her face. Her eyes float up to mine, and there's a glimmer of what might be interest, but then it fades.

I watch her for a beat, waiting to see if she'll say anything. Finally, she does.

"You look a lot like her, you know."

19

I tilt my head to one side in response.

"Does he tell you that a lot?" she asks, the hint of a smile on her lips. "That you have her features?"

"Are we really going to sit here and talk about my mother, instead of talking about how you just betrayed your family for a mob boss?"

Her eyebrows rise at this, and she leans back in her chair, away from me. The handcuff on her wrist keeps her from crossing both arms over her chest, so she settles for one, her fingers cupped around her opposite elbow. "He deserves this." Her tone is harsh and flat.

"But I don't, and neither does Clarity. Is revenge more important to you than the wellbeing of your nieces?"

This makes her wince, but she doesn't respond. Instead, she casts her glance over toward Royal, who is standing at Lotus's back, helping comb through the images on the laptop screen. Her hackles rise as she watches him. Merely looking at him fills her with revulsion. When she looks at me, she's practically snarling. "I won't apologize," she says.

"I didn't ask you to," I say, pushing out of my chair and joining the boys crowded around the laptop.

Lotus points at the screen, freezing the image there. "There! There she is."

Sure enough, Clarity is pictured on the screen walking casually toward the surveillance van, her hand over her eyes to block the sunlight.

"Finally," Royal says. The sag of his shoulders hints at the relief he's feeling at finally spotting Clarity in the satellite photos.

A detail catches my attention. She's not wearing her sunglasses in the photos. She must have left them here somewhere…

I cast around the hangar, and there they are, abandoned on one of the folding chairs. I jog over to retrieve them, placing the oversized frames on the top of my head before returning to where my team is huddled at the table. It's a small thing, but Clarity loves her shades. She'll want them back, and I'm going to make sure she gets them.

"Okay, so from there, she walks over to the van…" Lotus is narrating the footage as it unspools before our eyes.

"There's his car," I say as my eyes catch the vehicle pulling into the lot. "The plates are the same."

In the video, Clarity halts in place, watching as the car pulls to a stop and Arnoni steps out.

All we can see is her back, but it's obvious the moment she realizes who it is: her entire body tenses, but she doesn't move. Instead, she waits, for what, I don't know.

Arnoni takes a step toward her, his mouth moving in smooth words. We can't hear him, of course, but I can't help but strain to make out what he's saying. It's too bad I'm not a great lip reader. I make a mental note to work on it once we get my sister back.

As Arnoni takes another step toward Clarity, she shakes her head.

He advances another step, and my sister turns to run toward the hanger, her eyes wide.

But that's when Arnoni pulls the taser out of his jacket pocket.

Clarity's entire body goes stiff, and she hits the ground, immobilized.

"Oooh," Lotus groans, furrowing his eyebrows.

"That little… I'll, I'll…" I can't form words for how angry I am. No, I can. I want to murder that bastard, slowly, so he can feel his lifeblood leaving him. But I can't verbalize that. I'm pretty sure Royal would send me on the first flight to D.C. if he heard me talking that way. He's not a fan of unnecessary bloodshed, and I bet he'd disagree with me about whether killing Beppe Arnoni is exactly necessary.

I manage to keep my mouth shut, but he must sense what I'm thinking because he puts one hand on my shoulder, pressing gently until I turn to meet his eyes. "We'll make sure he pays a just price for hurting her. Trust me."

All I can muster is a curt nod, which he accepts. "Lotus, send this over to the embassy with a write-up so they know what they're looking at. And make it short."

"Yes, sir," Lotus says, leaning forward over the keyboard and typing quickly.

I let my head fall backward as I stand awkwardly behind Lotus, watching him type.

Royal's phone rings and he answers. "Haru?"

I close my eyes, hoping that she's found Arnoni's travel plans and that he hasn't left the area yet. If he's still here, it shouldn't be difficult to get Clarity back. He won't have all of the resources he would if we were on his home turf in Palermo.

But Royal's face doesn't lighten as he listens, and I know what he's going to say even before he hangs up.

"She's already gone." The words are sure, even as they leave my mouth.

"The plane he chartered left half an hour ago, mere minutes after he grabbed her."

"Ugh!" I stomp one foot on the ground, wishing I had my trench coat on so I could shove my clenched fists into its deep pockets.

The hangar door bangs open.

"What now?" I spin toward the door to see The Chin's bodyguard standing there, taking in the scene. His suit's rumpled and he has a bit of grass on one shoulder, but his small, stone-like eyes are bright and aware.

"What's going on in here?" he asks, voice gruff through his Russian accent.

"Igor!" The Chin yells. "Get me out of here."

I snicker. The Chin is mispronouncing his bodyguard's name.

"It's EE-gor," the man responds, the frustration clear in his voice. They've obviously had this conversation before.

"Same difference!"

Igor huffs and scans the room, his eyes moving over Lotus, Julep, Royal, and me, who are standing facing him, guns drawn. All except me. My stupid guns are still in the van.

"How much is he paying you?" Royal asks, his eyes not moving from the bodyguard's features.

"Not enough." And with that, Igor turns and leaves the hangar, leaving The Chin spluttering in the corner.

"Guess you're stuck with us," Lotus says, pointing a finger gun at The Chin, and winking.

I titter. It feels good to release some of the tension building up in me. I'm a woman of action. I'm not used to having to wait on another person to complete a mission. This state of suspension is going to be the death of me.

Chapter 4

"Loveday," Royal says.

I flop my head to one side so I can meet his eyes. "Yes?"

"You said you had a plane available?"

And this, finally, makes me smile.

With Royal's permission, I run, fleet of foot, out of the hangar and across the apron to where Pete's plane is parked on one side of a runway. I wish I was tall enough to take the steps two at a time, but the reality is that I'm so short I simply don't have the leg length for that, so I climb up the rollaway steps to the plane door and knock.

Kimberly opens the door, smiling when she sees me. "Brittney. What are you doing here?"

"I'm hoping to talk to Pete." I lean to one side so I can see past her into the plane. From what little I can see, either Pete or Adnan is sprawled out in the middle of the cabin floor, taking a nap. I can't tell which man it is, because from where I'm standing all that is visible is a pair of feet in black loafers and khaki pants.

"He's in the cockpit," Kimberly says, stepping aside to admit me.

In a flash, I'm inside.

It's Adnan who is sprawled on the ground with a pillow under his head and a soft, velvety blanket spread over his torso. A small puddle of drool has formed where his lips meet the cushion, and his hair has fallen forward over his forehead.

"Right this way," Kimberly gestures with one hand.

I walk past her to the cockpit, where Pete has turned in his chair to greet me. "Brittney," he says. "Didn't have luck getting Olympics tickets, I take it?"

I smile. "Something like that. Can you fly me to Palermo?"

His eyes widen at my abrupt request. "What, today?"

"Yes, today. Now. As soon as possible."

He closes his mouth, and clears his throat. "Um, yeah. We can do that. Just let Adnan get a little shut eye, and we'll be ready to go in let's say two hours?"

I nod. I'm not sure when the embassy agent is arriving to take my aunt and The Chin into custody, but it had better be sooner rather than later. "Great. I'll be back in two hours."

"Alrighty."

"And Pete?"

"Yeah?"

"I'll have four other passengers with me. We'll pay you, of course."

He nods slowly. "That's fine. Just fine."

"Thanks."

Kimberly is waiting expectantly when I step into the main cabin area. "Can I get you anything?" she asks, but I shake my head no.

"You're the best, Kimmy, but I'm not staying."

"No?"

"Nope, but I'll be back in a couple hours, and I'm bringing friends."

She smiles at this. "I'll be ready."

Chapter 5

Light from the dying sun hits my eyes as I step out of the plane and onto the staircase that leads down to the ground. I narrow my eyes and wait, allowing them to adjust to the flare of light from the horizon.

A black car is parked outside the hangar. The embassy agent has arrived. Finally. A man in a plain black suit steps out of the sedan and goes into the building.

I stroll across the concrete, taking my time. I have no desire to talk to my aunt any more before the embassy agent takes her into custody, and if I stall long enough, she'll be gone before I get back. That woman is no aunt of mine. Anyone who would sell out my sister, an innocent bystander, in the name of revenge is *not* family. Her actions over the past few months make her a traitor.

Outside the hangar, Darnay is standing against the building, speaking low into his phone. He doesn't flinch when the door swings open and the embassy agent steps out, leading The Chin to the car. The agent's movement is efficient as he guides the prisoner into the back seat and handcuffs him to the handlebar on the cab's ceiling. The car door slams closed, and The Chin is hidden behind a darkly tinted window rolled all the way up.

The embassy agent goes inside once more, but he doesn't come outside with the traitor in tow. What's taking him so long? It only took a minute for him to assume custody of the black market information seller, so why is it taking him longer to claim a teacher gone rogue?

My curiosity peaks, and I jog the remaining few yards to the hangar door. Opening the heavy metal door, I step inside. A gust of air billows around me as the door swings shut. The hem of my dress whooses in around my legs and a shiver runs up my spine.

Royal and the embassy agent are standing near the traitor, talking, as she sits in the folding chair looking up at them.

She's still handcuffed to her seat, but there's an expression I didn't expect on her face: hope. Her eyes flit between the two men as they converse in hushed tones.

And then Royal nods, and the traitor's lips curve upward in a smug smile.

The embassy agent gives a curt nod and pivots toward me, walking purposefully in the direction of the door. "I'll make sure to send you any information we get from the prisoner," he says over his shoulder to Royal before stepping outside into the waning sunlight.

I spin around, my mouth open in surprise. "Is he leaving?" I ask as I trot across the concrete floor toward where my dad is standing.

Royal nods. "He is."

"Isn't he forgetting something?" I gesture wildly toward the traitor, but refuse to allow my eyes to move in her direction.

Royal levels a heavy look at me. "She is coming with us to Sicily."

My eyebrows arch. "You've got to be kidding me. That's a terrible idea."

Behind Royal, Lotus winces from where he's sitting in a folding chair, elbows on his knees.

Julep is relaxed in the chair beside him, knitting. Where she got the yarn and needles, I have no idea.

Royal sighs. "It will be easier to take her along and question her about Beppe Arnoni rather than shipping her to the embassy and waiting for them to gather information to send us. Don't you agree?" His words form a question, but his tone is rigid. He's not really asking for my opinion.

Darnay re-enters the hangar, pocketing his phone and coming to stand beside Royal.

I chew on the inside of my lip, holding in the glare that threatens to cross my features. "If it'll save time..." It's been more than an hour since Clarity was kidnapped, and I'm anxious to get moving.

"It will." With that, Royal turns away from me.

"And once we're done questioning her?"

His body tenses, but he doesn't turn to look at me. When he speaks, his voice is quiet. "We'll make sure she's flown back to the U.S. and charged for her crimes."

I nod. "That's fair."

Starling gestures toward the paper bag of food abandoned on the table. "Anybody hungry?" he asks, a smile on his face.

"Yes!" Lotus pumps his fist. "I'm starving."

"Pack your gear," Royal says. "We'll eat on the plane."

Shooting a glance at Darnay, I march up to my dad. "Is he coming with us?" I ask, using a slight head tilt to indicate that I'm asking about Darnay.

"It appears so."

I purse my lips, my displeasure evident.

"Don't worry about Charles. He won't be any trouble, unlike someone else I know."

I scoff, but say nothing. I'm not thrilled about having yet another person to contend with—it makes the task of rescuing Clarity much more complicated—but it's not worth arguing about, so I let it go. Instead, I set about helping pack up my team's gear so we can leave as soon as possible.

Outside, Royal and Lotus go to the van to get all of our equipment, while Julep, Starling, and I remove any traces of ourselves from inside, around, and on top of the building. Julep sweeps the perimeter while I straighten up inside. Starling is tasked with removing the surveillance equipment the team used to gather photographs and video footage of the building and its occupants over the last three days.

We're ready to go in minutes. Having the ability to leave a place without a trace is a skill we've practiced frequently.

I'm just finishing my sweep of the floor when Royal leans inside the building. "Are you finished in here?"

"Just a minute," Starling says from his perch near the ceiling, where he plucks a tiny camera from the corner, pockets it, and climbs down the shelving unit he used to scale the wall. He gives me a nod, smiling with ease.

"Now we're done," I say.

"Great," he says, patting the door frame with one hand. "Take us to this plane of yours."

Chapter 6

Starling and I follow Royal out of the hangar to where Lotus, Julep, and Darnay are waiting, equipment cases in hand. Well, Lotus and Julep are holding cases. The cases Darnay is responsible for sit in a heap at his feet.

"Follow me." I march across the apron to the small luxury plane that's still parked several hundred yards away. Pete spots me through the windshield and waves.

Lifting my hand, I give a feeble wave in return. The weight of Clarity's absence is starting to press in on me. We haven't been apart for more than a few hours in all of our lives. And at this point I haven't seen her in almost a week.

My team, along with Darnay, follows me up the rolling, white staircase into the small plane where Kimberly is waiting, a smile on her face. She's either a total pro at pretending to like people, or she genuinely loves her job. I'm guessing it's the latter, since she's practically beaming as we all come clamoring into the cabin.

Kimberly takes one look at our heavy-laden arms and speaks. "There are storage cabinets at the rear of the plane for all of your cases." She gestures in the correct direction with one hand.

Darnay, who by all appearances seems not to have heard her, sets down the cases he was carrying and settles himself into one of the chairs in the front row nearest the cockpit. He closes his eyes, a faint smile on his lips. The man looks right at home in this fancy schmancy plane.

Without a word, Kimberly picks up the discarded cases and carries them to the back of the cabin, her movements practiced and efficient.

I glance at Julep, who's fidgeting with the watch on her wrist, apparently embarrassed at her former boss's cavalier attitude toward equipment storage, and Kimberly by extension.

My dad is leading the traitor toward the back of the cabin. She sits in the chair he indicates, and he handcuffs her hands together before buckling her seat belt over her lap. "If you need anything, let me know," he tells her in a low voice, before straightening to scan the plane's interior.

Beside me, Lotus cackles. "You flew here in this?" he asks, mouth agape. "This is *nice*." He flings himself into one of the cushy, captain-style chairs in the row in front of the traitor and fumbles along one side with his hand. "Dude. This thing's got a footrest." The small leather step swings upward and Lotus reclines his seat, putting his hands behind the nape of his neck, eyes closed in bliss.

The traitor's face contorts. She's less than pleased that Lotus is reclining into her space, even though there is ample room between the rows.

"You'll never want to fly commercial again," I say, grinning. It was pretty awesome flying here in this rather than in coach, which is where we usually fly. I'm not sure how much we make for each job we complete, but even if it's a lot, Royal doesn't spring for fancy accommodations. He's much too practical for that.

"Once you're seated I'll come around with refreshments," Kimberly says, smile firmly in place. If she's surprised to have a woman handcuffed to one of the seats on her plane, she doesn't show it.

"I'll need a minute with the pilot first," Royal says, leaving his case near the traitor's chair and turning toward the cockpit.

"Of course." Kimberly nods, moving to pick up the abandoned case, but Starling beats her to it. He picks it up, waits for Kimberly to pass, and stows it in the cabinet.

Julep and I follow him, finishing the job.

Once done, Julep sighs and sinks into the seat beside Lotus, pulling off her high heels and sighing with pleasure at the sensation of the plush carpet beneath her bare feet.

"Feet sore?" Lotus asks, opening one eye to look at her.

"You have no idea."

"Can't say that I do." He leans toward her and whispers in her ear.

Whatever he says makes Julep's face break into a warm smile, but she shakes her head.

Lotus whispers something else before leaning back in his chair and closing his eyes once more. Did he just offer to give Julep a foot rub?

Starling tries to catch my eye, jutting his elbow toward the empty seat beside his, but I shake my head and turn toward the cockpit. Curiosity about Royal's conversation with Pete compels me in that direction. I pass by Darnay, whose eyes are still closed. His even breathing indicates that he's asleep. My eyebrows rise. I thought I was good at sleeping anywhere, but Darnay is better.

"It'll take about six and a half hours to get to Palermo," Pete says to Royal as I approach from behind.

Royal is standing in the frame of the door that separates

the cockpit from the cabin, leaning against the wall, his hands in the pockets of his slacks.

"Did you all miss out on Olympics tickets, or something?" Pete asks as his eyes move between us.

Royal answers. "We're here for a school trip, studying the Russian monarchy. It's a coincidence that the Olympics is this week."

"School trip. Right." Pete nods, giving me a wink.

I grin in return. He's not a dumb guy, our pilot. He may not know exactly what we're up to, but between the last minute nature of my flight, my sudden change in appearance, and the fact that I hadn't originally contracted with him to fly us to Sicily, he's got enough information to know that we're no ordinary school group.

I peek around Royal just in time to catch Adnan yawning into one hand.

"Are you both fit to fly?" Royal asks, having also seen the co-pilot's slip.

"We are," Pete says, his manner easy. "Of course, once we get there we'll both need a nap." He chuckles up at Royal, who nods.

"Fair enough."

We head into the main cabin area, where Lotus, Starling, and Julep are stretched out in the luxury plane's soft, cushy seats.

Kimberly is bustling around in the small kitchen area in the back of the plane, across from the storage compartments. It looks like she's pouring sodas for the boys, and a stiff drink for Julep.

My eyebrows raise at this. I'm surprised Royal isn't saying anything about it, because he definitely sees her from where he's sitting in one of the front row seats, swiveled around so that he can see the entirety of the plane's interior. If I had to guess, I'd say he's letting it slide because she's an adult and we'll be on this plane for the next seven hours, and any alcohol in her system will be long gone by the time we touch down in Palermo.

But my assumption is wrong. Kimberly carries the low glass of amber liquid to Darnay, and sets it on the tray table over his lap.

Darnay takes the liquid and thanks her with a dashing smile.

Kimberly beams in response, apparently charmed by this man, who, mere minutes ago, gave no regard to whatever she said.

I cover my eyes with my hand to keep anyone else from seeing how hard I roll my eyes at Darnay, then look around the cabin. I can sit next to Royal and Darnay, in front of Julep and Lotus, or on the other side, next to Starling.

After surveying my options, I take the seat by Starling. We're teammates, and I can be cordial.

He shifts toward me in his seat, and a pang of guilt hits.

I scan the interior of the plane to make sure none of our teammates are watching us before I speak. Taking a deep breath, I begin. "I want you to know, I didn't come here because I don't trust you."

Starling's big, brown eyes fly to mine at this, his lips parted slightly.

I push on. I need to get this out so that we're clear on where we stand. "I came because I saw what I thought was my mom in the surveillance photos, and I couldn't pass up a chance to talk to her. You understand?"

He nods, his tone grave when he speaks. "If I thought my mom was still alive, I'd do whatever I could to see her again."

I swallow. "I'm glad you get it."

His eyes light. "So you're saying you trust me?"

My first instinct is to reply with snark, but I ignore it. It seems like as good a time as any to make peace with the boy beside me, so I try sincerity instead. "Yeah, I trust you."

He grins at this.

"Don't get carried away, now."

Starling laughs, tossing his hair.

I lower my gaze to my lap, but can't stop the smile that comes.

Kimberly delivers the prepared drinks to my teammates and moves in my direction, carrying a delicate china plate with a sandwich on it in one hand. "Here is the sandwich your friend brought for you. I've warmed it up since he said it was supposed to be toasted."

My eyes flit down to the sandwich. It's grilled with several types of cheese dripping down the sides, and the bread is crusty from being cooked in butter. It looks heavenly.

"Thanks," I say, taking the plate from Kimberly.

"Can I get you anything to drink?" she asks.

"Just a water. Thanks." I give her a pleasant smile, then glance at Starling, whose eyes are on me.

I set my plate down on the fold-up tray over my legs and gesture toward it with one hand. "Thanks for this."

He bends his head in response. "You're welcome."

I chew my lip, eyeing him. "How'd you know this is my favorite type of sandwich?"

His brown eyes lock on me, preventing me from looking away. When he speaks, his voice is low. "I pay attention."

I'm so caught off guard by this that my face heats, but I can't let him see that his words have gotten to me. "Have you been stalking me?"

This time Starling's eyes widen, and I don't stop the smirk that rises to my lips.

"No, not like that..." He says, but my laugh interrupts him.

"Relax," I say, waving the air with one hand. "Paying attention to detail is part of the job."

He opens his mouth to say something, but closes it again, his gaze falling to his own sandwich.

"Attention, everyone." Royal's voice causes me to spin my chair around to face him. He's standing at the front of the plane, having just closed the door that leads to the cockpit. "I intend to let you all get some rest, but first, I have an update on our itinerary."

Each of my teammates is still watching him. They're ready for whatever he has to say about The Chin, or about Clarity. Darnay is reclined in his seat, surveying us, twiddling his thumbs. He seems to be enjoying being in the thick of it with us after being out of the field for so long. In fact, the gleeful look on his face is creeping me out. I return my focus to my dad, who has crossed the plane cabin and placed sound-cancelling headphones on the traitor's ears. Then, his gaze moves to Kimberly. "Would you mind stepping into the back for a moment?"

Kimberly shakes her head, unphased by this obvious request for privacy. "Not at all." She walks to the rear of the plane, slipping closed a gray linen curtain behind her. The tap comes on. It sounds like she's washing dishes.

Royal bobs his head. The sound of running water should be enough to cover our conversation. Taking his seat, he leans forward, his forearms propped on his thighs. "I spoke to my contact at the CIA, who promised to do some digging into The Chin's recent movements, along with any communication he's made through traceable channels."

My eyebrows furrow at this. If he's smart at all, The Chin would never use any traceable forms of communication. But then again, I can't count the number of times I've observed criminals making decisions that made them easier to catch. Everyone makes mistakes sometimes, including black market information dealers.

"My contact was surprised to learn that The Chin claimed to have been hired by Nexus, since no one has heard anything about that operative for almost twenty years, but they promised to look into it. Frankly, they didn't sound hopeful. It's hard to pick up a trail that's been cold for that long." He sighs. "In any case, the whole situation is out of our hands. Other CIA operatives will take the case from here, and as always, they thank us for our service."

"Can you tell us anything more about Nexus?" I ask. I don't care if we're off the case; the mystery surrounding the operative Nexus is intriguing. I want to know whatever information Royal will share with us, keeping in mind that all of it is probably classified.

Royal's eyes find mine, and he studies me for a moment before responding. "There's not a lot to tell."

By this he means that there isn't much he can tell us without endangering national security. I swear, the worst thing about my job is the low level clearance I've got. Just once I'd like to know the whole picture surrounding one of our jobs.

"It was seventeen or eighteen years ago," Royal continues. "One of our agents was killed when a bio-weapon he had seized and was bringing to the States somehow became activated while in his custody."

"It was a nasty business," Darnay puts in. "No one could decipher how it had been deployed, so they did an investigation. Their conclusion was that someone had to have tampered with it while the agent wasn't looking, but there wasn't any evidence to prove it."

"That's rough," Lotus says, shaking his head. He's reclined in his seat, and his arms are relaxed so that his hands hang down on either side of the chair. One of his hands is suspiciously close to the armrest of Julep's chair, but her hands are folded in her lap. Still, if Starling, Royal, and I were to face the front of the plane, it would be easy for them to hold hands.

I try to catch Julep's attention with my eyes, but her gaze flitters over me before she leans toward the window beside her chair.

"How did you know the deaths weren't accidents?" I ask, returning my attention to the topic at hand.

Royal's expression is grim. "There were too many coincidences, and—"

"There are no coincidences in spy work," I finish for him. He nods. "Exactly."

"But you said the killings stopped, right?" Starling asks. The relief in his voice makes me wonder if he was worried about Nexus coming to kill us all.

"They did."

One question has been bothering me since Royal mentioned Nexus in the hangar, hours ago. "Why did they stop? Do you think they found and killed the person they meant to kill?"

Royal takes a deep breath, letting it out through his nose. "I don't know. You may be right; Nexus found and killed whoever it was they were after. Or…"

"Or maybe they were put in jail for some other crime," Lotus puts in, still relaxed in his chair.

"It's possible."

"If that's the case, maybe Nexus was just released from jail and is trying to get back in the game," I say. It's the interpretation of the information that makes the most sense to me. "Maybe we should ask the CIA to look into recent prisoners who have been released in the U.S.? And ask our allies to do the same?"

Royal takes out his phone and types a message. "Done," he says, looking up at me.

"The real question is, if Nexus has already killed whoever they were after, what are they up to now? Why steal the facial recognition software?"

"That," Darnay says, meeting my eyes, "is a question only Nexus can answer. MI6 and the CIA simply don't know."

Yet. We don't know the answer, yet.

Chapter 7

Royal is on the phone with Haru. He's listening to her talk with a look of mild amusement on his face. Finally, he speaks. "Just stay in the hotel, attend your classes with Truly, and we'll be back as soon as possible. All right?" He pauses to listen, and nods. "Good. Work on that, and stay in the hotel. Understand?" He hangs up and pockets his phone.

"Is she okay?" Lotus asks, scratching his ear.

"She's fine. I've asked Truly to keep an eye on her while we're away."

"Good, good," Lotus says with a head bob.

Royal turns to the rest of us. "I've procured a farmhouse for us. It's several miles outside the city, but it'll work for our purposes. The owner is an old friend. She asked that we help her milk her goats." A hint of a smile curls on his lips, which is the only indication that he's joking.

"Milk a goat? How do you...?" Lotus's words trail off as Royal breaks into a grin. "Oh, you're being funny now. I got it." Lotus shakes his head and sits back in his seat.

Beside him, Julep tries to hide a smile behind her hand. It's weird, thinking about her working for Darnay, now that she's been with us for the past few months. She's become such an integral part of our team that it feels like she's always been around.

Having Darnay here, on the other hand, is strange. I don't feel free to let my guard down around him. Instead, I'm always on alert, watching to see what he'll do or say. He's unpredictable, and it makes me uneasy.

And I'm not the only one who's a bit thrown off by Darnay's presence. Starling keeps sneaking glances toward the older man out of the corner of his eye, then shifting toward the window. It's kind of annoying that he's so starstruck. Hopefully he can reign it in.

I need all hands on deck so we can rescue Clarity as soon as possible.

Starling's eyes widen when he sees me watching him, but he doesn't look away. Instead, he sits up straighter, as if giving permission for me to size him up.

"Hey, Kimberly?" Lotus calls across the plane, jerking my attention away from Starling.

"Yes?" She moves toward him with graceful steps, and pauses at his shoulder.

"Is there a way to watch movies on this rig?"

The flight attendant smiles. "Of course." She makes a move toward the back of the room, where I presume she has stored the remote.

"Ahem," Royal says to get their attention. "I don't want anyone watching movies right now. It's late, and we should all try to rest, since we'll be arriving at Sicily in the middle of the night, and I don't know how much sleep we'll get once we're there."

"Yes, sir," Kimberly says, before turning to Lotus. "Can I get you anything else?"

Lotus purses his lips. "Got a blanket anywhere?"

The only noise in the otherwise silent plane cabin is the faint sound of Lotus snoring. It's not super loud, but it's there. For some reason, the quiet snuffle of it strikes me as funny, but I lift my hand to my mouth to quiet the giggle that escapes. In addition to Lotus, Royal, Darnay, and Kimberly are also asleep, and I don't want to wake them.

Beside me, Starling is doing a crossword puzzle on his phone. He glances over at me, and I make eye contact. We're quiet for a beat, staring at each other. His black hair is swept toward one side, with just enough product to give it a bit of texture without looking sticky. There's a shadow of a mustache over his upper lip that draws my eyes to his mouth.

"What's a six letter word for kiss?" he asks, voice low and smooth.

My eyes fly to his before skittering away toward the window over his shoulder. I run a hand through my own hair, which is staticy after being pressed against the airplane seat for several hours. "Um…" Something about having his eyes on me makes my brain fuzzy. I cast around for the word, but can't find it. I chance looking at his face again, and he's still watching me. "I don't know. Sorry."

A pleased smile forms on his mouth, and he looks down at his crossword, finger poised over the screen. "Hmm."

I ease my chair around toward the back of the cabin, where Kimberly is asleep in her seat.

The traitor is awake. She's sitting upright in her chair, watching. She must see me shifting in my seat, because her eyes catch mine. "Can you come here?" she whispers.

I bite the inside of my cheek, but stand. To Starling, I say, "Watch my back, will you?" The moment the question is out I wish I could suck it back in, because I'm all too aware that if he literally watches my back, he'll probably see my butt. There's not really a way to avoid that, since I just asked him to watch me as I walk away. Heat blooms in my chest, but I ignore it, not daring to glance over my shoulder at Starling.

"Any time," he says with a hint of amusement in his voice.

If I was a blusher, I'd be rosy pink right now. Thank God I'm not. The muscles in my face relax as I take the few steps to where the traitor is sitting, her hands still handcuffed in her lap. "What?" I ask, not bothering to hide the disgust in my voice.

Her mouth tightens into a thin line as she looks up at me. "I have to go to the bathroom."

"You can't hold it until we get there?" I look down at my watch. "We'll be there in three hours."

"No, I can't," she says, squirming in her seat. "Can you take these off me?" She lifts her bound wrists.

Julep and Starling are watching me from their seats. Julep's hands grasp her knitting in her lap, and the blanket Lotus got from Kimberly is tucked around her legs. I wonder when that happened?

Anyway, I could ask Julep to take my aunt to the bathroom, but shirking my duty isn't my style. I turn my gaze to the traitor, boring into her forehead with my eyes. If she has to use the bathroom, I'll take her. "Fine. Be right back." I walk to where Royal is sitting and use my best stealth moves to pluck the handcuff keys from his coat jacket pocket, which he's got slung over the back of the seat. The jacket slumps down over Royal's shoulder, and I freeze. His head shifts from one side to the other, but otherwise he doesn't rouse.

I exhale as silently as I can and tiptoe to my seat, where I lean toward Starling. "Can I borrow your tranq gun?"

He answers without hesitation. "Sure." That's one thing I like about him: the absolute trust he puts in his teammates, and his lack of need to ask superfluous questions. He reaches down to where his waist holster is sitting at his feet, retrieves the weapon, and holds the handle out to me.

"Thanks."

He nods. "I'm here if you need me."

My instincts rebel at this, but I push them down. Not relying on my teammates was a pretty big reason Royal benched me, and I'm determined to improve. "Thank you."

I glance at Julep, who is eyeing us, and give her a hint of a smile to let her know we've got it under control. She inclines her head and smiles in response.

At that, I pivot on the balls of my feet and cross to where the traitor is sitting. I keep my tranquilizer gun steady in one hand. "If you so much as breathe wrong, I'll shoot you. Understand?"

"Yes."

"And no closing the door all the way."

The traitor looks up at me with an exasperated expression, but doesn't argue.

I uncuff her and let her lead the way to the back of the plane where the bathroom is located. There's no way I'm turning my back on her while she's loose like this.

She complies by not closing the stall door, and does her business quickly. In a couple minutes, she's back in her seat and I'm returning the handcuffs to her wrists.

"Thanks for this," she says. "I appreciate it."

"Sure," I say without making eye contact. I turn on my heel, but her whisper stops me.

"It's his fault she died, you know."

Chapter 8

My aunt's words make me go still. I've thought the exact same thing a hundred times since I found out the reason my mom and me were on the road the night of the accident. They were fighting because he had just told her about baby Antonia. His baby.

It IS his fault my mother is dead. There's no way around that. But after all these years, I can't allow it to poison my relationship with the only parent I've ever known.

"I take it you agree." Her voice is louder now, more confident.

I spin to face her. "I'm not doing this with you. Not now, not ever." And I tromp past her into the kitchen to get a couple of cookies from the small storage area. They're large, oatmeal chocolate chip cookies. Normally, I turn my nose up at oatmeal cookies, because yuck, but since they're the only sugary food on this plane, I'll make due.

I settle into my seat and pull my legs up into the chair, folding them so I'm cross-legged. Then I hold Starling's gun out to him, and he takes it. "Thanks," I say.

"It was my pleasure," he says in return.

I'm bringing one of the cookies to my mouth when he

continues.

"Have you thought of a six letter word for kiss yet?"

I freeze with the cookie just beyond my lips, and hope he's not now staring at my mouth. I look up at him, and his eyes are on his phone, thank goodness. I give myself an inner shake. I've got to stop thinking about Starling as an attractive male and revert to thinking of him as a usurper. I can't go down the fraternizing-with-a-teammate road again. But a perusal of his features makes it hard to ignore the fact that he's hot, like really hot.

Focus, Loveday.

"It's smooch," the traitor says from her seat two rows behind us.

"Er, thanks?" Starling says in a quiet voice, and writes it down.

I turn in my seat to glare at the traitor, who winks at me. Winks! Ugh, I hate her. Not only is she a traitor, she's a smug one. I thump down in my seat and chomp on my cookie, chewing angrily. I can't believe Royal brought her along on our trip. Okay, maybe it will be handy to have someone with us who knows more about Arnoni's organization, but does she have to be so insufferable?

My stomach churns at the thought of Clarity, alone with Beppe Arnoni, wherever he's taking her. She's probably terrified right now, not knowing what Arnoni intends to do with her. He won't hurt her, I tell myself, but right now it's a small comfort. He won't hurt her. He won't, right?

"Royal?" Pete calls from the cockpit. "Can you come up here a minute?"

I sit up in my chair. Instead of sounding relaxed and at ease, his voice is tighter. It's not panic, but there's definitely something going on. I try to catch Royal's eye, but he motions with one hand for me to remain in my seat before walking up to the cockpit and ducking inside. He's only gone a minute when he returns, with Adnan following close behind.

"Have a seat," Royal says.

Adnan collapses into the nearest seat, rubbing his red eyes. "Thanks."

Royal pats the back of his chair with one hand before crossing to where Lotus and Julep are sitting. "Did you get some sleep?" he asks Lotus, who is leaning forward in his seat, watching with interest.

"You know it."

"And you're one hundred percent awake and alert now?"

A grin creeps over Lotus's features. "Yes, sir."

Royal nods. "Then get up to the cockpit. Pete needs a copilot."

"Are you serious?" Lotus says, voice loud with excitement. "Yes!"

Darnay jolts awake at this and frowns in the direction of the noise.

I cover my mouth with one hand to keep him from seeing me chuckle.

Lotus turns to Julep. "You hear that? I'm gonna help fly this plane."

"I did. That's great," she replies with a genuine smile.

"Get going," Royal says.

"Oh, right." Lotus jogs into the cockpit, but his voice carries to where I'm sitting. "This is awesome."

Pete says something in response, but I can't make it out.

Darnay leans over to Royal. "Is that safe? Can he fly?"

This time it's Royal who grins. "We're about to find out."

Starling nudges me with his elbow, and I meet his eyes. "He can fly, can't he?" he whispers.

"Yeah, he can. There's zero percent chance Royal would let him anywhere near the cockpit if he wasn't capable. He'd do it himself."

"Royal flies?"

"You've seen his desk."

Starling's eyes widen in recognition. "Oh, right. The airplane wing."

I nod. "It's from his first plane. I'd kill to know how it got so dinged up."

"I, too, wondered about that."

We smile at each other, and my heart jumps. I pull my eyes away and glance around the airplane, trying to distract myself from the boy sitting next to me. We need to get off this plane. Fast.

Chapter 9

"That was amazing!" Lotus yells into the inky black of the sky. He's standing at the top of the rolling staircase, gazing up at the twinkling stars, his arms held wide.

Behind him, Pete and Adnan stand in the doorway, one looking gruff and the other looking embarrassed at having fallen asleep at the wheel.

Starling and I are standing on the ground, watching as our teammates alight from the aircraft. Each of us has our gear in hand. Starling is wearing his black backpack and I've got my black duffle over my shoulder and my gun case in one hand.

"Shh," Royal says to Lotus from where he's standing a few feet away from me, and holds a finger to his lips. "It's almost midnight and I want to avoid attention, if possible."

"Sorry," Lotus says, covering his mouth. He looks down at Julep, who is standing below him on the staircase, and mouths something that makes her laugh her usual, brassy honk.

Royal shoots a stern look at them, and they both turn their focus to the steps at their feet, still smiling.

Next to him, the traitor is standing, shivering in her handcuffs.

Royal must notice, because he takes off his jacket and

drapes it over her shoulders.

She gives him a bitter frown, which he ignores. Still, she doesn't return the jacket.

"Thanks, Pete," I call up to our pilot.

"Any time, Brittney," he says with a smile. Then he ducks inside the aircraft, patting Adnan's shoulder as he passes. The co-pilot follows him inside.

After a moment, Darnay steps out of the plane, his expensive leather satchel over his chest. "What now?" he asks once he's on the concrete, standing next to Royal.

"This way," Royal says, gesturing with his head toward the small airport a few hundred yards away. The building is lit up, but there aren't many people around. There's one aircraft marshal standing nearby, who helped guide our plane down the taxiway to the apron near the airport terminal, but other than that the place looks pretty deserted. It's perfect for arriving unnoticed.

I turn in a slow circle, taking in the surroundings, but the only planes I can see are the handful parked near the building, down the way from ours. One of them must be Arnoni's. It strikes me as odd that there are so few airport personnel about, even at this late hour, but then I realize: Arnoni probably paid them to make themselves scarce. The fewer people around, the fewer people he has to pay off to keep their mouths shut about the teenage girl he's brought with him, whether she's unconscious or kicking and screaming. If Clarity was awake when they arrived, she'd be putting up quite a fight

The thought warms me, and I run to catch up with my teammates, who are walking along the side of the airport terminal, not speaking.

Once we reach the road, we stop.

There are three tiny European cars sitting along the curb,

waiting. The driver of the first car is leaning against his vehicle, hands in pockets. When he spots Royal, he stands and extends a hand, smiling. "Royal. Great to see you. How long's it been?"

Royal hems and haws. "Sixteen years?"

"That's too long," the Italian man says, and embraces my dad, who pats his back before letting go.

"Thank you for coming on such short notice," Royal says.

The man shakes his head, untroubled. "It's no problem. I was happy to get your call." He turns to the rest of us, and takes off his hat. "Welcome to Sicily. I'm Vico. Glad to see you all."

We murmur greetings in response, and Royal loads us into the three cars. He, Darnay, and the traitor are in the first car with Vico. Starling and Lotus take the second car, and Julep and myself climb into the third.

Lotus holds the door open while we climb inside, then closes it for us. "Ladies," he says with a wink before scuttling to his own car.

I furrow my eyebrows at this. Lotus has never held a car door open for me, or referred to me as a lady for that matter. But then I glance at the woman sitting next to me, her braids falling forward over her face as she digs a mint out of her bag. It wasn't for me, but he can't exactly single Julep out without getting in trouble with Royal.

"Hey, Julep?" I speak before I even have a chance to decide what to say.

"Yes?" Her brown eyes are soft as she looks at me. "Do you want a mint?"

"Sure." I take the round, white pill she offers me and pop it into my mouth. It can't hurt, since I haven't brushed my teeth in more than twenty-four hours. I run my tongue over my teeth, and the slime makes my stomach crawl.

"Was there something you wanted to say?" Julep's voice is eager, prompting.

"No, never mind." I'll ask her about her relationship with Lotus another time. Maybe after this mission. The last thing she needs is to be worrying about that right now. "Thanks for the mint."

Chapter 10

It's pitch dark outside of Palermo, and we're quiet on the drive down the winding street. Olive and cypress trees line the road, with breaks leading to driveways and side roads. Our driver doesn't say much of anything, which is fine with me. I'm exhausted. The last thirty-six hours have been draining, both mentally and physically. I'll be supremely grateful for the few hours of sleep we'll get once we arrive at the farm house.

Just as I rest my skull against the headrest, our car follows the two others onto a side street, and up a dark, steep hill. A two-story stucco house with a clay tile roof looms in the darkness. Lights glow through the front downstairs windows and the porch, where a woman is standing, smiling. She waves as our three cars park on the gravel drive abutting the house.

"Ciao, amici miei," the woman says once the drivers have parked the cars.

All of us pile out, standing in a tired clump.

Royal brushes off his suit and straightens his tie. "Ciao, Rosa." He smiles at the woman who greeted us. Then he turns to his car to help the traitor climb out, holding her still-bound hands. She looks up at the house, eyes wide with curiosity.

"Stay right here," Royal says, pointing a finger at the

ground at her feet.

She lifts an eyebrow. "What will you do if I don't?" It's a challenge.

"Shoot you." Royal's face is blank and his voice is deadpan. The words hit as he intends them to.

The traitor's face pales in the moonlight, and she takes a timid step backward toward the car to stand in the space between the car's body and the open back door.

Royal's eyes find me. "Keep an eye on her, will you?"

I nod. "Will do." My fingers go to the tranquilizer gun that I've got holstered at my waist, and unsnap the clasp so it's accessible if I need it.

Beside my dad, Darnay runs his fingers over his dark hair to smooth it down.

Lotus stands near the first car, stretching his arms wide and clamping his eyes shut. A small groan emits from his mouth.

Starling steps around the car toward him, stifling a yawn. Like me, he didn't get any sleep on the plane. "What a day," he says, his words breathy.

Julep, who is standing to my left, smiles warmly at the woman standing on the porch, and she beckons us forward. "Vieni. Vieni dentro!"

Royal and Darnay walk across the gravel drive to the porch, and the rest of us follow after. First the traitor, who is wary of me due to my role as her watcher, then Julep and the boys.

Royal and Darnay begin chatting with the woman in Italian. It gives me time to give her the once-over. She's short and a little round, her hair tied back in a long, silvery braid with wisps lining her tanned, wrinkled face. She's grinning and nodding, clearly thrilled that we've arrived.

My jaw hits the ground when she throws her arms around Royal, and he responds, giving her the most bear-like hug I've ever seen him give a person.

Then he turns and smiles at the rest of us, his arm still around the older woman's shoulders. "This is Rosa," he says. "I've known her for, gosh, thirty years?" He asks the woman something in Italian, and her head bobs in agreement. "This is her home, so I expect you all to treat her with the utmost respect and kindness."

Fatigue prevents us from responding with enthusiasm, so we murmur in agreement.

"Everyone, unload your gear and bring it inside. Once we're done, Rosa tells me she has some snacks for us in the kitchen. Let's get to it, shall we?"

We drag our things inside and pile them in the front room before tromping to the kitchen, where Rosa has prepared not snacks, but a feast. Steaming, homemade gnocchi soup is ladled into bowls and placed before us at the long, wooden farm table, and a platter of crusty slices of homemade ciabatta bread finds its way to my greedy hands. I hide the bread basket under the table.

"Oh no, you don't," Lotus says from his seat on the wooden bench across from me. "Give me some of that."

I smirk, but retrieve the basket from my lap and hand it over to him, swiping two pieces for myself.

"This is amazing, Rosa. Thank you," Royal says to the small woman, who is standing beside where he's seated at the head of the table.

"You're welcome," she says, a pleased smile on her lips. "My pleasure."

No one speaks while we eat. We're all too tired and hungry to make conversation. If someone were to see us eating so fast, they'd guess it had been a while since we'd all had a meal, but the truth is we ate during the flight over from St. Petersburg. Kimberly saw to that.

After we're finished, Rosa leads us upstairs to our rooms. Julep and I are sharing the first room on the landing. It's a small room painted a coral pink, with two full-size beds, a night stand holding a lamp, and not much else. But there is a nice sized window, and what appears to be a flower box.

"Thank you, Rosa," Julep says after setting her bag down on one of the beds.

Rosa's head bobs. "Prego. My pleasure."

She ducks out of our room and leads the rest of our team down the hall.

Royal brings up the rear, his hand on the traitor's elbow.

"Royal?" I ask, my voice low. "What are we going to do about her?" I don't dignify the woman with a look. Instead, my eyes remain focused on my dad's face.

"I've got the situation in hand," he says in a placating voice.

My mouth opens to respond, but he gives a faint smile. "Don't you trust me?"

I sigh. It's a loaded question. I don't know if I trust him to tell me the whole truth about some things, like my mother, or Clarity's paternity, which stings. And yet, my experience with Royal as a team leader has always been positive. He's always given us the support we need to do our work with the least amount of risk possible. Choosing to trust that fact isn't easy, but what other option do I have? When I speak, my voice is louder, sturdier. "Yes."

"Good." He leads the traitor down the hall after Rosa who has just re-emerged from the room next to ours, sans two teenage boys. Depending on how much insulation there is in the walls, we might have to be careful what we talk about, even behind closed doors. The walls in the dormitory are quite thick, but something tells me that won't be the case here. And sure enough, I can hear Lotus's enthusiastic ramblings through the wall. I turn to Julep, who gives an amused shake of the head.

"I hope you brought ear plugs," I say.

"I always do."

Julep gathers her things and leaves for the bathroom. "I'll be back in a few minutes."

"K." I sink down onto the edge of my bed, staring at my duffle bag. When I run my tongue over my teeth, they feel gunky and slick, but I'm too exhausted to dig out my toothbrush and trudge down the hall to use the sink. Instead, I flick out the lamp on the nightstand between the two beds, kick off my shoes, and crawl under the covers, pulling them up tight under my chin.

My thoughts turn to Clarity. The anxiety that built in my chest after she was taken has lessens slightly now that we're most likely on the same island. Arnoni's flight was from St. Petersburg to Palermo, so my sister isn't more than a few miles away from me. Even so, the harried, worrisome thoughts don't completely disappear. I'm pretty confident that Beppe Arnoni won't physically harm my sister, but I can't figure out what he wants with her. Yes, she's his granddaughter, but they have no history. They have no connection other than blood, which, in my experience, isn't the only way people become family to each other. I can't help but worry about what Arnoni will do once he realizes that Clarity will never stop fighting to escape him, to get back to us, her family in Washington, D.C. I'm not certain, but I'd bet he won't just let her go. That unknown, that question about what happens then, that fear is what's closing in around my heart, squeezing it into a smaller space inside my chest. Because whatever Arnoni does decide to do, it won't be for my sister's benefit. And I don't know if I, if we, will be able to stop it.

Chapter 11

The morning light streaming in the window hits my eyelids, pulling me out of sleep. I roll onto my back and pull the light, soft cotton blanket off my face. A sleepy glance at Julep's bed reveals that she's already awake and gone. I hop out of bed and dress in the only not-black clothes that I brought—a navy button-down and dark wash jeans. Pushing up the sleeves so they're bunched at the elbows, I peek out into the hallway. My fingers tangle in my gnarled hair as I walk across the rug. The clink of silverware on plates rings in my ears, making my stomach rumble. After a quick trip to the restroom, during which I brush my teeth and try to slick back my hair with wet fingers, I hurry down the wooden steps to the kitchen.

Everyone is seated around the table, eating bread with butter and jam, and sipping from steaming mugs. The warm scent of caffelatte fills my nostrils as I approach.

"There she is," Royal says when he spots me, his voice light and teasing. "Have a seat."

"It's not my problem all of you fools are morning people." I exaggerate the emphasis on the last two words.

"Like that's a bad thing," Lotus chimes in. "You missed an amazing sunrise."

"You were up at sunrise? What are you, a robot? You can't have gotten enough sleep."

Lotus chuckles. "No, but Rosa's rooster decided it was time for me to be up."

"Rooster?" I ask, recoiling slightly and eyeing an exterior door I didn't notice last night. It's a wooden Dutch door, and the top half is wide open, letting in a gentle breeze. "They don't come in the house, do they?"

"No, no chickens in the house," Rosa says, her eyes sparkling. She's clearly amused by my reticence to interact with the resident fowl.

But then a chicken jumps up onto the rim of the Dutch door and starts squawking.

The ear-splitting sound makes me squeal and jump backward toward the stairs, not taking my eyes off the large, fluffy black-and-white spotted bird.

Lotus cracks up at this, his guffaws filling the cozy, stuccoed room.

Royal and Julep both look like they're biting their lips to keep from following suit.

Starling's eyes are on me, his amusement obvious.

"Shut up," I say to the room at large, before screwing up my courage and pulling out the chair beside Royal and sitting down. The bread and butter on the table look scrumptious, and I'm famished. My eyes cut toward the chicken, who is still standing on the open Dutch door, watching us eat. It doesn't look like it's going to come inside, so I grab a piece of bread, slather it in butter, and take a big bite.

"Silly bird," Rosa says, leaving her seat at the table and swatting at the chicken until it gets the message and flutters outside. "Caffelatte?"

I swallow my bite before answering. "Yes, please."

Rosa pours me a cup of steaming coffee with milk and moves to the kitchen sink.

"Rosa, have you forgotten the rule?" Royal asks, shaking a finger at her.

"Are you bossing me around in my own kitchen?" she teases, hands on her hips.

Royal laughs. "Let us finish eating, and then the boys will do those for you."

"We will," Starling puts in. "We'd be happy to."

Lotus nods in agreement, his cheeks bulging with food.

Now that I'm wide awake, the chatter in the kitchen feels out of place. I can't wait any longer to begin our rescue mission. Instead, I blurt, "Rosa, what can you tell us about Beppe Arnoni? Where does he live?"

Rosa's eyes go wide in surprise.

The smack of Royal's palm hitting the table sends a jolt through me. "Loveday."

I swivel to face him. "What? We're here to rescue Clarity, so let's go do it. All we need to do is find out where they're keeping her..." I trail off at the stern look on his face.

"Believe me, I want to get her back as much as you do."

I shoot a disbelieving glare at him, which draws a frown in response.

"I do, but we can't just go into town and start canvassing the locals, asking questions about la nostra società. We have to be smart about this. I'll go into town today and talk to a friend in the U.S. consulate. The rest of you will stay here—"

"No way!" I say, splaying both hands out on the table top and leaning toward him, brow furrowed.

He continues without missing a beat. "You'll stay here, out of sight, until we have a bit more information. Then we'll discuss how to present ourselves in town. Am I clear?"

I huff and fling myself back in my chair, arms crossed over my chest.

"Loveday?"

"Fine." I fling the word at him without looking up. My teeth worry the inside of my lip.

"What about Loveday's aunt?" Starling asks. "What are we going to do about her?"

"She's locked in a room upstairs, safe. Darnay will keep an eye on her while I'm gone. I don't want anyone going in to talk to her. Understand?"

Again he looks my way.

I avoid his gaze in the hopes that he won't be able to read the thoughts criss-crossing my head. In the last two minutes, he's forbidden me from doing the two things I'm most eager to do. Too bad he won't be here to stop me.

Chapter 12

The minute Royal leaves in Rosa's car, I sneak out the front door. My head swivels back and forth as I walk, keeping an eye out for any sign of Rosa's chickens. Hopefully they don't wander from the back of the property, because their jerky movements and sharp beaks wig me out.

It's not a far walk into town, and if I remain inconspicuous like I've been trained, Royal will never know where I was. Behind me, a twig snaps and I freeze. Pivoting casually, I look around. There's a large, black-and-white spotted chicken standing at the corner of the house, eyeing me with its head cocked to the side. It has a red comb on its head, which I'm pretty sure makes it a rooster, but really I have no idea. Royal's idea of a pet is the animals we used to visit at the zoo, so my experience with domesticated creatures is literally zero.

I take a step back, but the chicken flaps its way across the yard toward me, its beady eyes peering up at me expectantly. The way it runs reminds me of the velociraptors in a creepy dinosaur movie I watched once, making me cringe.

"I don't have anything for you, bird," I say, my lip curled in disgust. "Go away." I shoo it with one hand, but it merely clucks at me and starts pecking the ground around my feet.

"Okay…" I turn away from the chicken with slow, deliberate movements, and run smack into Starling.

I push away from his solid body, issuing a curt apology before looking up to meet his eyes. My heart speeds in my chest, but I try to quash it. The look he's giving me doesn't help.

He smiles down at me with one eyebrow cocked, hands relaxed in his pockets. "Where are you going?"

"Nowhere," I say. "I'm just out here making friends with the locals." I wave toward the chicken with one hand, hopeful that the gesture will sell my story.

Starling's other eyebrow rises to meet its mate. "Really? You're out here making friends with Rosa's chicken?"

"Yep."

"Then why don't you give it a pat, eh?"

"Um…"

"Go on. I've been told that chickens don't bite, usually."

I cringe inwardly at this, but I can't back down now or he'll know I'm lying about my reason for being out in the yard, walking toward the road. "Fine." I squat and creep my hand out in front of me, toward the chicken, which, now that I'm looking at it properly, seems massive. Are most chickens this big? If so, shudder.

The chicken stills and watches my hand, which quivers as I inch toward the bird's side.

Beside me, Starling is still, waiting to see what will happen.

My fingers graze the chicken's wing. The second I make contact, the chicken jerks away, squawking and running across the yard and around the corner to the back of the house.

This surprise move makes me recoil, falling and landing flat on my back on the dry, dusty ground. Before I can catch my breath, Starling is standing over me, grinning.

"So, that's how you make friends with chickens? Very informative." His chuckle is low and warm.

"Shut up." He can laugh all he wants, but I'm never touching a live chicken again if I can help it.

"So, what were you really doing out here?" the boy asks as he extends a hand down to help me up.

I reach up to take it, but fake him out, hooking my foot around his leg and yanking it out from under him.

This does not have the result I expected.

Instead of landing on his back, he throws his arms out in an effort to catch himself and falls sideways, landing with his abdomen across my stomach.

"Ouch," I yowl, pushing at him, but he's too heavy for me to budge.

Our eyes meet, and I'm caught there, staring at him, trapped under his torso.

"Was this what you had in mind when you pulled that little stunt?" he says, his voice quiet.

My insides coil and quiver in response, but I can't do this. I can't get involved with this boy, the one who was brought to the Ivory Tower as my replacement. As Vale's replacement. It would land me in more hot water with Royal than I'm already in.

"Get off me," I say, shoving at him again.

This time, he obliges, standing and dusting himself off. A boyish smile crosses his face.

I don't stay to question it. Instead, I scurry to my feet and retreat into the house, my heart racing, and my skin warm where he touched me. Once I'm inside, I hide behind a curtain in the window next to the front door and peek out into the yard.

Starling is standing where I left him, gazing up at the

house, a wistful expression on his face.

And just like that, my unruly heart is in huge trouble.

Chapter 13

I don't know how much time I have before Royal returns from his trip into town, so I have to hurry. The problem is that Darnay is still in his room, pacing and talking low into his phone. From the sound of it, there's something going on at one of his hotels. Being the spy that I am, I press against the wall in the hallway to listen rather than retreating to give him privacy. You never know when you might hear something useful.

"Have you selected an employee?" Darnay asks eagerly, clutching his large, expensive smartphone in one hand and tapping his fingers on the surface of a wooden chest of drawers that sits in one corner of the room.

It sounds like he's facing away from the hallway, so I chance a peek around the door frame.

I was right; he's gazing out the window into the yard beyond, still drumming his fingers on the wood surface of the dresser.

Beyond him, there's a low door in the wall that leads to the small room where the traitor is being held. The panel is a medium wood grain with dark knots spotted along its surface. There's no window to offer me a glimpse of the woman inside, no way to see what she's doing in there.

I duck into the hallway just as Darnay turns to pace across the room.

"Then try a different one. Find an employee whose schedule allows us to complete the work within that time frame." He lets out an exasperated sigh and spins around. "I don't care if it takes you a month. I want this to go smoothly and without complications." With a jab at his phone, he ends the call.

I slide into the doorway and his eyes lock on me.

Darnay tenses where he stands, then seems to gather himself. He gives me a quick smile "Loveday," he says, turning to me. "Can I help you with something?"

I put on a pleasant smile. "I'm hoping you'll let me talk to the prisoner, just for a minute?" I bat my eyelashes at him, hoping a pretty face will convince him to overlook Royal's edict barring contact with the traitor.

It doesn't.

Darnay frowns before sauntering over to me and patting me on the shoulder. "Let us handle her, all right? You don't need to get mixed up with a back-stabbing woman like that."

The patronizing tone in his voice makes frustration rise in me, and I push his hand away. "Don't do me any favors. I'll judge for myself, if you don't mind."

The older man's frown deepens at this and studies me for a moment. He opens his mouth to speak, but doesn't get the chance.

Footsteps in the hall announce the approach of one of our teammates, and I take a step backward out of the room to stand in the hallway.

Julep is there, giving me a slight smile. She glances between Darnay and me before gesturing toward our room with one hand. "Can I have a word?"

I cut my eyes toward Darnay, whose frame fills the doorway I just vacated. It would be tricky to get past him now, because even though his public persona is one of buffoonery and clumsiness, he's not that simple. He was, in his day, a capable spy, which means he's got a good grasp on hand-to-hand combat and would likely know how to defend against any attack I could make. Plus, he's almost a foot taller than me and probably weighs eighty pounds more. My breath escapes me in a sigh, and then I follow Julep into our room.

Julep sits down on the edge of her bed. "Shut the door, will you?"

I comply, sitting across from her. The gap between the beds is so small that my knees graze hers as I sit down. "Where are the boys?" I ask. It's a stalling tactic, but I don't care. Whatever Julep has to say to me, it probably won't be something I want to hear.

"They're out in the yard with Rosa, learning how to milk a goat." She chuckles at this, and extends her arms behind her to lean back on her palms.

A smile rises to my lips. "I thought that was a joke."

"Me too."

We fall into a warm silence.

Julep doesn't move. From the concentrated expression on her face, I'm guessing she's trying to formulate the words for whatever she wants to say to me.

I sit still, waiting. My eyes rove over the coral-colored walls in our room, which glow in the midday sun. A watercolor painting of an Italian harbor, complete with fishing boats and fluffy white clouds, hangs on the wall in the corner. The waves in the image appear to move as I stare at it, but I know it's simply a result of the movement the artist managed to capture during the painting process.

"You know I worked undercover for the CIA," Julep says, bringing my attention back to her.

"Yes. You told us that, in Malaysia." My eyes grow heavy at the memory of that mission, but I don't allow them to fall to the ground. Instead, I focus on the woman sitting across from me. She's wearing a forest green blouse tucked into her khaki capri pants, and her braids are pulled into a ponytail at the base of her neck.

"Do you want to know what case I was working on? Before I quit?"

"Are you allowed to tell me? I assumed it was confidential."

"I can give you the big picture. No names or specific locations."

I lean forward. "Go ahead."

She gives me a wan smile. "I worked in Boston with my partner, Sean. We were trying to get a handle on who the higher-ups were in the Sicilian mob in that area."

My heart starts galloping in my throat. "Wait. You're telling me you've dealt with the Sicilian mob before?"

She nods. "Yes."

"Does Royal know about this?" My thoughts are whirling around in my head like a cow caught in a cyclone. If Julep has experience with la notra societá, this could give us the edge we need to rescue Clarity, sooner rather than later.

"We spoke about it this morning."

"So, what can you tell us about them? You've got to have some information that can help us get Clarity back."

Julep purses her lips. "Unfortunately, I don't know a lot about their organization here in Palermo. My dealings with them were strictly in Boston, and mostly through Sean. I posed as his girlfriend. He was the one who was trying to ingratiate himself to the leaders there."

"Why him?"

"Only men who are Italian on their dad's side can become full members. There wasn't a lot they would even say when I was around. Most of the interactions I had with members consisted of pretending to laugh at their inappropriate, misogynistic jokes."

"Gross."

"I know, but that was the job. And if something happened to Sean, I was supposed to be there to back him up." Her voice quiets, and she looks away from me, toward the open window. The breeze flutters in, making the white cotton curtains dance. Her eyes take on a faraway look. She's probably imagining Sean's death. Maybe it haunts her, in the same way Vale's death haunts me when I allow myself to dwell on it.

After a moment, she seems to shake it off. Julep's focus returns to me and she gives a half-hearted smile.

"So, why are you telling me this?"

She pushes off the mattress with both hands and sits up, her palms resting on the edge of the mattress on either side of her. "I guess I'm just trying to tell you that the Sicilian mob is dangerous."

I roll my eyes at this. "You think I don't know that?"

Julep shoots a look at me, her eyebrows scrunched down over her eyes. "I don't know if you do. You seem to want to go running in there, guns blazing."

I spring up from the mattress. "But—"

"No. Listen. Please." She stares me down, unblinking, until I close my mouth and slink down onto the mattress. "Thank you. I know that, more than anything, you want to get Clarity back. But you have to understand that Royal does too. And so do Lotus and Starling and I. We care for her too. She's important to all of us. And that's why it's so important for us to take this slow. To gather information, formulate a plan, and move forward as a team. We're stronger together than we are alone."

Her words hit me like a punch to the gut. All of the thoughts and guilt and fear that have been swirling around in me for the past six months bubble up to the surface of my mind, and my eyes betray me by forming tears. I blink them away, but Julep sees.

She reaches out and puts a hand on my knee. "What's wrong?" Her voice is calm, soothing. "Tell me."

It all comes gushing out. I can't stop it, and I don't want to. "I don't know if I can work with a team anymore. It's my fault that Vale died. I asked him to help me bring down that helicopter, and they shot him. He bled out in my arms because I couldn't shoot down the bad guys by myself. I needed backup, and it cost the boy I loved his life. I can't ask anyone else for help, because if I do, I'm afraid it'll kill them. I can't lose another person I love."

Julep's eyes shine with sympathy. "Oh, honey. It wasn't your fault Vale died. We were all there, and it was chaos. They were shooting, we were shooting... Besides, Vale knew what he was getting into when he asked to be considered for field work."

I press my hands to my eyes to stop the tears. My anguish slides into frustration. "Did he, though? We've never had an operation go sideways like that before."

"He'd been on the team for several years, right?"

"Two years, yeah."

"And he ran the comms for you all that time?"

"Yes. It's the reason Royal brought him on, so we'd have extra hands to support Clarity, Lotus, and me in the field."

"And has he ever helped with a job when one of you was shot at?"

I purse my lips, frowning down at the carpet, hesitant to acknowledge the truth of what Julep is asking. Finally, I grind out an answer. "Yes."

Julep smiles faintly, not a happy smile, but a comforting one. "You see? Vale knew exactly what he was signing up for. And another thing: if Royal had known how dangerous it would become, he would have declined the job. I think he's got a bit of a blind spot when it comes to Mr. Darnay."

My head bobs in agreement. "I've noticed that."

Julep tilts her head and her braids fall forward over one shoulder. She trails her fingers through the tiny, tightly wound plaits as she speaks. "Why is your instinct to blame yourself for Vale's death?"

I suck the inside of my lip between my teeth, mulling over her question. "Because I'm the one who made the call to put him in the field. If I had told Royal he wasn't ready, Vale would still be alive."

"I don't think that's it. From what I've seen, Royal has the final say on pretty much everything."

I can't help it; I bristle at this. "Don't remind me."

Julep points one finger in my direction. "There it is."

"There's what?"

She takes a deep breath, but doesn't look away from my face. "I think the real reason Vale's death bothers you so much, aside from your feelings for him, is the fact that you weren't in total control of the situation. You, alone, couldn't take down the bad guys, and in the melee someone was killed. I think your biggest issue, the thing you hate most, is feeling out of control." She watches me for a beat, measuring my response to her words.

I lean forward and pat her leg. "Good talk." I stand, turning toward the door.

"Loveday," she says. "Don't shut us out. We're a family, and part of that is helping each other when we're struggling."

She's right.

I clamp my eyes shut to forestall the second round of tears that threaten to spill.

A message comes through on our watches.

Royal
Meeting in ten minutes.

The few seconds it takes to read the message are all I need to regain my composure. "Looks like he's got something."

"Yes, it does." Julep stands and pushes her hair behind her shoulder.

"And about shutting you out?"

"Uh huh?"

"I'll try not to."

"Good."

Again I turn to go, but she catches my sleeve with her fingers. "One more thing."

"Yeah?"

"Royal told you to stay away from Megan. So you better listen."

"Yes, Mom."

She relinquishes her hold on my blouse with a snicker. "I am not anywhere close to old enough to be your mom!" she exclaims, wagging a finger at me.

"You sure?" I ask with a laugh.

Julep swats at me before slinging an arm around my shoulders to give me a squeeze. "Let's go downstairs."

I nod in affirmation, and we stroll down to meet Royal. I'm hoping with all my might the consulate people were able to tell him where Arnoni lives, and give us information we can use to rescue my sister, and fast.

Chapter 14

Starling and Lotus are already in the living room, sitting on the wicker sofa when Julep and I enter the room.

Starling takes one look at my red, puffy eyes and stands. "What happened? Are you okay?"

"I'm fine, thanks," I say, smiling at him. Julep's pep talk helped lift the weight off my shoulders. Besides, it's not the time to talk about my problems. I'm dying to know how Royal's meeting with the staff at the consulate went, and if they had any useful information to give him.

Starling sits down again, still eyeing me with concern.

It's unnerving, the way he's looking at me, so I turn my attention to the newsfeed on my watch. Even so, my stomach flutters at his attention.

A car pulls up the drive and shuts off. The car door shuts with a thud, and footsteps crunch on the gravel drive.

Lotus leans back on the sofa and looks out the window. "It's Royal," he says.

The man himself strides into the house, locks the door behind him, and makes for the stairs.

I jump up off the couch and go after him. "Royal, Dad, what's going on? You're acting like there's someone chasing you… Wait, is someone chasing you?" I halt on the landing and call down to Starling, Lotus, and Julep. "Check outside, and see if anyone followed him back!"

They jump up at my command, and I run up the remaining stairs after Royal, who has disappeared into the room he's sharing with Darnay. It didn't occur to me before now that it would be weird for them to share a room, but it's weird. I'm sure if there were other rooms available, my dad would have preferred some privacy. In fact, Rosa tried to give up her room for him, but Royal refused to put her out.

When I enter, Darnay is sitting on one of the two full-size beds with his eyes trained on the inner door, his expression curious. He glances at me and pauses, probably noting my puffy eyes and blotchy skin.

Royal is standing in the open inner doorway with his back facing Darnay, blocking the view so that all I can see is a bit of the dimly lit room beyond. I'm sure he's doing it more to keep the traitor in than to keep me out, but I can't resist creeping forward to peer around him.

The traitor formerly and for about five minutes known as my Aunt Megan, is sitting on a camping cot against the wall. Beside the bed, there's a low wooden night stand holding a small lamp and a glass of water. There's a food tray with a few bread crumbs and bits of fruit on the floor at her feet. Above the cot, there's a small window open to let in some fresh air. It's not large enough to crawl out of, though. This observation makes me wonder how often this room has been used to detain people who were hostile to American CIA agents here in Palermo. New respect for Rosa blooms in my chest. She may appear unassuming, but she's really a hard-core ally to the United States for allowing Royal, and undoubtedly others, to use her home as their base of operations.

"Where would Arnoni keep Clarity?" Royal asks, his piercing blue eyes bearing down on the traitor.

She glares up at him, lips pouting, and doesn't respond.

The traitor looks at me, and her eyes widen at my appearance. "Are you okay?"

I cross my arms, and grunt in response.

Royal turns to me, taking in my appearance, but says nothing. He'll bring it up later if he deems it necessary. Instead, he shifts his weight from one foot to the other, his focus again on the traitor. "It will go better for you if you help us. I can talk to the prosecutor when you're tried and ask him to give you a lesser sentence."

"No! She deserves to rot in jail." My angry words hang in the air between us.

The traitor's mouth drops open, but no words come out. She must know there's nothing she can say to adequately defend her actions over the past months.

Royal casts a glance over his shoulder at me, and his grim expression makes it clear that he agrees. However, he's always saying that you catch more flies with honey than vinegar, so I guess that's what he's going for right now. I force my face muscles to relax—glaring at my aunt probably won't help—and purse my lips to avoid blurting out anything else. As long as I don't interfere with his interrogation any more, I'm confident Royal will allow me to stay.

The traitor looks from Royal to me and back, sneering. "I'll never help you. I'm an only child because of you."

"And you wish to do the same to Loveday, your niece?" Royal hooks a finger in my elbow and pulls me forward to stand at his side in the small room.

The traitor's eyes move to meet mine, and a flicker of guilt flashes across her face.

I can use that to my advantage. Taking a slow breath, I lower my shields and allow the anguish of being torn asunder from my sister to register on my face, in my eyes. "Please," I say, my voice barely over a whisper. "I can't even remember my mother, and being without her is a constant ache. Please don't take my sister from me too. You know how much that hurts." It's a little melodramatic, I admit, but it's all true. I can't imagine the pain of never seeing Clarity again, and it can't hurt to show a little bit of that to the woman sitting in front of me.

She bites her lip as she considers my words.

Beside me, Royal puts his hands in his pockets. The movement catches the traitor's attention, and she scowls up at him again. Seeing this, he shifts into the outer room, leaving me in the doorway alone.

I take a step forward and kneel down in front of her. It puts me at a physical disadvantage; she could lunge and tackle me, but the softening expression on her face makes me doubt she'll try anything. Besides, if she does, I can take her. And even if she did get the best of me, Royal and Darnay are both within striking distance, should a well-aimed tranquilizer dart be needed.

"Please, help us."

We stare at each other for a moment, me and this woman who could be my mom's twin, before she nods. "Okay," she whispers. "I'll help, but not for him." Again, she shoots a glare over my shoulder toward where Royal must be standing behind me.

"Thank you." I wait, crouched at her feet, for her to continue.

"Mr. Arnoni's men often congregate at the barber shop on the edge of the park in town. If they're holding Clarity somewhere, they're likely to be talking about it there." She pauses, tilting her head to one side in thought. "If I had to guess, though, I bet they took her directly to Mr. Arnoni's house outside of Palermo. Beppe spends a majority of his time there, and doesn't come into town unless there's a problem his guys can't fix without him. I'd start there, if I were you."

I give her a flash of a smile before standing and turning toward Royal. "Did you get all that?" I ask.

"I did."

I slam the inner door shut and stalk out of the room. If she thought helping us would soften me toward her, she was wrong.

Royal and I head back downstairs.

I settle onto one of the chairs and wait.

He stands in front of the large window, looking outside, unmoving. After a moment, he turns to us. "As you all know, I was at the consulate this morning, talking to a contact there about Arnoni and la nostra società." His mouth tightens in a thin line. "Truthfully, they were reticent to talk to me about the mafia at all because of its large presence here in Palermo. Of course, once I told them we were investigating a kidnapping of an American citizen, they acquiesced."

"They were inclined to acquiesce to your request?" Lotus says with a grin.

"Now is not the time," Royal says, but his mouth curves upward in amusement.

"Shush," Julep says to Lotus, putting a finger to her lips in a playful gesture.

Lotus winks at her before returning his attention to Royal.

"So, you know where Arnoni's likely to be holding Clarity?" I ask, edging forward in my seat, a cream-colored cushion on a large, wicker chair.

"My contact gave me Arnoni's home address, and the

addresses of businesses in town where they suspect the organization has a presence. Our guest upstairs narrowed it down to one business in town, a barber shop. Apparently, many of Arnoni's men frequent the place when they aren't extorting money out of local business owners."

"Great," Lotus says. "So when do we go?"

"It's not that simple," Royal says slowly. "For one, my guy at the consulate said that we should be wary of involving the police, because the mafia pays several of the officers to look the other way for them."

"Okay, so we don't use those guys," I say. "That's pretty simple."

Royal shakes his head. "The turnover rate in their department is staggering, apparently, so the staff at the consulate are never sure who they can trust. It's a tricky situation. Plus, it's complicated on our end as well."

I study him for a moment, not sure what he's talking about.

"Julep?" Royal asks, turning to her.

Julep, who is sitting primly in a chair with her ankles crossed, speaks. "Several guys in Arnoni's crew will likely remember me from Boston if they see me. Plus, Arnoni saw me in the hangar during the auction. If any one of them spots me, they'll know something is going on. It's too big a coincidence."

I bite my lip. "He's seen me too, but I was wearing a wig, contacts, and had a Texan accent."

"I'm aware of your encounter," Royal says. "Clarity told me all about it after your last trip here."

"Not surprising," I say. "Then what do we do? What's our next move?"

Royal turns to the boys, who are both sitting on the couch, Starling sitting upright and Lotus leaning forward on his elbows.

A slow grin rises to Lotus's face. "It's up to us, baby!" He elbows the boy beside him. "Starling and I will go in, right? Right?"

Royal nods. "You two will pose as college students on vacation, that way your presence around town won't arouse suspicion. You'll keep eyes on the business where Arnoni's men congregate. Lucky for us, there's a grassy area right across the street from there, and it'll be easy for you to watch from that distance. We'll also plant listening devices inside so we can pick up their conversations. It's a barber shop, so it won't be difficult for one of you to go in and plant a bug while you're inside."

"Whoa," Lotus says, sitting up. "You all know how I feel about strangers cutting my hair." His hand runs over his growing afro, then he turns to Starling. "This one's all you, bro."

Starling nods. "I can do that. My hair's getting shaggy anyway." Starling runs a hand through his straight black hair, drawing my attention. Personally, I think Starling looks really good with his black hair falling over his forehead, but I keep this fact to myself.

I blink and force myself to look back at Royal.

"So it's settled," Royal says, nodding. "We'll go in an hour. Everyone go get ready."

The boys rise to standing, adjusting their clothing once they're upright.

"Wait a second," I say, holding up a hand to catch Royal's eye.

"So close," Royal says with a half-hearted chuckle. His piercing blue eyes land on me, and he waits.

I stand, hands on hips. "I want in on this. Arnoni's only seen me once. I'm confident I can change my appearance enough that he won't recognize me. Besides, it's not realistic for two college guys to be dinking around in the park by themselves. They'd want a girl around so they can show off."

"That's true," Lotus says. "If I was going on vacation, I'd definitely be on the lookout for a hot girl." He points toward me.

I grin. "Thanks?" I say, laughing.

Starling's eyes meet mine, and his intense gaze on me makes my insides heat.

Julep smiles and gives an amused shake of the head. "Loveday is right. All the guys I know love showing off. If Loveday isn't there, any number of local girls might distract them, being that they're both attractive."

Lotus hits his fists together in front of him. "Yeah we are," he says, beaming.

Starling smiles, confident, but says nothing.

Royal's eyes lock on mine, and we remain there, him measuring my readiness and me willing him to agree. The creases at the corners of his eyes furrow in thought.

I don't move from where I'm standing. I don't want to give him any reason to deny me. If he tries to keep me out of the effort to rescue Clarity, I'll go off the rails. I have to be involved in this.

Royal exhales before folding his arms. "Fine, but you are to obey orders at all times, answer all communications in a timely manner, and don't go rushing into anything. Can you do all of that? Because if not, I'll lock you in the inner room with your aunt while the rest of us work." His mouth quirks, so I know he's kind of kidding—about the last part, at least.

"I'll behave," I say with a simpering smile.

"Good. Julep and I will watch Arnoni's home, outside of town. A local business was gracious enough to rent us their van, although I'm sure they'd be surprised to know that we're using it for surveillance rather than florist deliveries."

"Taking up horticulture?" I ask with a snicker.

"Maybe," Royal responds. "If we get bored in the van."

"Not likely," Lotus murmurs, using a head scratch as a way to eye Julep surreptitiously.

Starling smirks; he caught it too.

"Everyone go get ready. We leave in twenty minutes."

"Yes!" I'm off up the stairs before he can change his mind.

The boys clunk after me, and we go into our separate bedrooms to change clothes. I kneel down at the foot of my bed and open Clarity's wig box to see what my options are, but the wig on top immediately calls my name. "Hello," I whisper as I pull it out. "You will be perfect."

Chapter 15

Starling sits next to me in the van, his still form radiating confidence.

I catch myself feeling relieved that the boy next to me, unlike Vale, doesn't need assurance of his abilities in the field. But the thought feels traitorous, and I bite my lip to quash it.

Royal pulls the van to the curb around the corner from the barber shop and twists in the driver seat to look at Starling. "You're on," he says.

"Yes, sir." Starling casts a quick glance at me, his eyes flitting over my strawberry blond midi-style wig. "See you in a few."

"You know it," I say, and then he's stepping out of the door.

Royal pushes a button and the door slides shut.

I smile into my hand at Starling's face. He got one look at me in this wig and his jaw dropped. My eyes cut toward Lotus, who's sitting behind me in the van. "You ready for this?" I say, trying out a super sweet voice.

He grins. "You know it." He sits forward in his seat and flicks my shoulder.

"Ouch," I say, but the laughter that follows negates my protest. "You better watch out, or I'll buzz your hair in your sleep."

Lotus's eyes widen in mock offense. His hand flies up to cover his tight curls, which are getting long enough that they're starting to droop in his face.

"I'll wait for your signal," Starling says into the top button of his shirt, where his communications device is located. It was actually Darnay's idea to put it there, since Starling couldn't wear an earbud to have his hair washed and cut.

"Give us five minutes to get in position," Royal says as he pulls the van away from the curb and down the cobblestone street. He navigates around the block and pulls to a stop, idling the van. Twisting in his seat, he catches Lotus and I in his line of vision. "You're up."

Lotus gives an exaggerated salute, and we climb out of the sliding door.

From the front seat, Julep pushes the button to close the door, and they pull away.

It's a little tricky in the long, flowing floral dress I borrowed from Clarity's suitcase, but I manage not to fall on my face on the sidewalk. I straighten the skirt, then reach a hand up to run my fingers through the strands of my wig. It's pretty different from the one I was wearing during my first trip to Sicily with Clarity, so anyone who saw me then won't recognize me now. Even though It's only been nine months, it feels like a lifetime has gone by since my sister and I strolled down these streets toward the city's archive building, and were told that Clarity's birth certificate was nowhere to be found.

A sigh escapes me. It's the only outward expression I allow of the ache I feel at the absence of my sister.

Lotus nudges me with an elbow. "You okay?"

I nod, and he smiles. "Then let's get to work."

I return his gesture. Game on.

We stroll along the sidewalk, smiling and sending furtive, playful glances toward each other. Honestly, it feels really weird flirting with Lotus, but it's the job, so I keep it up. We've never posed as flirting teenagers, but we're both professionals, so we can do this. It occurs to me that it'd be much easier to flirt with Starling, who I'm actually attracted to, but I'd never admit that out loud.

Lotus bounds ahead of me before looping around and grabbing my hand. "Hey girl, it's hot out here. Let me buy you some gelato." He's got his walk set to full swagger.

I giggle, putting on my best flirtatious smile. "Deal, but I get to keep my hand."

Lotus laughs. "Deal."

I hitch up my long dress, enjoying the swish of the airy cotton as I move.

We amble into the gelato shop, and the tinkle of a bell brings the worker out of the back room. He's a teenager, probably a couple years younger than me, with olive skin, wavy caramel hair and sleepy brown eyes. His demeanor perks up when he sees me, and he steps up behind the counter with a smile.

I give him a megawatt smile in return before floating my eyes upward to survey the menu. The list of flavors—from watermelon to pistachio—makes my mouth water.

"Everything looks so yummy," I croon, leaning forward so the boy behind the counter can smell the sweet perfume I put on before we left the house.

Out of the corner of my eye, I see him giving Lotus the once-over before returning his attention to me. "What can I get you?" he asks in accented English.

I focus on the bank of ice cream behind the glass case. "Can I pretty please have a scoop of watermelon, orange, and chocolate? In a cone?"

"Sí." He scoops the gelato into a crisp, golden brown cone and hands the towering dessert to me gingerly over the counter. He's given me the largest scoops I've ever seen.

"Thanks," I grin and take a small, careful lick. "Yum."

The boy behind the counter must realize he's staring at me, because he flushes and looks away.

I titter into my gelato.

Lotus orders a scoop of pistachio and pays before opening the door for me and leading us outside. "Want to walk through the park?" He wiggles his eyebrows at me, which prompts a genuine laugh. Lotus doesn't often get to act during jobs, owing to his role as our getaway driver, but he's loving it.

I incline my head toward him, and he leans in, pretending to whisper something funny in my ear. But really, he asks, "How am I doing?"

I laugh again, louder this time, and give him an encouraging smile.

He beams, slings an arm over my shoulders, and we cross the street into the park.

There's a dusty, navy blue Fiat at the curb, which we ignore. It's our getaway car, in case we need to make a hasty exit. Lotus has the keys in the pocket of his cargo shorts.

The barber shop is at the other end of block, across the street from the park, so Lotus and I amble over the cushy, green turf in more-or-less the right direction. It's a weekday, so the park is mostly empty, but for a young mom and her child playing under a shade tree to our right. The little girl squeals in delight as her mom zooms a toy over her head, making airplane noises as she does it.

A pang goes through me at this. I don't remember anything about my mother, much less sweet moments like this one. And the woman who I thought was my mother, returned from the dead, turned out to be a lying, backstabbing…

I push the thought away and focus on our mission. Now is not the time to get all worked up about the traitor we've got locked in a bedroom at Rosa's house. There will be time for that later, once we've rescued Clarity and made our getaway from Sicily. I won't feel completely at ease until we've got an ocean between us and Beppe Arnoni.

The white rays of summer sun make the grass sparkle as Lotus and I skim over it, eating our tasty dessert. The cold, sweet gelato on my tongue is a fantastic contrast to the warm air on my fair skin. I loop around the park bench we scoped out earlier in the day, and take a seat in the middle, ankles crossed. From here, I can see the entire interior of the barber shop, as well as Starling, who is in the bakery next door buying a loaf of crusty ciabatta bread.

Lotus stands at my side, bouncing on his feet and eating his ice cream cone much more quickly than I am.

"We're in position," I whisper, before taking another lick of my gelato. "Mmm, this is delicious."

"Good," Royal says. "Starling, proceed."

"Confirmed. I'm heading inside," Starling responds over the earbuds. He pays for the bread, pockets his change, and strolls down the sidewalk to the barber shop.

"We've got eyes on you," I say. "Royal, we've got it from here."

"Copy that. We're heading over to Arnoni's residence now."

"Over and out," Lotus says with a snicker.

All he gets in response from Royal is a grunt.

Over the comms, the barber greets Starling. "Buon pomeriggio. I'll be right with you."

"Thanks," Starling says. The chair in the waiting area of barber shop creaks as he sits down, surreptitiously planting the tiny, lady-bug sized listening device under its seat. He leans over his watch and types a quick message.

Almost instantly a message comes through on my watch.

Starling
I dropped off the box at the post office.

Lotus and I glance at each other, and he winks at me.

Anticipation courses through my chest.

Once Starling pulls this off, we'll finally be on our way to rescuing Clarity.

Inside the shop, the barber is chatting away with the man whose hair he's cutting. I have no idea what he's saying, but the translator the consulate is sending to Rosa's house this evening will help us with that. Royal's contact called this morning to let us know they'd found a police officer we can trust, and we asked them to send him tonight, once we return from our mission.

Royal could do the translating for us, but he and Julep are busy surveilling the Arnoni residence, watching for signs of Clarity. For now, it's a waiting game.

I finish up my cone and lick the sticky residue from my fingertips. "That was so good."

"It sure was." Lotus plops down beside me and takes my hand, lacing his fingers through mine. It feels foreign and strange, sitting this close to him and holding his hand this way, but I smile and lean my head on his shoulder. It's the job, and we're doing it for Clarity.

Lotus and I keep our eyes on Starling for the next half hour while he waits for his turn with the barber. To any passersby, we look like a couple of teenagers laughing and flirting on a park bench. They'll never know we're actually teen spies staking out a mob-run business.

When it's Starling's turn in the chair, I sit up straight, eyes craned on the barber shop through the lenses of my dark sunglasses.

The barber turns to retrieve a clean pair of scissors from the top drawer of his rolling cart, and Starling plants a bug underneath it while the older man's back is turned. He makes it look so easy, I have to smile. Then he sits and relaxes into having his hair washed. "I could get used to this," he says with a laugh.

The barber chuckles, but doesn't speak as he continues washing Starling's hair.

Since the listening devices are in place and the task almost complete, I produce a Frisbee® from my drawstring backpack. "Want to play?" I ask Lotus. "We can keep an eye on him while we toss this puppy around."

"Can you play in that?" he asks, pointing to my dress, which skims the ground when I stand.

"Watch me," I say, pulling the skirt aside to reveal the slits in the sides, which make it more than possible for me to move, and run, in this dress.

"All right then," Lotus says, jogging away from me. "Ready when you are," he calls.

"Incoming!" The Frisbee® zooms through the air toward Lotus, who jumps up to catch it. He pumps his fist before making a return throw.

I catch it easily, and stop to adjust the spaghetti strap of my dress.

"Almost finished," the barber says to Starling.

I can see him in my peripheral vision, sitting in the barber's chair, facing away from the mirror. The barber works quickly, styling the dark hair with expert fingers.

"Isn't it a beautiful day?" I call to Lotus. It's my way to signal to Royal that we're almost done here.

In my ear, Royal says, "Thanks for the update."

I toss the Frisbee® to Lotus, who has to dive over the grass to catch it. When he sits up, there's a grass stain on the front of his white button-up shirt. "Oops," he says, and unbuttons it. Standing, he walks over to me and shrugs the shirt off, hanging it over the park bench.

I pretend to ogle his muscled arms and abs through his white undershirt, and he gives a cocky smile. "Like what you see?" he asks, voice low.

I act embarrassed at being caught staring, and turn away, covering my smile with my hand.

Through my earbud, Starling thanks the barber for cutting his hair, and pays.

"Grazie," the man says. "Buona giornata."

"Buona giornata," Starling responds with a slight accent. He doesn't sound half bad.

"Watch your—" Lotus yells.

It's too late. The Frisbee® beans me in the butt, and he busts up laughing.

Feigning indignation, I spin to face him. "It's not funny."

"Sorry," Lotus says, jogging over the grass toward me, feigning embarrassment. "I'm so sorry."

I pout, but say, "It's okay."

We're about to resume our game when Starling approaches us.

"Hi. I'm Derek," he says with an easy smile. "Can I play?"

My eyes turn to him and I freeze. The barber's given him a modern quiff—long on top with a fade on the sides—and it looks *good*.

Lotus elbows me, and the jolt wakes me up. "Um, sure," I say. "I'm Brittney. This is Mark."

"Hi, Brittney. Mark." Starling fist bumps with Lotus, a satisfied smile on his mouth. Did he see me looking at him? Crap.

My heart flips as I avert my eyes, pretending to dig for something in my purse. I pull out a tube of lip balm and apply it, before looking at my teammates. "Actually, I need to find a bathroom. You two go ahead."

Both guys look at me, their expressions concerned. "You okay?" Lotus asks.

"Can I get you anything?" Starling asks, a smug smile on his face.

"I'm fine, and no thanks," I say, waving them off. "Be right back." I shoot a cheery smile their way before scurrying across the road to the bakery. I have to get away from them for a minute and cool down. For the first time since Starling joined our team, I'm genuinely glad that he's here with us, but it's not because he's a good spy, although he is that. It's because I think my traitorous heart is developing feelings for him, and it has got to stop.

Chapter 16

Now that we've planted the bugs in the barber shop, we're focused on surveilling Arnoni's residence. Although Royal still plans to listen to and translate all of the sound the tiny listening devices record of the barber and his customers, it's far more likely that Arnoni is holding Clarity at his residence outside of town.

To that end, we've parked the florist van we borrowed on a hill behind the house, and set up cameras so we can see the occupants' comings and goings. It's the best we can do until Haru hacks into their security system and gets us access to the cameras Arnoni's got dotting the perimeter of his property. I'm hoping she'll be able to access any cameras he's got in the house as well, but so far no luck. For the time being, we're stuck with the footage we record from up on the hill.

It's my turn to keep watch, so I've borrowed Rosa's bike and am pedaling through town. The rubber wheels skim over the cobblestone streets, making my ride a little bumpy. Since it's after 01:00, the streets are all but deserted, and the cool air on my skin sends a pleasant shiver through me. The afternoon was hot, so the soft breeze that has risen during these hours of darkness is a welcome relief.

As I pedal, the buildings in town, which are sandwiched together like cream-colored building blocks, begin to space out. Front yards grow larger, and vegetable gardens appear. The moon is full above, and casts its blue glow on everything, as far as my eyes can see. For a fleeting moment, I smile up at it before focusing on the road ahead. The moon has been my constant companion for many years, since I started working with Royal, because much of our work is done at night. As a result, it's a soothing presence. I wonder if Clarity is sitting at a window, looking out at the moon now, too. I hope she is.

When I'm about a quarter mile away from Arnoni's house, I dismount from my bike and walk, careful not to make any noise. I pass the olive-tree lined drive that leads to the great house and push the bike farther up the hill toward an empty field covered in green growth and a few trees. Hidden above the bluff, I find the van. On the roof, there's a small antenna pointed toward the house below.

"I'm here," I say, tapping on the vehicle's sliding door.

It opens, and Julep smiles out at me. "Boy, am I glad to see you. I'm starving."

Smiling, I lift a small food container out of the bike's basket and hand it to her. "Rosa sent this for you."

Julep takes it, grinning. "Thank you. Thank you. Thank you," she says, ducking inside and motioning me to follow.

I prop the bike against the side of the van and hop inside, shutting the door behind me.

Inside, the setup is much like the one in the van in St. Petersburg. It's remarkable, really, that Royal can outfit a van for surveillance so quickly, no matter his location. Practice makes perfect, I guess.

Along one wall there's a bank of monitors, each showing a different angle of the Arnoni residence. Four cameras show the building's perimeter, and four camera angles show common areas within the home. An icon on the lower right corner of several of the monitors indicates that there is sound, but that it's turned to a low volume. From the looks of it, Haru was finally able to hack into the security feeds in the house.

"This is great," I say, scanning the feeds. "Have you seen anything interesting yet?"

Julep purses her lips. "Neither Royal nor I has seen Clarity, or Arnoni for that matter, but there aren't any cameras mounted in the upstairs portion of the house, so it's possible that she's there. Around dinner time, one of Arnoni's men took a dinner tray upstairs, looking none too happy about it. He could have been taking it to Clarity, or someone else. There's no way to know for sure, since we can't see anything up there."

"So, basically, we need to get eyes in the house, somehow."

"It would help. We can pull the architect's blueprints at the city records office tomorrow, but if Arnoni has anyone in that office, they'll alert him and he'll know someone is poking around his home."

"And he won't take kindly to that," I put in, frowning at the monitors. "We need to figure out a way to get in there without arousing suspicion, so we can map out the house and confirm Clarity's location. Then we can go back in and get her, once we know what's waiting for us."

"Royal agreed," Julep says, bumping me in the shoulder with her own. "You've got a good tactical head on your shoulders."

"Thanks," I say with a faint smile. I sink down onto the crate she was using as a seat. "Go ahead and eat. I'll take over here."

"Thanks," Julep says, opening the food container and

taking a whiff. "Oh, this smells amazing."

"It was. Seafood spaghetti and fresh bread. Just thinking about it makes me want some."

Julep tears off a piece of the bread and holds it out to me. "Here. Have some."

"You're the best," I say, taking the bread and popping it into my mouth. "Mmm."

My companion eats quietly while I sit, chewing on my bit of bread and watching the monitors. "We've got to figure out how to mount cameras in the upstairs of that house. But how?"

"That's the million dollar question," Julep says, then takes another bite of her spaghetti.

"You're telling me."

We sit in silence until she's finished eating. She wipes her mouth with a napkin and stands. "I think I'll bike to the house and get some sleep. It's late."

"Do it. I'll be fine here. Royal is sending someone for the next shift in a few hours anyway." I tap my fingers on the long, narrow shelf that holds the monitors.

Julep squeezes my shoulder with one hand. "Thanks for bringing me that food. It was delicious."

"Don't thank me, thank Rosa. She insisted."

"I like that woman more every minute." Julep smiles wide.

"Me too."

She ducks out of the van, takes the bike, and pedals away.

I put a wireless earbud into my free ear and scroll through my phone, looking for music. The metal I've been listening to for months doesn't appeal tonight. Instead, I choose the instrumental soundtrack to my favorite Marvel movie and settle in. It's going to be a long four hours.

We're at the breakfast table the next morning when a loud

knock sounds on Rosa's front door. Everyone on the team looks up, wondering who it could be. Starling is on shift in the van, but he's not scheduled to return to the house for another two hours. Even if it was him, he wouldn't knock.

And it can't be the Sicilian police officer we were expecting last night, because he never showed.

Royal stands, motioning for the rest of us to remain quiet.

I ease out of my chair and follow him, my hand at my waist holster in case I need to draw my gun in a hurry. I know he said to stay put, but there's an unexpected visitor at the door, and in our line of work that's usually bad.

We creep out of the kitchen and down the hall to the front door. It's solid, without a peep hole or window, so we can't see out. The only advantage to this is that whoever is outside also cannot see inside the house.

I take a deep, silent breath, preparing for whatever is about to happen.

Royal's eyes meet mine, and he signals for me to remain behind the door, out of sight.

I nod and step toward the wall behind the door, my pulse quickening.

He unclips the strap over his gun and removes it from its holster, holding it steady in his left hand so it'll remain hidden behind the door until he needs it. Then, he unlocks the deadbolt and pulls the door open in a gentle motion.

"Buongiorno," comes a man's voice from outside. "I'm Officer Berto Calisto. A friend at the U.S. consulate said you were in need of a translator?" The man tries to step inside, but Royal stops him with a hand to the man's chest.

I get a good look at our visitor now. He's an Italian man, about thirty, with long, curly brown hair, dark eyebrows and eyes, and a prominent nose. His skin is nicely tanned, and he's wearing a green canvas jacket over a black polo, and distressed jeans. I clock the holster under his left armpit, but don't move to engage. I'll wait for a cue from Royal.

"Whoa, sorry," the man says, taking a step back, hands raised in front of him.

"Who, exactly, sent you?" Royal's gaze is steady as he watches the newcomer, appraising him with practiced suspicion.

"Signore Campbell, from the consulate?"

"Do you have proof of identification?" Royal asks, not moving from where he stands blocking the man's entry into the house.

Over my shoulder, out of sight, Lotus and Julep have drawn close, weapons in hand.

"Sí, no problem." The man pulls a badge and photo ID out of the pocket of his jacket and shows it to Royal

Royal studies the photo and the man. "We were expecting you last night."

Calisto bows his head. "I'm sorry. I was detained at work."

Royal studies him for a long moment before nodding. "Please, come in. Thank you for helping us."

The newcomer breaks into a toothy grin as he steps into the house. "It's my pleasure." His eyes land on us, standing at Royal's back with our weapons drawn. "Who are these young people? And with guns, too?"

Royal motions for us to put our weapons away. "My team. Loveday, Julep, and Lotus. This is Officer Berto Calisto."

"Nice to meet you," I say.

"Hi," Lotus says, offering his fist to the man.

The man responds in kind, a laugh breaking from him when Lotus bumps his fist. He then turns to the rest of us. "Nice to meet you all."

Royal leads him down the hallway into Rosa's home office, where he's set up his laptop. "All of the audio we've recorded so far is in this file." He pauses, meeting Officer Calisto's eyes. "How much did Mr. Campbell tell you about our operation?"

The officer gives a mild head shake. "He told me that you're here to recover your seventeen-year-old daughter who's been kidnapped by Beppe Arnoni." He lets out a low whistle. "Why did Arnoni take her, anyway? I've been working to bring down the mafia here in Palermo for ten years, and I've never heard anything that ties them to human trafficking. If they're going down that route..." He rubs his forehead with his thumb and forefinger.

"It's not like that," Royal says. He pauses a beat, his expression unreadable.

I'm staring at him, waiting to see how much he'll tell this guy about Clarity. My heart is pounding in my chest at the thought of another person hearing about our figurative dirty laundry. Heck, I'm the only one who even knows about Clarity's biological connection to Royal. Surely he wouldn't air that little secret now, not with Lotus and Julep right behind me, watching the proceedings.

"Beppe Arnoni has reason to believe that my daughter is his granddaughter." He speaks the words in a slow, matter-of-fact tone.

Officer Calisto's eyebrows shoot up. "Is she?"

"Yes."

At this, the officer's jaw drops open. "Wait a second. I keep tabs on every single member of the Arnoni family, and I've never heard about another teenage granddaughter. He's got one, Milena, but as far as I know..."

"Arnoni believed my daughter died in the earthquake, along with—"

"Carmine and Giada." Calisto looks shocked, but confident that he's guessed correctly.

"Yes."

"So, how did this girl end up with you?"

Royal takes a slow breath. He's clearly losing patience at all of these questions, but he indulges the new guy by giving one more answer. "I was here in Palermo when the earthquake struck, and volunteered to adopt the baby. I was friends with her mother, and she wanted me to take the girl, get her away from the mafia and Beppe Arnoni."

Calisto opens his mouth to ask another question, but Royal holds up a hand. "That's enough for now. Let's get you started listening to our audio surveillance, shall we?"

Calisto purses his lips, as if holding in more questions, but then breaks into a smile. "That's why I'm here, right? Just point me in the right direction and I'll get started." He takes a pair of wireless headphones out of his jacket pocket and sets them on the desktop.

"Flag anything that might allude to where they're keeping my daughter. We're reasonably sure she's being held at Arnoni's home outside of town, but I'd like to have proof before we proceed. And if you can think of any way for us to get inside the house, other than a tactical assault, I'd like to know about it. Can you do that?"

"Sí, definitely," Calisto says as he sinks into the pale pink and green floral desk chair and places the headphones in his ears.

"Grazie," Royal says, patting the man on the shoulder with one hand. He turns and ushers us out of the room to give Calisto space to work without being hovered over, as if we're news helicopters being called off a car chase.

Royal sits down at the kitchen table and weaves his fingers

together on the wooden surface in front of him. His head falls forward as if it's grown too heavy for his neck to support, and his eyes fall to the knotted table top. It's a rare moment of uncertainty that makes my heart clench in my chest.

I slide into the chair beside him and put a hand on his elbow. My lips part to speak, but I wait until my dad looks up to meet my eyes. "We're going to get her back," I say. "And then we'll make sure that Beppe Arnoni can never come after her again."

Royal sighs and sits up in his chair, letting his hands fall to his lap. "You're right. We will." Setting his jaw, he stands. "Lotus, it's your shift in the van after Starling, so head over there at 21:40 to relieve him. Until then, everyone stay close to the house. I want to keep as low a profile as possible since it's uncertain how long we'll be here in Sicily. The fewer people who remember us, the better."

Chapter 17

Starling, Julep, and I are sitting in the living room, playing Uno with a deck we borrowed from Rosa. The older woman bustles around the house cleaning, gardening, and spending time with her menagerie in the backyard. It doesn't even phase her that we're here, invading her space. In fact, I suspect from her bubbly demeanor that she loves having us.

It's fun playing with Starling, because he hasn't been warned by Lotus about my penchant for cheating. Uno is not the easiest game to cheat at, but there are ways. When it's my turn, I wait until Starling is zoned out on his own cards, then I lay two of my own on the discard pile.

Julep snickers into her hand.

Hearing this, Starling looks up at her. "What are you laughing at?" he asks. "Got a great hand or something?"

She shrugs. "You'll see."

I glance up at the clock on the wall. Lotus's shift in the van is almost over, and Royal has just gone to relieve him. I'd better wrap up this game before he gets back and clues Starling in to the reason I've won every hand.

"Uno," Julep says.

"What?" I say, peering at her. "How'd you get down to

one card?"

"While you were focused on your own strategy, some of us were getting rid of our cards."

A smile rises to my lips. "Crafty. I like it." I lay down a Draw Four, which draws a good-natured groan from Starling. "You're killing me," he says, leaning forward to take a bunch of cards from the pile on the glass top covering the wicker coffee table.

Julep eyes the deck, then her final card.

I grin. "You can't play it, can you?" Laughter bubbles up in me at the feeling of impending victory.

Julep draws several cards before getting one she can play, and then it's my turn.

I hold my final card high in the air and slam it down on the discard pile. "Bam. I win."

Starling shakes his head. "Easy, killer. It's just a game."

"Just a game?" I ask. "Then why does it feel so good to beat your sorry butt?" I stand and do a little victory dance, which causes Julep to give her loud, trumpet-blast of a laugh.

"What's going on in here?" Officer Calisto asks, leaning into the room around the door to the kitchen.

"Just beating everyone at Uno. Why?"

Calisto smiles. "I think I've got something."

My body snaps to attention at this. "Show me."

Starling and Julep both jump up from their spots on the wicker sofa, also eager to see what Calisto has found.

"Right this way." He leads us through the kitchen to Rosa's office, sits at the laptop, and plays the audio file he's been translating. It plays for a few seconds, and a man speaking Italian can be heard over the clip of scissors, his tone boastful. Then Calisto pauses the recording and looks at us, clearly expecting a response.

"None of us speak Italian," I remind him. "That's why you're here."

"Right. I forgot." He face palms. "In that case, I'll explain. The man talking in this file is one of Beppe Arnoni's top guys in their organization. He's responsible for assigning tasks to their minions. In this clip, he's talking about sending someone out to Arnoni's for a specific job. He calls it 'babysitting duty.' Now, I don't know what he'd have to babysit out at the house..." His brown eyes are on mine as I take in his words.

I'm about to respond when the front door opens and shuts with gusto. "Honey, I'm home," Lotus calls. "Where's lunch? I'm starving."

"Is that how your mama taught you to talk?" Julep calls. "I bet it wasn't."

Lotus's laughter precedes him into the office. "But seriously, when is lunch? I've been without food in that van for hours, and I'm so hungry I could eat... What's the biggest animal you've got around here, anyway?" He aims this question at Calisto, who chuckles.

"Probably a wild boar."

"Bacon. Excellent." He pats Starling on the shoulder. "She didn't rope you into playing Uno with her, did she?"

Starling glances at Julep, his forehead wrinkled in confusion.

"Not her. Her." Lotus points at me with eyebrows raised.

"What do you mean, rope me in?" Starling asks. The corner of his mouth tugs upward at this.

"She didn't tell you? She cheats."

"I do not!" I say, defending my own spotty honor. But I can't help the smile that breaks across my face.

"You do too," Lotus says, the amusement in his voice making his words increase in volume. He turns to Starling.

"You have to keep an eye on her, or she'll do it every chance she gets."

Julep laughs, her hand covering her mouth. "You should have seen her... Discarding multiple cards, playing sixes and nines interchangeably. It was epic."

"No way!" Starling says, his voice rising to match the volume of the rest of us. "You're kidding. No."

I shrug. "Constant vigilance, new guy."

Lotus laughs harder at this.

Starling eyes me. "Impressive. But it won't happen again."

My eyebrow cocks. "Want to bet?"

"Hey. Hey, let's focus, shall we?" Julep says, gesturing toward Calisto, who is still sitting at the laptop, staring at all of us with his mouth agape.

"Right. Yes. The audio I just listened to seems to support the idea that your missing teammate is indeed at Beppe Arnoni's house. There's no other reason for Arnoni's right-hand man to station several men at the house, since Arnoni himself is away from home for the evening."

"That lines up with what I saw on the video feeds," Lotus puts in. "One of the thugs they've got out at the house was taking a dinner tray upstairs, but it wasn't to Arnoni, since he and his wife had already left the house."

"Perfect," I say, my mind humming. "So we know Clarity is at the house. Now we just need to figure out a way in."

All afternoon, my team brainstorms ways to get into the house to confirm Clarity's location and the layout of the upstairs, since it's not on any of the security feeds.

"We pose as florists, since we already have the van," Julep suggests.

"We cut their cable and go in as TV repair men, like in that one movie," Lotus says.

"I'll just sneak in one night and look around," I put in, my words edged with urgency.

Royal shakes his head each time, shooting down our ideas but putting forth none of his own.

By the time we sit down to dinner, I'm on edge. All of this waiting around is killing me.

"We're going to have to be patient," Royal says, finally. "I know it's not what you want to hear." His blue eyes are sad as he looks at me.

I exhale in frustration, and push back from the table, leaving my mostly-untouched dinner. "I need some air." The front porch is empty when I step out into the cool evening air and sit gingerly on the porch swing. The seat sways underneath me, so I push off with my feet.

My body grows heavy, so I lay down on the seat, allowing the slow swinging back and forth to relax my muscles and my mind. I put one hand behind my head and watch as the first stars begin to come out, shining in the indigo sky.

The front door opens and I move to sit up, but Starling stops me.

"You look comfortable," he says, holding a hand out. "Don't get up." He strides over to the swing and gestures toward my feet. "May I?"

I nod, my eyes never leaving his form as he lifts my feet and slides onto the swing underneath, letting my black-socked feet rest across his legs.

He takes a deep breath, watching the sky. "We're going to find a way into that house," he breathes without looking at me. His long fingers are warm on my shins, giving me something to focus on besides the restlessness that's rattling around in the pit of my stomach.

"I just wish it wasn't taking so long." I sigh, finding it hard to relax fully with his hands on me. I swing my legs off him and sit up, leaning back in the seat and tucking my feet underneath me.

Starling continues to move the swing with gentle pushes of his feet on the ground. He stretches his arm along the back of the seat and his fingers brush my shoulder once.

I intake a sharp breath at the feather-light touch, but it doesn't happen again. It must have been an accident.

After a moment, he turns his face toward mind. "Why do you call yourself Loveday? I've been wondering."

A smile creeps over my mouth. "She's a character in an old book. *The Little White Horse?*"

He shakes his head. "I've never heard of it."

"I picked it originally because the story was one of my mom's favorites, at least, according to my dad. But as I've gotten older, I realize it suits me. I'm a lot like the character, Loveday Minette."

"How so?"

"Well…" I chuckle. "She's strong, independent, and a little impulsive."

Starling grins. "No, that doesn't sound like you at all."

I laugh at his teasing. "Right?"

We fall into a comfortable silence, and my gaze returns to the sky. There are more pinpricks of light in the deepening blue canvas now. "What about you?" I ask, turning to the boy beside me on the swing. "Do you have an interest in birds? That's what starlings are, right?"

His smile is sad when he responds. "They are. When I was little, my dad and I used to go out into the country to watch them move. It's truly beautiful the way they fly in a group, their shape constantly changing."

"So, the name reminds you of your dad?"

"It does, but it also reminds me of one of my goals." He stops talking abruptly, and swallows.

We've somehow wandered into intimate territory, and I'm not sure if I should push him to continue, so I remain silent.

The porch swing glides back and forth, suspended on chains that emit quiet creaks as they move.

I'm pretty sure the conversation is over, but then Starling speaks. "Growing up, I never felt truly part of a family. I didn't have a lot of friends, so that's one of my goals: finding a group of people I can belong to, like a starling amongst his flock."

I suck in a breath, not sure what to say. If it were Lotus, I'd crack a joke about how he'll never fit in anywhere because he's such a dork, but that response feels all wrong now. I bite the inside of my lip, and whisper. "You have a home with us, if you want it."

Starling's eyes meet mine, and he smiles softly.

I return the gesture before turning to face the sky.

My stomach is in knots.

Something has shifted between us, and I don't know what it means.

Chapter 18

Since Haru was able to access Arnoni's security cameras and tap us into his system, Royal has put the kibosh on surveillance shifts in the van.

Instead, we're taking turns hovering over his laptop screen, monitoring the footage from Rosa's home office.

Currently, I'm alone in the office, hunched over the computer. It's pretty boring stuff, actually, since there aren't any cameras upstairs in the Arnoni house, where we're pretty sure they're keeping Clarity.

I arch my back and throw my arms wide, emitting a high-pitched groan as I stretch my tightly coiled muscles. Pushing to a stand, I amble into the living room, where my teammates are gathered.

Royal and Darnay are seated on the couch, the former with a book open in his lap and the latter poring over his phone.

The boys are sprawled in the floor playing a card game, and I'm pretty sure Julep is upstairs taking a nap.

I sink into a seat near Lotus and peer down at his cards, not saying anything.

He looks over his shoulder at me and smothers his cards

into his shirt. "No cheating!" he says, eyes wide. "Or helping him," he adds, gesturing to Starling with a lift of his chin.

I smirk. "I wouldn't dream of it," I tease.

"Sure," he says, drawing out the word in disbelief. Then he turns back to the game.

As soon as Lotus's back is turned, I wave at Starling to catch his attention, and signal that he should pick up any twos he finds, because Lotus needs them to win the game.

Starling chuckles, smiling at me, and shuffles through the cards in his hand.

Across from me, Royal closes his book and sets it on the wicker side table. "Lotus, Starling, let's brainstorm for a minute. Put the cards down, please."

"Yes, sir," Starling says, picking up the discard pile and adding it to the cards in his hand.

"But I was so close," Lotus exclaims, handing over his cards as well.

Royal opens his mouth to speak, but he's interrupted by Rosa, who walks into the room carrying a spare apron. "Who wants to help me make a pizza?" she asks, standing in the doorway between the kitchen and the living room.

I glance at my dad, who nods. "Go ahead. We'll fill you in at dinner."

At this, I jump up. "I'll help you, Rosa. I love pizza."

Rosa grins. "Grazie. Come with me."

"Don't let her burn it," Lotus crows after us.

"I've never seen her burn anything at the Ivory Tower," Starling says in retort.

"I was just kidding," Lotus says. I can almost hear the eye roll he gives Starling from where I am in the hallway.

"Okay, first, we make the dough," Rosa says as she squares her body in front of the smooth, marble countertop and slides the large glass bowl over toward me.

I grip it in both hands, a little nervous. Cooking at home is one thing, but with Rosa, here in a foreign place, it's totally different.

She must catch the way I'm clinging to her bowl, because she puts one arm around me and squeezes. "Don't worry, cara. I'll walk you through it."

I give her a thankful smile. "Okay. Just tell me what to do."

An hour later, I'm amazed at everything we've made. The pizza is sizzling in Rosa's large oven. There's a delicious dish of eggplant, celery, tomatoes, pine nuts, raisins, and vinegar called caponata that Rosa's just finished putting together. And the part that I'm most excited about: raw red prawns that Rosa says are so fresh they're best eaten raw with a little lemon juice. Yes, please!

"La cena è pronta. Dinner's ready," Rosa calls into the living room.

The galloping of my teammates into the kitchen sounds like the stampede scene in *The Lion King*. Chairs scrape and bump as Royal, Lotus, Julep, Starling, Darnay, and Officer Calisto find chairs at Rosa's long table.

Royal stands behind his chair, waiting for everyone to get situated.

"Do you think they're hungry?" I tease Rosa, bumping her arm with my elbow.

"It's a good thing I have such a large table," she quips in return. "Take a seat."

"Thank you."

I scan the table and my heart jumps. The only vacant seat is right next to Starling. Of course. I walk across the room and slide into the chair.

"Rosa," Royal speaks as his gaze moves over the table laden with food. "You've outdone yourself."

Rosa beams at this, batting her hand in his direction. "Di niente."

"Will you make a tray for our guest? I'll take it upstairs."

"Sì, right away." She bustles over to the cabinet, retrieves a plate and glass, and puts together a plate for the traitor, which Royal takes with a quick, "Thank you, Rosa," and leaves the room.

Rosa comes to the table and takes her place at its head. "Eat," she says, "before it gets cold."

That's all it takes. All of us reach for the platters of food, taking a portion and passing each dish around the table so everyone can serve themselves.

I load my plate with shrimp, but take a slice of pizza and some caponata as well. Honestly, I'm here for the shrimp. Crustaceans are the best.

Beside me, Starling shifts, turning his torso toward me. "Hey, you've got some... I'll get it." He reaches over with a napkin and brushes it across my cheek.

The gentle look on his face makes me freeze, and my pulse picks up. Stupid, traitorous emotions.

"Flour," he chuckles, pulling the napkin away.

"Thanks," I say, embarrassment keeping me from meeting his eyes.

Across the table, Julep is watching us, her eyes narrowed slightly.

Royal re-enters the kitchen and takes his seat at the table, pulling his napkin into his lap.

I clear my throat and look over at Rosa. "Grazie, Rosa. It's delicious!" But inside, my heart is racing completely out of my control.

"Officer Calisto," Royal says, pausing with his handful of bread in midair. "What can you tell us about Arnoni that might be useful? What family does he have? Guests in and out of the house?"

This change of course grabs my interest and slows my galloping pulse. I focus on the taste of Rosa's delicious food in my mouth, and the words being exchanged by my teammates between bites.

Calisto swallows before speaking. "He doesn't have a lot of family. He's grooming his son, Nestore, to take over the organization when Beppe retires, so he's probably not going to be willing to help us. Nestore's wife and children aren't involved in the organization, but they benefit from it. Plus, they have bodyguards. Apparently there was an incident with the little boy in the marketplace a few months ago."

I snort, which draws Calisto's attention. "You know what I'm speaking of?" he asks.

"Yeah, Clarity and I were the incident. We caught the kid pick pocketing a tourist and intended to take him to the police."

Calisto's eyebrows rise. "Ahh, I see. So you've tangled with the mafia before?"

"Well, we let the kid go when he told us who his grandfather was. Arnoni himself paid us a visit the next morning, basically threatening us if we made a fuss about the whole thing."

Calisto narrows his eyes. "Do you think Arnoni would recognize you if he saw you now?"

I shake my head. "No. I was wearing a wig and a totally different style of clothing. Plus, I was using an accent."

"That I want to hear," Lotus says. He turns to Julep. "You should hear her accents. They're hilarious."

"You're no Johnny Depp either," I retort.

"True," Lotus says with a shrug.

"Focus, everyone," Royal says, reining us in. "Back to the task at hand." He looks at Calisto. "Please continue."

Calisto smiles. "As I was saying, it would be difficult to approach any of the members of the Arnoni family without arousing suspicion. The rest of the members of the organization are from other old Sicilian families."

"None of them have teenage daughters?" Starling asks, leaning forward, elbows on the table. There's a sly smile on his face.

Calisto opens his mouth to respond, but Royal interrupts him. "I'm not having one of you pretend to woo someone to get inside the Arnoni residence alone. That would be a very dangerous predicament to get into." He shakes his head. "No, we're going to find a way to do this as a team. There has to be a way."

Julep exhales loudly. "It's really frustrating to me that I can't simply apply for a job with the Arnonis, since undercover work is my specialty." She frowns, teeth clenched.

Royal swivels his head to focus on her. "Don't beat yourself up over this. You had no way of knowing that your work in Boston would affect this particular mission. In fact, none of us could have predicted this. Besides, I don't want to get involved with Beppe Arnoni, or his household."

I bite the inside of my lip. I can't argue with the thoughts that are rising in my mind. I saw how protective Beppe Arnoni was of his grandson. If I had known Clarity was his granddaughter, I never would have let her walk around Palermo without some type of disguise on. At the time, I understood her desire to appear to the people of Sicily, her people, as herself, but now it seems like such a stupid mistake.

Calisto's eyes light up, as if he's hit on an idea. "I think I've got something."

"Go on," Royal says.

"Ferragosto is a week from Thursday. It's a national holiday. Every year Beppe Arnoni hosts a huge party at his house, with food, fireworks, live music… It would be the perfect time to get into the house. What do you think?"

Royal considers this. "How many people are usually at this party?"

"Several hundred. It would be easy for two of your people to sneak in."

"What's Ferragosto?" I ask. If this is our opportunity, I have to know everything I can about this holiday. Because there is no way I'm letting Royal send anyone into that house without me.

"It's a celebration," Calisto says, "of when Mary was taken up into heaven at the end of her life. It's been a Roman holiday for centuries. It's a huge event here in Sicily. There are feasts, parades, and boat and horse races all over Italy on that day. Here in Palermo, Beppe Arnoni's party is the largest, but others all over the city will be hosting celebrations as well."

"I could totally sneak into a party," I say, voice casual. "It wouldn't be the first time."

Royal levies his gaze at me. "I know you're capable, Loveday, but I'd still rather have a valid reason for being there. The last thing I want is for you to be caught crashing a party at a mobster's house."

"Who says I would get caught? I haven't yet," I fire back.

"I could go with her," Lotus says. "Keep an eye on her."

"Says the guy who's been locked in an arts and crafts closet!" I say, deadpan.

Julep snickers at this. "I love that story."

"It was one time!" Lotus says, laughing. "Can't a guy live down his only mistake?"

"Not a chance," I say, grinning.

Starling leans into me. "I need to hear about this closet."

I smile up at him, bobbing my head. "We—"

"Focus, everyone," Royal says, his voice raised to be heard over the rest of us.

"Sorry," I mutter to Starling. "I'll tell you later."

"Thanks."

"Royal?" I ask, trying to sound as nonchalant as possible. My fingers smooth out the cloth napkin in my lap.

His eyebrow raises. He's not buying it. "Yes, Loveday?"

"I'd like to be one of the people you send into that party, no matter what our cover is."

"Noted," Royal says, then turns to Calisto. "What other families are involved in the mafia? Is there anyone we could contact who could get us an invitation to the party at the Arnoni's?"

Calisto drones on about the other families involved in the mafia, but my attention is elsewhere. I can't get the fact that Clarity is an Arnoni out of my head. Their blood runs in her veins. What if, while she's with them, she starts to feel that it's where she belongs? What if, by the time we get to her, she's decided to stay here in Sicily? I mean, I'm one hundred percent sure she'll refuse to be involved in the mafia, but I can't be sure she won't want to get to know her grandparents, uncle, aunt, cousins… There's a whole other side of her family tree that she knows almost nothing about. It's a whole group of people who could draw her in, and keep her from returning to Washington, D.C. with me, maybe forever.

Chapter 19

I need to talk to traitorous Aunt Megan again. We need as much information about the interior layout of Beppe Arnoni's house as possible, and she's the only person I know who may have once been inside.

I drum my fingers on the table, glancing over to the sink, where Lotus and Starling are once again doing the dishes.

Rosa stands from the table and makes her way toward the back door to check on her animals before night falls.

"Rosa, wait. I think I'll come with you." Royal pushes out his chair and stands.

Now's my chance. "Dad?"

Royal stops, his mouth open slightly at my use of this familiar moniker. I don't use it often, so when I do it makes him suspicious. It occurs to me that I should start using it at random times just to throw him off, that way he won't suspect my motives every time I call him by his informal title. But, honestly, he's not wrong. Unlike Clarity, I do tend to only use it when I want something.

"Yes?" he asks, looking at me with expectant eyes.

"Can I go up and get the traitor's dinner tray?"

Royal's mouth tightens as he looks at me. "Yes, but take

Julep with you."

"I don't need an escort," I say. "I can handle myself."

Julep, who was helping clear the table, pauses, her eyes rising to look at the both of us, squaring off across the table.

Royal crosses his arms. "Take Julep, or don't go at all."

I smother a glare, managing a stiff nod instead. "Yes, sir."

Royal takes a key from his pocket and gives it to Julep before following Rosa out into the yard. The sound of Rosa's warm, friendly voice carries into the house through the open top-half of her Dutch door.

I sigh. The requirement of a chaperone for this visit chafes at my pride; I can handle myself if my aunt decides to make a move. But my irritation is deeper than that. I was hoping to ask my aunt a few questions about my mom during this conversation, and I don't feel like doing that with Julep watching over my shoulder.

"I'll stay out of your way," Julep whispers so the guys can't hear her over the running water from the faucet.

"Thanks," I say, smiling at her.

The two of us trek up the stairs together, and Julep unlocks the door to the inner room.

I sweep into the small alcove and notice that Aunt Megan has already eaten every bite of the dinner Royal brought up. "Can I get you anything?," I ask.

The woman on the cot looks up at me with a grateful smile. "No, thank you. I've had enough."

"All right." I scoop to retrieve the tray, then retreat to stand just inside the small room.

True to her word, Julep remains outside in the larger bedroom, a few feet away. Her hand is poised on her gun holster, and her eyes never move away from the traitor as she moves.

The woman on the cot motions toward the tray. "That pizza was delicious. Thank Rosa for me."

Even without turning around, I can feel Julep's gaze boring into the back of my head. I glance over my shoulder at her, giving a slight shake of my head. She gives me a prompting look, but I ignore it. I'm not telling this woman that I helped make the pizza she enjoyed so much. I don't need her approval.

"I need to ask you a few questions," I say, my voice polite and businesslike.

She clasps her hands in her lap. "I assumed as much. Go ahead. I'll help if I can."

I'm so anxious to get answers that I start talking almost before she's done. "What do you know about Beppe Arnoni's house? Have you ever been there?"

Her expression falters, then she shakes her head. "I've never been to his house. Whenever we spoke, it was either on the phone, or in my classroom in town."

My shoulders sag. "You've never even been on the grounds?"

She frowns. "I'm sorry."

I cast around for another approach. Maybe she knows more than she realizes. "Did he ever mention his house to you? Any details?"

This draws a vigorous head shake. "He was always very private about his family. I was surprised that he actually told me who I was looking for when he sent me to the States to look for his granddaughter."

"So, why did he send you to look for Clarity?"

She bites the inside of her lip. "He said I could do it as a personal favor for him, since his grandson was having such a hard time in my class. Really, that boy was a huge handful, but try telling that to Beppe Arnoni. He implied that if I didn't, I'd be physically harmed."

"He threatened you."

"Yes."

"And you've never been anywhere near his house, nor do you have any clue about the interior layout, security, or anything?"

She drops her head. "No. I'm sorry."

I sigh, pinching the bridge of my nose between my thumb and pointer finger.

She reaches out, whispering my name.

I recoil. "Don't call me that."

The woman flinches and draws away, but finds the courage to speak under my withering glare. "I didn't think about what losing Clarity would do to you. I was blinded by hatred of your father. I'm sorry."

My instincts tell me she's not lying. I glance over my shoulder to where Julep is standing. I'd like to talk to her a little more, but now isn't the time. I'll have to wait until I can do this without an audience.

"Thanks." I spin and leave the room. "Lock up, will you?" I ask Julep as I brush past her.

"You know it," she responds, closing the inner door as I step out into the hall.

All that's left for me to do now is wait.

After breakfast, Julep announces she's going for a walk, since it's not her turn to monitor the video feeds. "I need some fresh air," she says, stretching her arms wide. She sneaks a glance at Lotus as she leaves the room.

Starling, who is sitting on the wicker sofa working on another crossword on his phone, doesn't look up. "Enjoy!" he calls after her.

I attempt to read the book in my lap, a science fiction story about a teenage girl and her murderous AI, but I can't focus. I'm clocking the minutes, waiting for Royal and Darnay to leave the house. They're supposedly going to return the van to its owner, but they're taking forever in the office, scanning through the video footage I already watched early this morning.

After only a couple of minutes, Lotus stands up and moves toward the kitchen. "I need a snack. Anybody else hungry?"

"No, thank you," Starling says, nose still buried in his phone.

"No," I say when Lotus's eyes fall on me.

"All right," he says before going into the kitchen. It's quiet for a minute, and then the hint of a squeak from the back door opening and closing reaches my ears. It sounds like Lotus has snuck out of the house to join Julep. I shake my head.

"You heard that, huh?" Starling asks, his voice low.

My eyes rise to meet his. "Lotus isn't very subtle."

Starling chuckles at this. "No, he isn't." He goes back to his phone, typing with his thumbs.

"What are you doing over there?" I ask.

Starling's eyes lift to mine. "Crosswords."

"You like those, huh?" I want to kick myself as soon as the question leaves my lips. What a brainless thing to say. Of course he likes them. I've seen him working on them a few times over the past few weeks.

Amusement lights his eyes. "Yeah, I like them. The ones I do, they're cryptic crosswords, so you have to work out the clues themselves, first. It's a good brain exercise."

"Brain exercise. Neat." Neat? I should swear off talking, right now.

He chuckles. "Want to give it a try?"

"I'd better not, seeing as how I'm about as sharp as a sock today."

"Now, now. We can't have the witty banter all the time."

"Who says?" I ask in mock horror.

Starling shrugs, and we fall silent again.

My eyes fall to my book, but it's impossible to focus. The words swim across the page. I glance toward the office, but can't see inside. The door is almost completely closed. Why won't Royal and Darnay hurry up and leave already?

Finally, the office door opens. Royal and Darnay tromp into the living room, talking quietly about their planned visit to the consulate while they're in town today. Darnay looks dapper as usual in a cream-colored suit, crisp white shirt, and burgundy tie. His brown penny-loafers shine in the morning sunlight streaming in the window. Royal looks more casual in his gray slacks, pale blue button-up with sleeves rolled up to his elbows, and his top button undone.

"Don't go anywhere while we're gone," Royal says to no one in particular, but his eyes are locked on me.

"Don't worry. I won't," I say, holding up my book. "I'm reading."

Royal watches me for a beat, as if he's weighing the likelihood of me actually reading a book the entire time he's gone. Whatever he sees must satisfy him, because he follows Darnay out the front door, locking it behind him.

As soon as Royal pulls the van out of the drive, I put my tattered Captain America bookmark in place and hop up, leaving my book on the now vacant chair. I stalk past Starling, avoiding looking at him, and jog up the stairs.

"Where are you going?" he calls after me.

"Nowhere," I respond. It's none of his business. Plus, I'm not sure how he'd feel about breaking Royal's rules, so it's better if he doesn't get involved. I creep down the hall to the room Royal and Darnay are sharing, but the door is locked. Lucky for me, I know how to pick quite a few different types of locks. This one's easy—the doorknob has a hole in the center of it—so all I have to do is retrieve a paperclip from my utility belt, and the door is open in seconds. I slide into the narrow space and close the door carefully behind me so if anyone else comes upstairs they won't know I'm inside.

The interior of the room is shadowed, the curtain over the window pulled closed.

I push the soft curtain aside and check outside, making sure the van is nowhere on the road. It wouldn't do to be caught in here if Darnay and my dad had to come back to the house for something. The coast is clear, so I turn my attention to the inner door. Picking the lock on this second door is almost as easy; all it takes is a couple of the small tools I keep in my belt, and the lock clicks open. I return the tools to their place before turning the knob and pushing the door open.

The traitor is sitting cross-legged on the cot, eyes wide. "You're not Mr. Darnay," she says, the surprise apparent in her voice and in the pink tinge on her cheeks.

"No, I'm not." I stand in the doorframe, arms across my chest, hovering between the two spaces, unsure of what I'm doing now that the door is literally open to me.

Silence hangs in the air between us.

The traitor shifts on the cot, sliding her feet down to the floor, and tries again. "Are you here to take me to the bathroom? I could use it."

I could take her, but I don't have any weapons on me. My sidearms are stowed safely in my case under my bed. I'm pretty sure I could subdue the woman before me if she tries to escape, but I'd rather not take the chance. "I'll take you. Give me one minute." I lock the door again and sneak down the hall to my room to retrieve my tranquilizer gun. There's no sense in risking it if there's a quick and easy way to put her down if she tries anything funny.

Starling catches me red handed, coming out of my room with my tranq gun gripped in my right hand. "What are you doing up here?" he asks, eyes appraising me before sliding down the hall toward Royal's room, where the door is ajar.

"The prisoner needs to use the bathroom," I say, standing up straight and meeting his skeptical gaze.

"That's all?" he asks. He's standing in the middle of the hallway, feet hip-width apart, arms crossed over his chest. His black T-shirt pulls at his shoulders, drawing my attention.

He clears his throat, and I almost jump. Almost.

I force my eyes up to his face, instead of where they want to go, which is anywhere else.

"Are you sure you're not up here carrying out a grand scheme?"

I holster the gun and put my opposite hand on my hip. "What do you take me for? An amateur?"

"Hardly," Starling says, looking at me with appreciation in his eyes.

"Cut it out," I say. "Don't look at me like that."

"As you wish," he says, uncrossing his arms and holding his hands up, palms out. "But I think I'll tag along."

"So we can all chat about girly things in the bathroom?"

"Oh, please," he says. Then, "Lead on."

He follows me up the hall and into the now unlocked room.

I hesitate at the inner door, because if he sees me picking the lock he'll know this is an unsanctioned activity. But there's no help for it. "Hold this." I hand him my tranquilizer gun

125

before taking the tools out of my pocket and picking the lock.

"Did Royal forget to leave the key?" the boy beside me asks, watching over my shoulder. The nearness of him sends crackles of electricity through me. It's as if his body and mine operate on a shared frequency, and when we're in close proximity my nerves hum in recognition of a like body. I wonder if he feels it too.

I square my shoulders and focus on the task at hand, tightening my grip on the lock-picking tools between my fingers. "Something like that," I say as the door swings inward.

My aunt's eyes are even bigger this time. "He's not coming with us, is he?" she asks, her face pale with embarrassment.

I shake my head. "No. We'll both wait outside." I emphasize the last word with a glance at our tall, dark, and woodsy scented companion.

"I'm so disappointed," he deadpans.

I snicker at this. "Let's go. And no sudden moves."

My aunt stands. "I won't." She leads the way down the hall and into the bathroom.

I step in behind her, scanning the room for anything she could use as a weapon. There's nothing here that an untrained civilian could use in any effective way. The bar of soap sits on a washcloth by the sink rather than in a dish, and there are no razors or shaving equipment anywhere in the cabinets. There isn't a plunger or toilet brush either. Even the curtain rod is bolted to the wall. Satisfied, I take a step back. "We'll be right outside."

"Thanks," she says as I swing the door closed, leaving it cracked an inch.

I lean against the wall, my hand on my tranquilizer gun, my head resting against the cool, faintly textured, yellow wall.

Starling does the same, mere inches from where I'm

standing. His arm brushes mine for a second, and tingles run up my arm. He adjusts, and we're no longer touching. It's like he's trying to tease me into… No. I have to focus. I can't go there right now.

"You didn't just come up here to escort your aunt to the bathroom, did you?"

I turn my face to look up at his without lifting it from the wall. "She needed a bathroom break. I obliged."

His deep-set brown eyes study my vivid green ones. "But that's not why you came up here."

I swallow. "How do you know that?"

He reaches up one hand to run it over his freshly trimmed quiff, and looks at me. "It's exactly what I would do, in your situation." His voice drops to a whisper. "If there was someone who could tell me anything about my mom, anything at all, I'd do everything I could to spend time with that person."

A pang shoots through me at his words. They're a reminder that I'm not the only one who lost my mom at an incredibly young age. In fact, of all of us, Haru is the only one who still has both of her parents at all.

In the bathroom, the toilet flushes, then the sink begins to run. My aunt is almost done in there, which means this conversation with Starling is nearly over.

I look into his eyes, trying to convey my sincerity when I say, "I'm sorry about your mom. It sucks."

He nods in agreement, and his mouth opens.

The bathroom door swinging open cuts him off. My aunt steps into the hallway. "I'm finished. Thank you." Her eyes linger on us for a second, but then she moves past us into the room whence we came.

We follow her inside, the electricity I'd felt between us diminished.

Dutifully, the woman walks into the inner room and sits on the cot.

"Can we get you anything else?" I ask from where I stand in the doorway. "A glass of water?"

She gives me a faint smile. "That would be great."

I look at Starling, who nods. "I'll be right back," he says, and leaves the room. His footsteps echo along the hallway, but go silent once he reaches the stairs.

I focus on my aunt, willing myself to ask the question that's at the tip of my tongue.

Her head tilts as she looks at me. "What is it?" she asks.

I let a breath out through my nose. "What was she like?" I whisper.

The woman smiles. "She was beautiful, but she was also loving and kind. She enjoyed cooking. She was always trying new recipes." Her eyes start to sparkle as she talks about her sister, my mom.

I relish in this conversation. Every bit of information about my mother is like gold to be squirreled away and remembered at a later date. I don't want this woman before me to stop. I wave my hand for her to continue.

"One time in high school she tried to make homemade ravioli, but she cooked them too long and they burst. It turned into a sticky, gooey mess. We tried to eat it, but…" She trails off, making a disgusted face.

I laugh, and try to picture my mom as a teenager, worried about if her ravioli is going to come out all right. It's a far cry from the worries I've been experiencing over the past year. The stark differences between my mom's teenage years and mine are painful reminders that my life is radically different from hers, and not all of it is good. When she was my age, my mom still had both of her parents. My mouth sinks down into a frown.

My aunt seems to sense this change in my emotional state, because she changes course. "She was funny, your mom. She was good at making people laugh. She had lots of friends in high school, and in college too, but then…" Her voice dies, and her expression grows hard.

"Then?" I prompt her, leaning my shoulder against the door frame.

"She met your dad." This is said with a shrug. "They got serious really fast, but she kept finding excuses not to bring him home to meet us. We thought she was afraid to introduce him to us, like there was a reason we wouldn't approve." She purses her lips, and pulls one foot up onto the cot and underneath her.

"What happened when you did meet him?"

"It went great. At least, my parents and I thought so. We all met for dinner, and your dad was charming, handsome, and friendly. He was a few years older than my sister, but it didn't seem to matter to them. I remember thinking he was pretty smooth." Her fingers trace the seam of her jeans as she talks. "But after that, whenever she would come home, whether it was for a simple visit or a holiday, he didn't come with her. We didn't understand it. And, slowly, she became distant with us. I knew it was his fault. I just didn't know why."

"He was trying to protect you, all of you," I say. "Our job, his job, it's not without risks."

When she looks up at me, her entire expression has changed. Her eyes are narrowed, eyebrows pushed together, and mouth drawn down in a frown. "You don't think I know that? I lost my sister, because of him. Because they had a fight about his job. She was upset, so she was bringing you to stay with me for a couple days, and she died. That fight, it killed her. And I'll never forgive him for it."

The sound of a car door shutting outside catches my attention, and I cross to the small window to look down at the drive.

Royal and Darnay are stepping out of a taxi and coming toward the house.

I duck down so they won't see me. "I have to go," I say, moving toward the door. "Thanks for talking to me." I bite my lip, unsure of how much I should say to this woman who is still so obviously angry about the death of her sister, even though it happened more than sixteen years ago. "And try not to hate my dad. He loved her so much, and he didn't mean to kill her." I close the door and lock it before she can respond, and then I'm out of there.

I run smack into Starling in the hallway, who holds up a glass of water. "I guess we don't need this?" he asks.

"No," I say. "I need some air." I brush past him and run down the stairs, hoping to get outside before Royal and Darnay see me. I need some time to process everything my aunt just told me, and I'd much prefer to do it alone.

The hall is shrouded in darkness as I creep out of my room and tiptoe down the hall, past the boys' room. The faint sounds of snoring emanate from inside, making me wonder which one of them is the snorer. The hope that it's Lotus and not Starling rises to the front of my mind, making me pause. I really have to stop thinking about things like that. I give myself a mental shake and push forward.

A cricket stops chirping as I tiptoe down the hall. I pause again, but the house is silent.

My knuckles make a light knocking sound as I tap on Royal's bedroom door. He opens it, hair mussed and eyes blinking to clear away the sleep. "What is it?" he asks, stifling a yawn.

"Sorry, did I wake you?" I ask, feigning ignorance. I know I woke him; it's 03:00 in the morning.

"Is there a point to this early morning visit?" He leans his forearm against the doorframe, bracing himself against the stained wood.

"I've been thinking. We need a way into Arnoni's house, right?"

His head bobs. "Yes." The word is slow, hesitant, like he's reticent to hear whatever I'm about to say.

My eyes flit over his shoulder to where Darnay is sprawled out in his bed, asleep, and past him to the inner room, behind which my traitorous aunt is, no doubt, also sleeping. I pull them back to Royal's face to see that he's already frowning. He must have followed my gaze, and with it, my train of thought. He opens his mouth to speak, doubt etched into the lines of his face.

I reach out for the hand at his waist, and grasp it. "Please. Just think about it. She has a relationship with Arnoni. Maybe she could take me to the house and find some pretence for going inside, even for five minutes. It would give me all the time I need to get a look around, and see where exactly they're holding Clarity."

His mouth is a grim line. "You're talking about a woman who teased you for months, making you think you were seeing your mother again. She led Arnoni to your sister, knowing that he would kidnap her with no plan to ever let her go, and now you're asking me to let you go into that house alone with her? No. Absolutely not."

My shoulders sag. "I don't know another way. She's our best option."

"I refuse to believe that."

"Why? Just because she doesn't like you? I could control her. Besides, I don't think she'd do anything to physically hurt me..." I trail off, not even sure I believe the words I'm saying.

"No. Don't ask again." He pushes off the door frame and lets loose another yawn. "We'll go through the surveillance footage again tomorrow and study their habits. We'll find a different approach."

I grit my teeth. "Fine. Okay." I turn to go, but his hand on my elbow stops me.

"Loveday."

I swivel to face him, my eyes pricking in frustration. "What?" I whisper-yell.

He studies me, his eyelids drooping over tired eyes. The lines around his mouth are fuzzy in the dark. "We'll find another way. One that is less risky. And we'll get her back. Just be patient."

"You know that isn't my strong suit," I whisper, quieter this time.

Royal squeezes my elbow. "I know." He leans forward, as if he's about to give me a hug, and I stiffen, not sure what to expect.

He must see my tense response, because he withdraws into the shadow of his room. "See you in the morning," he whispers, and then the door closes behind him.

Without Clarity, it feels as if the space between us is widening more each day, and soon it'll be so large we won't be able to bridge the gap. Without her, it seems, my relationship with Royal, my father, is crumbling. It's one more reason I have to get Clarity back, before the expanse is so large there's no way to cross it, and my connection with Royal is severed forever.

Chapter 20

My eyes start to glaze over as I stare at Royal's laptop screen, noting any movement that goes on inside the Arnoni residence. We're studying their schedule. We have to know every detail: times that it's likely one or both Beppe and his wife leave the residence, what rooms they're in at any given hour of the day, how many other people are at the house, security measures, the works. The Ferragosto celebration is our best bet for getting into the house to rescue Clarity, but we've got to think of a way to get inside before next week so we can scope it out. It'll be infinitely harder to bust Clarity out if we go in sight unseen.

I'm typing everything into a spreadsheet on the laptop when someone on the screen catches my eye. It's a teenage girl. She can't be much older than me, but she's much more stylish, caramel brown hair coiffed in effortless waves, designer sunglasses and bag, high heels strapped to long, tanned legs. Reaching down to the spacebar with my thumb, I pause the footage. "Officer Calisto?" I call into the other room, where he's chatting with Royal about their experiences with the criminal element here in Palermo. It's a conversation I would love to be in on, frankly, if circumstances were different. I bet Calisto's getting more details about Royal's work than I've gotten in my entire life. But this surveillance, rescuing Clarity, is vastly more important. So I sit at the desk taking detailed notes while the footage scrolls across the laptop screen in harshly contrasted color.

"Si?" Calisto pokes his head into the office.

"Who is this?" I wave him forward and point at the laptop screen.

He leans down to peer at the screen for a moment before standing again, resting his thumbs in his brown leather belt. "That's Arnoni's granddaughter, Melina. She's about nineteen, I think?"

"You said she's not involved in the mafia, right?"

He shakes his head. "No."

I snap my fingers. "She's our in, our way into the house." I turn to face our Italian friend. "What's her friend situation like?"

"Er, what do you mean?"

"Sorry. Let me try another way. Does she have a lot of good friends? And what are they like?"

He shrugs. "She spends a lot of time with a girl whose the daughter of one of Arnoni's associates, but other than that... Many of the young people leave Sicily to attend university elsewhere, and most of Melina's friends have gone."

I sit in rapt attention. Every detail he gives me is vital to the success of the plan forming in my brain. "Why did she stay here?"

"I'm not positive, but I think it was because she is very close to her Nonna. In addition, her boyfriend lives and works here. He's quite a few years older than her, attended university abroad, then returned to join his father's business."

"So, she doesn't have a lot of friends, is what I'm hearing."

"That is correct."

"Perfect." I'm out of my chair and brushing past where Calisto is standing before he has a chance to ask me what is so perfect about Melina Arnoni's situation here in Sicily.

The chattering in the living room grows louder as I draw close. Darnay's horsey laugh is the most pronounced.

I burst into the room with a flourish, and all eyes swivel to me. Royal, Julep, Starling, and Darnay stare up at me, waiting expectantly.

"Where's Lotus?" I ask, scanning the room for him. "He's essential to my plan."

"He's out helping Rosa milk her goat." Amusement dances on Julep's face as she points toward the back of the house.

I smirk. "That will never not be funny."

"I know, but I think he's hoping she'll teach him how to make goat cheese. And you know how much he loves that stuff."

I laugh. "Oh, man, do I know."

Royal clears his throat. "Can we get to the reason you burst in here and interrupted our conversation?" He eyes me, curiosity behind those baby blues.

"Sure." I pause, grinning for effect. "Drumroll, please?"

Starling cocks his head, but plays along, drumming his fingers on the glass top of the coffee table. He finishes with an imitation of crashing cymbals, then looks at me.

"Thank you!" I clasp my hands together in excitement. "I know how we're going to get access to the Arnoni residence," I say, arms flung wide.

"How?" Royal asks as he leans forward, resting his forearms on his knees.

"Yes, do tell," Darnay adds, smiling up at me with a cheeky expression.

I force down the urge to roll my eyes, choosing to ignore him instead. "Calisto, here," I pause again, smacking the man standing beside me in the chest with the back of my hand, "has just informed me that Arnoni has a granddaughter about my age who is in desperate need of friends. I am going to be that friend."

Julep's eyebrows push inward and she opens her mouth to speak. "How to you plan to do that? Force her to be friends with you?"

I grunt. "Of course not. We'll follow her around for a few days to learn her schedule, and then we'll stage a meet-cute. I'll ingratiate myself to her and convince her to take me to her grandparents' house. I'll tell her I'm interested in Italian architecture or something." I wave my hand. "That's not the point. The point is that she needs friends, and I need a way into the Arnoni house. We can use her situation to our advantage."

Royal sits back in his chair and steeples his fingers. "It's a stretch, but it might work."

"It's definitely going to work," I say. "Trust me."

Starling lifts his hand. "I have a question."

"Shoot."

He bites his lip before continuing. "You aren't exactly... friendly with strangers. How are you going to pull this off?"

I glower at him. "I'll have you know I'm perfectly capable of being charming and sweet."

He snorts. "That, I'd like to see."

"Too bad for you. You're not who I have in mind."

"You're getting ahead of us," Royal says.

"Sorry," I say. "It's just that I'm excited about this. We've been waiting around for what feels like forever trying to make headway in this mission, and I've finally figured it out."

"Don't keep us in suspense," Julep says, smiling. "Go on."

"Per Royal's instructions, I can't go in alone, so I'm bringing a friend."

Julep shakes her head. "I can't go with you, remember? One of Arnoni's men could recognize me from Boston." She pulls her long braids forward over her shoulder and runs her fingers through them, frowning.

"I know. That's why I'm not bringing just any friend, I'm bringing a boyfriend."

As if I had timed it, the kitchen door opens and Lotus strolls into the room, a bucket of goat milk held in one hand. "What's everyone—"

Before he can react, I grab him by the front of his black tee-shirt and pull him toward me, landing my lips on his.

Lotus freezes, his entire body tense against my fingers.

Julep gasps.

And that's when I feel it: kissing Lotus feels like kissing my brother, and it's awful. No, it's not just awful, it's truly horrible. Like, that is never ever happening again in my lifetime kind of horrible.

I push him away, spluttering. "Yuck."

Lotus merely blinks at me, not believing that I've just kissed him in front of our entire team, and then some. "What... what was that?" he asks, mouth agape.

I shake my head. "That's not going to work. Not at all. Have a seat."

Lotus's eyes are wide as he scoots away from me, not daring to look away. He sinks down onto the couch beside Julep and murmurs something to her that sounds an awful lot like, "That was really weird." The bucket of goat's milk makes a low thunk as he sets it down on the floor.

Julep pats his knee in response, and whispers, "Pretty much."

Beside them, Darnay is hunched forward on the couch with his hand clamped over his mouth. From the mirth in his eyes I can tell that he's doing his best to stifle a burst of gleeful laughter.

Royal clears his throat, and stands. "That was an interesting demonstration," he says, glancing at Darnay. The sight of his friend in such a state cracks his calm demeanor, and both of the men burst into guffaws of laughter.

"His face," Darnay says, slapping his knee. "I can't believe it."

"I know," Royal says through a loud chuckle.

"She took me by surprise, is all," Lotus says, scratching the back of his neck furiously. "I can try it again if you..."

"No!" Julep and I yell at the same time. "There is never going to be a reason to repeat that," I finish.

Even so, my heart speeds up. I'm losing my audience. "Wait. This can still work. Just not with Lotus." My eyes lock on Starling, and the room goes quiet.

His deep-set brown eyes meet mine and a jolt of electricity crackles around the room, making goosebumps rise on my arms.

I'm frozen in place as he stands without taking his eyes off me. He seems shockingly tall and handsome at this moment, and I fight the urge to retreat from him. If I'm going to get Clarity back, I need to get into that house. In order to have any chance of getting into that house, I have to have a plan. And Royal insists I take a partner. Starling, this devastatingly gorgeous boy who is moving toward me with a sense of purpose in every movement, is my best shot at that. I take a deep breath to slow my thudding heart, and remain where I am in the middle of the room.

Starling moves closer to me and squares his body up to

mine, a hair's breadth away. "Are you sure about this?" he whispers. His soft breath caresses my face.

My tongue sticks to the roof of my mouth, which has gone completely rogue and refuses to cooperate, so I merely nod in response.

Gingerly, Starling lifts his hands and cradles my face between his warm fingers. "Ready?" That one word sends anticipation scorching through me.

I nod again, and he bends to meld his lips with mine.

I sink into him, wanting to forget that we have an audience. The sensation of Starling's mouth on mine sends longing through my entire being. All I want is to press closer, deeper into his embrace. My hands ache to push upward into Starling's thick, black hair, but I will them to remain where they are at his sides.

The hairs on the back of my neck stand up, and not in a good way. The awareness of someone standing just beside us, peering down at me breaks me out of the kiss. I swivel my face to look up at none other than Royal, who is watching me with a probing expression. His eyes slide downward from mine to where Starling's hands are still cupping my jawline.

Starling clears his throat and steps away from me, dropping his hands to his sides.

Tension mounts. If Royal doesn't go for this, if he sees more than a professional interest between Starling and me, he'll shut my idea down before I can blink. I force my body to remain still, relaxed, under his gaze, willing Royal to agree to my plan.

After a beat, Royal speaks. "That will work." He claps a hand on my shoulder, weighing me down. "Make it so." And then he leaves the room.

"Royal, wait!" Darnay calls, standing and striding out of the room after his friend.

Calisto shrugs and follows them, casting a quick glance at us.

My gaze turns to Julep and Lotus, who are both staring up at Starling and me from their spots on the couch, eyes wide.

Julep takes a long sip of her ice water, sets it on the coffee table, and stands. "Do you two need to be alone? Because..." She trails off, her eyes hopping between Starling's face and mine.

"No," I say, too quickly, in answer to Julep's question. "We're professionals. This is all part of the job." I smooth my black tee with both hands.

Julep nods, slowly, her skepticism clear in her voice. "Right. Part of the job."

Lotus quirks an eyebrow at Starling and me, the bucket of goat's milk still gripped in his hand. "Yeah." He motions toward the kitchen with his free hand. "I'm gonna go help Rosa make some cheese." He shuffles out of the room, careful not to slosh the creamy liquid in the bucket out onto the floor.

Starling clears his throat, watching me.

I give him a half-hearted smile. Frankly, I don't believe a word I'm saying either.

Chapter 21

The first part of my plan is the easy part: watch Melina Arnoni for a few days to learn her schedule. Calisto told us that Melina works at her boyfriend's olive oil plant, in the little shop attached. Her job is to facilitate tastings for hungry tourists, plying them with olive oil and bread pairings, along with ample amounts of wine in an attempt to get them to buy and carry home expensive bottles of freshly pressed olive oil.

Lotus has already insisted that we should all go to one of these tastings, because it sounds fancy, and also because Lotus loves free food.

Julep was quick to point out that it isn't actually free; you're expected to buy something after the tasting is over. At this point, Lotus shot a pointed glance at Royal, who didn't blink in return. "I'm not buying a thirty dollar bottle of truffle-flavored olive oil just so you can eat some free bread and cheese."

"You're no fun," Lotus retorts, sticking out his thick bottom lip in a faux pout.

Julep bumps him in the arm. "Once we get Clarity back, ask him again. He'll be so happy he won't even notice you picking his wallet clean."

Lotus grins. "Good idea."

"Don't encourage him," Royal says to Julep, but the tone of his voice suggests amusement rather than the exasperation that was there a minute before.

"It's true. Once we get Clarity back, we should celebrate," I say. "Once we're at a safe distance from our soon-to-be enemies, the Sicilian mob." I turn to Julep. "They don't have a strong contingent in D.C., do they?"

Julep purses her lips. "I don't think so."

My eyes narrow. "Royal?" I ask, concern edging my voice. "What's going to prevent Arnoni from sending someone to Washington, D.C. to kidnap Clarity again? It's not like she can hide in the Ivory Tower forever."

Royal studies his palm for a moment before casting his eyes toward Calisto.

"Ideally," the man says slowly, "we will arrest Beppe Arnoni for kidnapping, which will result in him being put in prison for quite a length of time. I'm hopeful that, once he is behind bars, the rest of the organization will not be as motivated to come for your sister a second time."

"That seems like a pretty big, 'if.'" My gaze slides from the officer to my dad.

He looks at me, his eyes mirroring the worry that I know is apparent in mine. "We'll find another way to keep her safe."

I'm quiet, hoping he'll elaborate, but he doesn't.

Now, in the quietness of the car, I look over at Julep. "We'll be able to keep Clarity safe once we get home, right?"

She looks over at me and frowns. "It won't be easy, but we'll find a way. Trust Royal and Calisto. Between them, they have plenty of experience in these types of situations. I'm sure they're working on a plan this very moment."

142

That night, after dinner, Rosa puts the boys to work doing all of the dishes. They're standing side by side at the sink, Lotus doing the scrubbing and Starling doing the drying. I haven't done dishes since we got here, and I can't say I'm disappointed. They're easily my least favorite housekeeping chore.

Darnay excuses himself from the table to make some calls, and disappears up the stairs. Calisto has long since left for home, and Julep has retired to the living room, where she's sitting listening to music with wireless earbuds while she knits a pair of socks. Apparently her grandma is super picky about the socks she wears; she'll only wear them if Julep makes them. So Julep makes a bunch of pairs of soft, fuzzy socks each summer and sends them home to her ninety-year-old grandma down in Georgia.

I'm still sitting at the table, pushing the last bits of my dinner around my plate. The scene from earlier this afternoon replays in my head: the kiss, the wide-eyed stares, the probing look Royal gave me afterward. It plays on a loop, over and over. At times, I want to speed up the memory so I can relive it as many times as possible. Other times, I wish I could slow it down and savor each detail of that mind-blowing kiss.

Royal's hand on my shoulder breaks me out of my reverie. "Take a walk with me," he says, and nods toward the door. From the set of his mouth and the pronounced creases around his eyes, it's not a request.

"Okay." I scrape the food debris from my plate into the garbage, hand the plate to Lotus, and follow Royal outside.

We step out into the late evening, and a cool breeze floats around us, ruffling my hair. The sun is sinking toward the horizon, but it's not yet gone. Streaks of fuschia and cerulean blaze across the summer sky, catching my eye and drawing me to a stop on the back step. "Look at that," I say, my voice breathy.

"It's beautiful," Royal says, but his tone is dismissive. He hasn't asked me out here to talk about the sunset. There is something else on his mind. The man steps down off the step, and Rosa's rooster comes skimming over the ground toward him, his tiny head cocked to the side and his beady eyes swiveling toward Royal's hands. "I don't have anything for you," the man says to the chicken, who remains where he is, unfazed.

Inwardly, I recoil away from the scruffy bird. The disgust must be apparent on my face, because Royal's mouth eases. "He won't hurt you."

"Sure," I say, but I tiptoe around the bird all the same.

Royal leads me around the house toward the road.

We walk in tense silence between the trees—olive, cypress, oak—their leaves bathed in the last orange glow of the setting sun. The pebbles on the path crunch underneath our shoes. The sound reverberates in the quiet of evening, punctuated by the last calls of birds settling in their nests.

My eyes rise to the indigo dome above us, but it's still early. There aren't any stars winking into the blue just yet. They're biding their time, until the sun forfeits its last vestiges of dominion over this day.

"About earlier," Royal says, and I lower my chin to meet his eyes.

"Yes?" I won't say more, because I'm not sure where he's going with this conversation and I don't want to provide him any ammo. I can't get benched again on the night before we put our plan to rescue Clarity in play.

"I don't have to describe for you the consequences of getting emotionally involved with a teammate, do I?"

My teeth clench. I will never forget the aftermath of my relationship with Vale, his death, or the gut-wrenching turmoil I've experienced over the past nine months. "No."

"Because that kiss, it looked an awful lot like the real thing."

"It wasn't. It's just that I haven't known Starling as long, so it's not weird like it was kissing Lotus."

"Are you sure?"

I stop on the path, hands on hips. "I'm positive. I won't make the same mistake again."

Royal's head dips. His eyes skim the ground before rising to meet mine. "It's been a long time since I was a teenager, but I still remember wanting to be close to someone. I know you must feel that—"

"Dad! It's not about that. It was just a kiss. Nothing more."

His expression softens, and my heart warms. "I'm trying to protect you," he says, his voice soft. "Sometimes I forget that you're still so young. That all of this, it's not normal for people your age." His voice hitches in his throat. "Do you even want this life? Because you can get out. Go to college. Get a regular job. Do normal adult things."

I shake my head, smiling. "You're forgetting that I'm the one who forced you to let me in. Remember? Two eleven-year-olds scooping your bump and grab from right under your nose?"

He smiles at this. "I was so proud of both of you, I couldn't see straight."

It's been a long while since I've heard those words from him. "Thanks, Dad."

He puts an arm around me and squeezes gently. "Let's go back, shall we?"

"Yeah."

We turn and meander in the direction we came.

I lean into him. "Dad?"

"Yes?"

"We're getting Clarity back from those brainless toads."

A half-smile cracks his serious features. "Yes, we are."

Chapter 22

Julep stands at the front window, watching the road. Our taxi is on the way to the house to pick us up for a quick shopping trip in one of the city's most famous streets. She convinced Royal that if I want to ingratiate myself to Melina Arnoni, I have to look the part of a rich college student on vacation, and the black on black on black I brought won't do it. So, he agreed to this outing.

I'm sitting on the couch jiggling my knees. "I've never gone shopping without Clarity," I say. "She tells me what looks good on me and what to steer clear of. She's the one who's good at shopping, not me."

"I'm not too shabby either," Julep says, smiling at me over her shoulder.

My head tips. "You're not. You always look great."

Her smile brightens. "Thanks."

Julep's attention goes to the window. Her fingers pull the gauzy white curtain aside so her view of the drive is unobstructed.

The house is quiet. Lotus insisted on dragging Royal, Starling, and even Darnay on a hike around the area. He said the lack of physical activity, coupled with all of the delicious food Rosa's been cooking up, was making him go flabby. His fifty push-ups per day weren't cutting it. The thought of Darnay going on a hike strikes me as funny, and a smile flashes over my face.

"This will be your longest time using one alias, right?" Julep asks. "Aside from being Brittney the concierge girl back in D.C.?"

"Yes. And Brittney doesn't count. That wasn't important."

Julep snorts. "I bet Summer thinks it is." She swivels toward me. "What are you going to tell her when you get back, anyway?"

I shrug. "I have no idea. I mean, she saw me climbing out of the waterfall, and she's the one who arranged my flight to St. Petersburg, so she knows something is up. Maybe I could tell her I'm a secret shopper who got lost in the hotel's service tunnel?"

This draws a laugh from Julep. "Sure. Try that and see what she says."

"I know it's rough. I'll figure something out."

A car's tires crunch up the gravel drive.

Julep turns to me. "The taxi's here. Let's go."

We leave the house together, careful to lock up after ourselves. My eyes flit to the upstairs window where my aunt is standing, watching us leave. Royal saw to her needs before the boys left for their hike, so she should be fine for a little while. I'll breathe easier once she's out of our custody, but Royal insists on keeping her here for now, in case we end up needing her for something else. What that could be, I can't imagine.

My expensive heels click on the wooden stairs as I make my way down. I can't remember the last time I had to get so dressed up for a job. Most of my work involves black from head to toe, rather than the printed silk, button-up dress I'm wearing. I wanted the solid black, but Julep insisted I try another color. So instead, I chose the black with bright red poppies in a painterly style. The shoes we selected are stilettos in a matching red, with shiny gold soles. The cross-body purse is equally expensive—shiny patent leather on a chunky gold chain.

It's a much louder outfit, visually, than I'm used to wearing, but that's the goal—to draw Melina's attention. The only part of the persona that feels like me is the wig. It's a blunt, chestnut brown, A-line bob. It's the only wig of Clarity's that I haven't worn yet on this trip. I catch sight of myself in the reflection in one of the glass frames that line the staircase, and the sight of myself in this particular wig sends me back to another time, when Clarity and I were tasked with infiltrating a gentlemen's club to retrieve some documents stolen by a congressman's power-hungry aid. Why he insisted on going straight to that tacky place after work every night was beyond me, but we made quick work of him and retrieved the documents without too many ruffled feathers. Clarity walked out of that trashy place wearing a bright-green feather boa. I think it's still in our room somewhere...

I shake myself out of the memory and continue down the stairs.

The voices of my teammates carry up toward me, and I resist the urge to peer down over the railing.

Julep says that since I'm dressed up, I should embrace it and make a grand entrance. I can't say that the idea was altogether unsavory, so here I am, having waited until the rest of my teammates were downstairs to get changed into this getup. It's not my normal M.O., but receiving a compliment or two never hurts, especially since I'm wearing something much more feminine than I normally do.

I step off the last stair and walk into the living room. My eyes go immediately to Starling. He's dressed in a nice pair of gray slacks, a pinstripe shirt with sleeves rolled up to mid-forearm, and shiny black shoes. He's in the middle of a whispered conversation with Lotus, but he stops talking abruptly when he sees me. His eyes pull me in as they survey my outfit and land on my face. The muscles of his jaw clench, and he stands. He crosses the room in long strides and stands in front of me. "You look... different," he says finally. The look in his eyes betrays his admiration for me.

My heart jumps and I look away. "Thanks."

Outside, a car pulls into the drive, catching our attention.

Darnay and Royal come marching into the room, still in mid-conversation.

"I'll call you once I get to London," Darnay says over his shoulder to Royal. "To check in."

"Do that." He pats Darnay on the back. "It's been like old times, having you here."

"Indeed it has." Darnay gives Royal a quick man-hug and bustles out the door, suitcase in hand. "Er, goodbye everyone," he calls to us, but he's already almost running to the waiting vehicle. He slams the door and the car pulls away, churning the pebbles along the drive.

"What was that about?" I ask, turning to look at Royal.

"He got a call about some urgent business in the states," my dad answers. "He didn't elaborate past that, but he hinted that it had something to do with one of his properties on the East coast. Apparently there was a security problem of some kind that needs his immediate attention." He ends with a shrug.

"For a former spy, he seems to have a lot of those." My eyes narrow as I look out the window toward the road, but

Darnay's car is long gone.

I catch Starling doing the same thing. "He does tend to leave in a hurry, doesn't he?" the boy says, his gaze moving to meet mine. "You'd think with all of the money he has, he could pay someone to take care of things like this for him."

It's my turn to shrug. "Guess not."

Royal clears his throat, bidding to get our attention.

Once all of our eyes are on him, he speaks. "Are you both ready to go?"

We nod.

"And you understand your roles, your objectives?"

My hand rises to adjust the purse chain on my shoulder. "Dad, this was my plan, remember? I know what we're trying to accomplish here."

"Right. Just checking. And you're properly prepared?" He glances at the small purse I'm carrying, and I catch his meaning.

"If you're asking me if I'm packing, yeah. Julep showed me a trick or two about concealing weapons under a dress." I am definitely packing. I've got my tranquilizer gun, a handgun, and my karambit knives stored in various holsters underneath my black dress. If there's one thing I've learned from Julep, it's that a woman can carry an amazing number of lethal weapons under her clothes.

"Yes, I did," Julep says, grinning.

Lotus holds up a hand and Julep high fives him.

Royal inhales. "Once you're in town, you have to be on your game every second, no mistakes."

In a move meant to show ease at the situation I find myself in, I take Starling's hand, intertwining our fingers. His hand feels large and warm around mine, and he squeezes gently. "We're ready for this," I say. "Don't worry."

"All right."

"Good." We're saved from any further parental advice by the arrival of our driver. It's Royal's old friend, Vico, who Royal assures us is 100% trustworthy, having driven for other American assets in the past.

"We'll see you when we see you," I say as I walk toward the front door, pulling Starling along behind me. I don't say more because I'm not sure when I'll see them. If this goes according to plan, we'll be out late with Melina.

Royal catches my arm as I step outside, and I turn to look at him one more time.

"Be careful," he whispers. "I can't lose both of my girls."

The worry in his eyes makes me draw back. I don't know how to respond to it. Usually, he saves the mushy stuff for Clarity. With me, it's all business all the time.

"You're going soft," I say, smiling, trying to lighten the mood.

"Don't worry, Royal," Starling says, moving closer to me and slinging his arm over my shoulder. "I won't let anything happen to our girl."

"Our girl?" I ask, eyebrow arched.

He merely smiles down at me. "Just getting into character."

"Right."

"Have fun," Julep calls after us.

"And don't forget to bring me some truffle oil," Lotus yells.

"Go do some push-ups," I shoot back, suppressing a laugh.

Starling and I cross the yard, his arm still around me, and we climb into the car. From this moment on, we're a madly-in-love couple of college students on a summer getaway. It's game on. But as we drive away from Rosa's house, I'm not sure how much of it is an act, and how much of it is real.

Chapter 23

Starling slings his arm across the back of the car seat, behind my head, but I reach up and push it away. It's hard to focus with his hand so close.

He pulls it into his lap and twiddles his thumbs, but even so, he takes up a lot of space in our small car. I'm hyper aware of how close we're sitting, and edge closer to my door, pretending to be fascinated by the landscape outside the window.

Outside the car, the harsh morning sun creates stark shadows between the trees that grow along the road. Vico maneuvers the car along the winding road with expert precision, unbothered by the growing silence in the back seat.

Beside me, Starling fidgets with the collar of his shirt, adjusting it once more to make sure it's neatly folded.

I drum my fingers on my thighs, not sure what to say to him.

The silence between us is awkward, which doesn't bode well for our mission. I've got to break the ice. "So, are you ready for your first undercover work?"

His mouth flattens. "I am, but I have to say, it's strange. I feel like I'm just getting to know you, and now we have to act like... like we're dating. Shouldn't there be rules or something?"

I laugh at this. "Rules? That's..." I trail off when I see the serious look on Starling's face.

"Okay. Rules. Number one: keep our back story in mind. Stick to the facts we've established."

Starling nods in agreement. "I like that one. Keep focused." He bites his lip and sneaks a glance at me. "Rule two: anything we say in character cannot be used against us later."

A laugh escapes me in a short blast. "What would I use against you?" I smirk at him. "Are you planning to profess your undying love for me in the middle of the tasting?"

He exaggerates a pause, stroking his chin as if he's thinking about the possibility. Then he wags a finger at me. "No. No, but I can see you taking any compliment I give you and holding it over my head for the next decade."

"If it's cheesy, yeah." My eyes scan the road ahead. "We'll be in town in about five minutes."

Starling reaches over and puts a hand on my knee.

"Hey!" I say, sliding it away.

"What? I'm just getting into character."

"You used that line earlier. No cheese, remember?"

"See? You're doing it already." He reaches over and pokes at my side with one finger, making me squeal and pull away.

"I warned you," I say between peels of laughter.

Seeing my exaggerated response, he grins. "Found your weak spot, haven't I?" He digs his finger into my side, sending tickles across my abdomen.

"Stop, stop," I say, still laughing, but he stops, all the same.

"Okay, that's another rule," I get out once my laughter stops. "No touching unless we're actively on the job. We need to keep the boundary lines in sight."

Starling's eyes widen at this. "Like you did when you kissed me yesterday? Don't get me wrong, it was an amazing kiss, but it definitely wasn't necessary." A smile plays on his lips as he speaks.

I smother my hand over my mouth to hide the returning smile that rises. "It was a field test. After the fiasco with Lotus, I had to make sure we had chemistry."

His mouth curves upward, and he lifts his eyebrows. "So you're saying we have chemistry?" He asks in a teasing voice.

"I'm a good actor," I say. Lucky for me, he doesn't point out that my acting couldn't save that awful kiss with Lotus. "It won't happen again."

"Pity," Starling says, pinning me against the fabric seat with his gaze.

My pulse speeds up as he looks at me, and for a fleeting moment, I see something in his eyes, a flicker of longing that makes my head start to spin. I bite the inside of my lip, willing myself to remain focused on the task at hand. "No joking like that," I deflect. "We have to stay focused. I want my sister back."

"Loveday," he says, and the sound of my name on his lips makes my heart jump into my throat. I force my eyes up to his.

"We will get Clarity back. You can count on me in this. I won't fail you."

I nod. I believe him.

We drive through Palermo and out the other side, through the rolling hills. The brush that grows along the ground is dry and brown, but soon we enter a beautifully scrolled, wrought iron gate under an archway that reads Baldinotti, and the landscape changes. Instead of bare, golden brown hills, olive trees in neat rows extend as far as I can see in either direction. This is a massive olive oil operation, and the Baldinottis own far more land than I expected. No wonder Melina Arnoni decided to stay here and work for them.

Reaching up, I switch on the tiny device in my ear.

Starling lets out a low whistle, doing the same. "That's a lot of olive trees."

"You're not kidding."

From the driver's seat, Vico says, "The Baldinottis own one of the largest olive oil factories in all of Italy. Their business has been around for a hundred and fifty years. They're one of the largest exporters of olive oil in Italy."

"Wow," is all I can think to say.

"I bet it's beautiful," Julep sighs through the comms. "I may have to drive out there later to take a look."

"I can drive, if you want," Lotus says, his voice bashful.

Royal grunts, and the line goes silent.

"We're almost there," Vico continues from the front seat. "Are you two ready?"

I turn to Starling and meet his eyes.

He gives me an encouraging smile.

Unbuckling my seatbelt, I slide across the seat and nestle myself into his side, pulling his arm down over my chest. My shoulders relax against him. Starling feels solid and comfortable at my back.

"We're ready," he says, breathing deeply. "We're pulling up to the building now."

"We'll have eyes on you," Royal says. "Proceed."

Vico drives up to a large, rectangular building with levels that follow the contour of the hillside. It's exterior siding consists of warm, reddish wood panels broken up by dark windows at regular intervals. In the front of the building, there's a lower entryway made completely of windows. Inside, the shop and tasting area sit off to one side.

There's a man in plain-clothes sitting on a bench just inside the door. From the cut of his build, I make him as Melina's bodyguard.

Melina is inside, chatting with an older couple and smiling wide. She's clearly enjoying herself. From what I can see, there isn't anyone else in the shop yet. It's a good sign. It'll be easier to talk to Melina if she's not busy tending to a lot of other customers.

"I'll be here waiting," Vico says, looking at me expectantly.

I realize I must have been staring at the shop. "Oh, thanks," I say. "I'm not sure how long we'll be."

"No problem," he says, holding up a science fiction novel with a large spaceship on the cover. "I come prepared."

"Excellent," Starling says. "That's a good one."

"You read science fiction?" I ask, turning to him.

"There's a lot you don't know about me," he says, and pushes open the car door. He slides out and turns to offer a hand, which I take. I try not to think about how nice his hand feels in mine as we walk up the wooden stairs to the front of the olive oil factory. I've got to focus.

Starling holds the door open for me and I thank him in my newly-practiced English accent. Over the last few days, we both tried to affect a bunch of different accents, but Starling wasn't great at them, so we decided to have me put on his accent. I think he enjoyed hearing me repeat everything he said, based on the sheer amount of smiling he's been doing recently.

"We're going inside," I whisper.

"We see you," Julep says in response.

I can't hear the faint buzz, like that of an angry swarm of bees, but I know the drone is nearby, capturing our movements.

I remind myself that I'm supposed to be British, not American, so to keep my volume and enthusiasm at a lower level than I might otherwise choose.

Melina beams at us as we enter the shop, hand in hand. "Benvenuto," she says. "Welcome. I'm Melina."

"Thank you," I say. "I'm Mia, and this is my boyfriend, Leo."

"You have a great accent. You're from London, right?"

I smile and look up at Starling, who answers. "Yes. We've lived there all our lives."

"How lovely," Melina says. "What are you in the mood for today? Can I help you find something?" She stands patiently, enthusiasm enveloping her like a halo.

"Actually," I say, feigning hesitance. "We heard you do olive oil tastings? We're interested in participating in that. We're both getting into cooking, and have heard that olive oil is a good choice."

"You're right," Melina nods. "Olive oil is a healthy, versatile oil, great for cooking." She goes through a short spiel about the benefits of olive oil in cooking, and then leads us across the shop. "Here are a few of the different kinds of olive oil we offer here at Baldinotti. Are there any you're interested in in particular?"

Starling's still holding my hand, and his thumb draws slow circles over my skin. It's tough to ignore it as I scan the labels of the neatly organized bottles of olive oil on the shelf behind Melina. I'm still reading them over when Starling says, "I'd like to try the chipotle one."

"Ah, so you're a spicy guy, are you? I'll be happy to add that one to the tasting. It goes really well with red meats and vegetables." She turns to me. "How about you?"

"I'd like to try the truffle oil." Lotus will kill me if I don't bring some of this back for him, and his insistence has me curious to try it.

"Nice choice!" Melina says. "It's one of our best sellers." She plucks one of each of the flavor-infused bottles off the shelf and walks behind a high, wooden counter with a smooth travertine top. "Mr. and Mrs. Hall?" she calls to the elderly couple, who are perusing a rack of homemade-looking jars at the other end of the shop. "I'll start the tasting in about five minutes."

Starling and I have the charm dialed up to ten, but Melina isn't taking the bait. We're almost through the tasting and she's been friendly and professional, but hasn't shown any interest when we've subtly suggested meeting up later. I'm starting to get frustrated, but I can't let it show. We can't push too hard, because we don't want her instincts telling her we're creeps or weirdos. We have to get her to trust and like us so we can move to the next step in our plan.

"Keep trying," Royal says over the earbuds.

I give Starling's knee a squeeze.

He finishes chewing the bite of bread he's working on, and speaks. "We've just arrived in the area," he says, "and we're not really interested in going to all of the touristy restaurants the concierge at our hotel has recommended. When you go out to eat, where do you go?"

Melina smiles indulgently and leans over the counter toward us, her shiny brown hair brushing her shoulders. "You're right. So many of the touristy restaurants aren't the best. My boyfriend and I like to go to a little place down by the water. It's called, Le Onde Dell'Oceano. It's in a pretty old home on the beach, and run by an older woman and her family. If you decide to go, make a reservation. They're always busy."

"Thanks. We will," Starling says. He picks up a piece of the fresh, crusty bread Melina's given us, and dips it in the chipotle-infused olive oil. "This is delicious," he whispers to me. "Have you tried it yet?"

I shake my head, my mouth working on a bite of crusty bread as well. I swallow before responding. "I've been too busy enjoying the truffle and herb ones."

"Here, try this." He dips a small piece of bread in the oil and holds it up to my mouth.

It feels intimate, letting him feed me something, but we're supposed to be madly in love, so I go with it, accepting the bite with a smile.

"You two are so cute," Melina says. "How long have you been together?"

"A couple months," I say, at the same time as Starling says, "Two months, four days, and about eighteen hours."

My eyes swivel to his face, and he ducks his eyes. That is far too specific to be just random. I count quickly in my head and realize that he's citing the first day we met, back at the Ivory Tower, down to the hour.

"Aww, you're so sweet," Melina coos. "Like my boyfriend and I were when we first started dating." She sighs and gets a faraway look in her eyes.

I'm still staring at Starling, who pulls his gaze up to meet mine. There's an eagerness in them that I haven't seen before. What is he playing at?

I can't take it, so I focus on the last slice of bread on the plate in front of me, tearing it into small pieces so I can try each of the oils Melina has put out for us one more time. I'm planning to buy three or four of them. Royal did say we could bring some back, after all. I add up the cost in my head. It's kind of a lot for four bottles of olive oil. Better not check with him first. That way he can't say no.

After a few more minutes, Melina wraps up the tasting, neatly stacking the dirty plates and carrying them to the counter next to a closed door. I'm guessing it leads to a kitchen area or something similar.

"I hope you enjoyed the tasting," she says. "Can I ring anything up for you?"

"Yes, please," I say, holding up four bottles of oil.

"I take it you're a fan," she says, winking at me.

"Yes."

She taps on her tablet, and Starling stands still while she scans his handsome, smiling face. The facial recognition software on her tablet beeps to let her know the payment has gone through, and she puts the device down on the counter. "Thank you. Come again."

It's one of those phrases people use to be both polite and noncommittal, which in this case is a clear rejection of our attempts to see her outside of work.

I sigh. We'll have to go about this another way.

Starling takes the heavy paper bag she offers, and reaches out with his other hand to claim one of mine. Our fingers intertwine and he gives them a light squeeze. "Let's go home," he whispers, and I nod in agreement.

"Come on back, and we'll figure out our next move," Royal says.

"Okay," I say, trying to keep the nerves out of my voice. But as I slide into the car, I can't ignore the ache in my heart. We've got four days to get into the Arnoni residence to scope it out before the Ferragosto celebration, and it's starting to feel impossible. Hold on Clarity, I think, leaning my head against the car window. We're coming. I don't know if I'm saying it for her, or for me.

Chapter 24

By the time Vico pulls into the drive in front of Rosa's house, my frustration with the time it's taking to mount what should be a simple rescue operation has boiled up inside me until my entire body feels hot. I step out of the car, my muscles tense, spoiling for a fight. Walking around the vehicle, I find myself right behind Starling. His tall, muscled form blocks my path. I pause, fighting the urge to fling myself at him and pick a fight. I might be able to take him, if I catch him by surprise, and if I don't let my emotions make my fighting sloppy.

But my instincts stop me. It is not a good time to get into a slugfest with this boy. He's the one person I'm relying on to help me build a solid cover for when we go into town, so starting an argument would be tantamount to firing a torpedo at the plans we've been careful to construct over the past few days.

So I shoot past him, ignoring the way he moves behind me, unruffled by my angry demeanor.

I burst into the house and stand in the entryway, trying to calm down by controlling my breathing. Inhale, one, two, three, four. Exhale...

Starling comes into the house and closes the door gently

before coming to stand at my back. He reaches out to put a hand on my shoulder, but I flinch, so he withdraws. I can't afford to make him mad at me right now.

"Loveday," he says, voice low. "Have I done something...?"

He's interrupted by Lotus, calling from the kitchen. "Hey, they're back." He comes strolling into the living room wearing an apron. "How'd it go?" he says, but at the sight of me, he stops abruptly in the middle of the room, holding his bread-dough covered hands away from his sides. "Royal?" he calls without looking away from me. He's seen me like this before and doesn't want to be on the receiving end of whatever rant I'm about to unleash.

Royal comes into the room, munching on something. He stops beside Lotus and swallows his bite, studying me. "You're frustrated it didn't work."

My eyes fall to the floor, and I blink to stop the pin pricks that rise behind them. I don't dare speak, so Starling answers.

"She seemed to like us, but customer service is her job, so it's hard to gauge. I think if we ran into her again, she'd warm up to us more."

Royal nods. "Cultivating an asset like this takes time."

"We have four days." I throw out the words, emphasizing the last two. Frustration edges each one. I need to find an outlet for it before I do something I regret.

"I'm aware of the timeline," Royal says in a maddeningly calm tone. His eyes float from me to Starling, and back. "May I make a suggestion?"

With one hand, I gesture for him to go ahead.

"Sparing."

"Sparing?" Starling and I say it at the same time.

Royal smiles, and it gives me the willies. "Yes. You haven't had a chance to spar with each other, and it'll help blow off some steam."

"Yes!" Lotus exclaims. "Wait for me." He scurries into the kitchen, and I can hear him telling Rosa, and whoever else is in there, that Starling and I are going to duke it out.

Julep comes out of the kitchen, eyes wide. "Really?"

I point at Royal. "It's his idea."

She nods slowly. "All right. This I need to see."

"Can you record it for me?" Lotus asks her in an eager tone. "I have to finish helping Rosa."

Julep laughs at this. "Sure thing."

Starling nudges me with his elbow, so I upturn my face to meet his eyes. "You want to do this?" he asks, lips parted slightly.

I take a deep breath. "I think it's pretty obvious that I need to use up some energy. Doing some sparing will definitely help with that. And Royal's right; I haven't seen what you've got." I nudge him in return with my elbow.

A slow smile spreads over his face. "Okay, you're on."

We turn to Royal, who is still standing in the middle of the room, waiting.

"Where do you suggest we do it?" I ask. "Here?" I glance around at the living room, with its warm, yellow walls and wicker furniture. "There's not much room in here." And there are several lamps that look like they'd break if they were knocked over. I don't want to wreck Rosa's things.

"No, I have a place in mind. Follow me."

I'm confused. Where else would we go to spar? There aren't really any large rooms in the house, and the terrain outside is rocky and rough. It would make for a pretty intense workout.

166

But Royal doesn't go outside. Instead, he walks down the hall and stops in front of a narrow door. I'd noticed it before, but always assumed it was merely a hall closet, so hadn't given it much thought. He opens the door, and sure enough, it's a small closet, with a pole and a couple of light jackets on hangers.

I start to speak, but Royal cuts me off. "Hush," he says. "Just wait."

I cross my arms over my black and red designer dress and watch, pinching my tongue between my teeth.

Royal pushes the jackets to one side, revealing a button on the back wall of the narrow space. He presses it, and the wall slides open to reveal a staircase down to what must be a basement.

My eyebrows furrow. I've been all around the outside of this house, and there are no signs of a basement. No windows, storm cellar doors, nothing. "Huh," is all I can think to say.

"Come on," Royal says, before ducking into the closet. He flicks on a light, which illuminates a set of concrete steps. "Watch your head." He stoops and walks down the stairs.

"After you," Starling says, motioning for me to follow my dad.

I walk down the stairs after him, and find myself in a large, concrete, soundproof room lit by hanging light panels that buzz quietly. One wall of the room is lined with storage cabinets, beside which are propped several folded sparring mats. A long, metal bench lines a third wall.

In the corner, there's a dusty punching bag suspended from the ceiling.

I turn to Royal, mouth hanging open. I'm practically vibrating with excitement. "Why didn't you tell us this was here? This would have been helpful, like, days ago."

He smiles. "I was waiting until you really needed it. This room was a great source of comfort to me when I was here, all those years ago."

"Wait, this isn't where…" I trail off, disgust apparent in my voice.

"NO. No," Royal says, cutting his eyes at Starling, who is standing just behind us.

"Okay. Okay," I say again, with more gusto this time. "Let's do this." Spinning on my high heels, I turn to Starling. "Meet you back here in ten minutes?" I'm grinning now. This is going to be excellent. Not only will I get to punch out my frustration, I'll get a good measure of Starling's hand-to-hand skills while I'm doing it.

He laughs at the sudden lightening of my mood. "I'll be ready."

"Good." And with that, I'm clicking up the stairs into the main house, glad I had the good sense, even in my hurry to reach St. Petersburg, to pack exercise clothes. There's no way I'd spar anyone in the dress I'm wearing. It's far too flowy and easy to grab.

In ten minutes, I'm downstairs wearing a tight black tank, black spandex shorts, and black tennis shoes. One good thing about being built like a gymnast? I don't need a sports bra. I'm a lean, mean, sparring machine.

I hop onto the mats Royal has spread out on the floor, and a cloud of dust flies up into the air.

"Gross," I sputter, covering my mouth and nose with one hand.

"No one has been down here in quite a while," Royal says, laughing. "Rosa hasn't had occasion to host anyone for several years."

"I guess not," I say, stepping more gingerly on the mat this time. The dust may be of use later, so I'm careful not to send any more of it flying.

With rough fingers, I fluff up my flat hair. My scalp tingles with pleasure at being able to breathe again. "Are there gloves down here, and everything?"

"There should be," Royal says. "In one of the cabinets."

I walk across the room and open the cabinet doors. They creak at the movement, but they've done their job. Everything inside the cabinets is clean and dust-free. I find a pair of all-black gloves that fits me pretty well, and strap them on. Taking a boxing stance, I throw a few punches at the hanging punching bag, reveling at the adrenaline coursing through me. This exercise is exactly what I need.

"Did I miss anything?" Lotus says as he runs down the stairs. Seeing that Starling isn't here yet, he slows. "Guess not." His eyes go wide as he looks around the room, surveying the space and equipment. "This is cool," he says. "Very cool."

"This house holds lots of secrets," Royal says cryptically.

"Oh yeah?" Lotus asks, walking over to where Royal is standing near the mats. "Like what?"

"In due time," Royal replies.

"So, it's kind of like the room of requirement in Harry Potter," I say. "Things appear when we have need of them."

This draws a hearty chuckle from Royal. "Something like that."

The sound buoys in my chest, spreading its warmth through my limbs. Royal read the entire Harry Potter series to Clarity and me when we were kids. "Classics," he'd called them. And he had been right. Clarity, especially, had loved the magic of them, and spent days afterward carrying around a chopstick and saying spells, hoping to make something transform, or even explode.

"What's going on down there?" Julep calls, poking her head into the room at the top of the stairs.

"Nothing, yet," Lotus calls. "Come on down."

"I think I will." She comes strolling down the steps, wipes the metal bench off with one hand, and takes a seat, crossing her legs.

Movement at the top of the stairs draws our attention.

Starling appears wearing a black tank and black athletic shorts over black tennis shoes. "Am I late?" he asks as he comes down the stairs.

Royal looks at his watch. "Right on time. Why don't you stretch out some, and then we'll begin."

"Yes, sir." Starling steps onto the mat and begins doing some stretches.

Starling's immediate compliance to orders draws an amused head shake from me. He's such a military guy, but born or bred? I oblige Royal as well, moving over to the mat and stretching my arms and legs until I feel loose and ready to begin.

Royal hands Starling a pair of gloves. "These should fit you."

They do.

"Ready?" Royal asks.

"Ready," Starling and I say together.

"Good. The rules are simple. No head or groin shots. And try not to hurt each other too badly. Both of you are important for the rest of our mission here in Sicily."

Lotus nods his agreement, teeth clenched. "Yeah, so no biting, Loveday."

Starling's eyes widen. "Have you…?"

I grin. "Maybe. Maybe not."

Starling shakes it off. "I'll worry about that later."

"Yeah, when you're on your back and I'm on top."

His eyebrows shoot up at my accidental double entendre.

I simply laugh. "You know what I mean."

"I do," he says, voice low.

"Touch gloves," Royal says, unamused by my slip-up.

We comply, then move to opposite corners of the mat.

"Ready? Begin."

Starling and I move toward each other and begin circling in slow, careful movements. I'm sizing him up, wondering if he'll strike quickly or wait for me to engage. But I don't have time.

He lunges toward me, throwing a solid punch, which I'm just able to parry. It's a good thing my reflexes are fast.

His outstretched arm shoots past me, and I land a punch on Starling's side.

He flinches and moves away from me.

From the sidelines, Julep cheers. "Go get him, girl!"

I remain focused, eyes on my opponent.

He comes for me again, and I'm ready. Our bodies come together in a flurry of punches and jabs, each of us only able to land a few hits here and there. We're both defending like pros. My wheels are turning. Starling appears to be a great boxer, but how will he do with Krav Maga? I adjust my stance and attack.

Starling is ready for me. He blocks my kick and grabs my leg.

I attempt to knee him in the abdomen, but he swivels to the side and we both go down.

It's a scramble as I attempt to gain my feet before he gets a hold on me.

He sweeps his leg, but I summersault over it, landing in a squat. Before I can turn to face him, Starling is on me, forcing me to the ground and attempting to get me in a half nelson. His chest presses against my back as he attempts to reach my neck with one hand. But I know how to defend against a half nelson. I pull his fingers back and swivel away from him, flipping onto my back and jumping to my feet.

Starling grabs for my legs, hoping to pull me back down to the mat, but I stomp the blue pads, sending dust flying into the air. The cloud distracts Starling, whose hands shoot up to protect his eyes.

My diversion has worked, giving me time to scramble out of reach.

"Yes!" Julep calls.

"Get her," Lotus cheers.

"Who's side are you on?" Julep says with a salty voice.

"Bros before… You know," Lotus responds, laughing.

Royal doesn't quiet them down. He says that we have to be prepared to fight in all situations, many of them bursting with distractions.

My eyes never leave Starling, and we start circling each other again.

Now that I know he's an aggressive attacker, I wait for it.

He doesn't disappoint.

I block his punch and pivot around him, trying to get behind him, but he's quick. He spins to face me before I can execute my plan.

Instead, we're back to throwing punches and kicks, hoping to ground each other and win the match.

He gets me on the ground one more time, but I manage to get out of his pin.

"You're a scrappy one," he says, smiling at me.

"Have to be," I respond, hands held up in front of my face.

Once more he lunges, but I'm ready for him. I parry his blow and spin around behind him. In one thrust of movement, I fling myself on his back and throw one arm around his neck and the other behind, locking him in a naked choke hold.

Starling scrambles to get me off him, but my arms tighten, holding myself in place.

Lotus hoots from the bench. "Come on, man. Get her off."

"She's got you now," Julep taunts.

I smile. I do have him, unless he decides to slam me against the storage lockers. But I'm confident he won't do that.

Realizing that he can't pry me off his neck, Starling tries to push my legs down, but they're locked in place around his waist, my feet hooked around each other. His movements slow, whether from lack of breath or from resignation to losing the match, I'm not sure. Probably both. Starling stills, dropping his hands so that his fingers wrap around my outer thighs, gripping so I can't unwind. "Okay, you asked for it," he says, voice breathy. He starts to lean back…

"No!" I yell, but it's too late.

We flop backward onto the mat and land that way, with him smashing me into the blue vinyl, still wrapped snugly around his torso. He relaxes the fullness of his body weight on me, pushing the air out of my lungs in one fell swoop.

I'm frozen there, underneath him, gasping for breath.

"Not what you had in mind?" he says, managing a chuckle between ragged breaths.

I unhook my arms and legs from around him and starfish onto the mat. "Get off me," I rasp.

He rolls off to one side and rises onto his hands and knees, breathing hard.

My air returns and I suck in large gulps of sweet oxygen

before rolling over and pushing to up to a squat.

I inch into an attack position, preparing to lunge at Starling, my blood pulsing in my veins. This match has been a thoroughly therapeutic experience, but I'd like one more shot to get a clean win.

From the bench, I hear Lotus whispering loudly. "See that? She's going to—"

"That's enough for now," Royal interrupts, stopping me mid-pounce.

My eyes swivel to where the man stands beyond the edge of the mat, watching me with a knowing expression.

"All right," I say, conceding. I push to a stand, hands on hips, still taking rough breaths. Sweat drips down my back, and I swat at it with one hand.

"Shake hands," Royal says. He always makes us do it when we spar, to assuage any hurt feelings. But really, I think all of us know not to take anything that happens on the mat personally.

Starling makes his way over to me, and extends a hand. "Well fought."

I shake his hand. "Thanks. You too." It was a good fight. We're pretty evenly matched, he and I. Someone has trained this boy well.

"Did that help you? Are you feeling less… frustrated?" Starling whispers.

"Yeah, thanks," I say, smiling up at him. "You're pretty good."

He grins at this. "Coming from you, that's quite the compliment."

"Don't let it get to your head," I shoot back, still smiling.

"Too late."

I laugh at this, and it feels good. I'm finally starting to feel like Starling and I could be more than teammates. Maybe we can even be friends.

After my sparring match with Starling, Lotus and Julep wanted in on the action. We ended up sparring in different combinations, testing our skills against each other, until all four of us were sweaty and too exhausted to throw another punch. Then the boys, imagining themselves to be gentlemen, let Julep and I use the showers first.

As I step out of the shower, I'm immensely grateful for this small act of chivalry. My entire body is warm from the piping hot water, and my fair skin is pink across my chest. I stand on the floor mat, toweling off, enjoying the quiet buzz of the fan over the shower stall.

It's time to put in place the next phase of our plan to get into the Arnoni house for a scouting mission.

Picking up my phone, I search for the number I want, and dial Le Onde Dell'Oceano, the restaurant Melina Arnoni recommended.

"Ciao. Come posso aiutarla?"

"Parla inglese?" I cross my fingers. I can understand some Italian, but I don't speak much of it.

"Sì. How may I help you?" The man's voice is friendly, but detached. He has clearly answered a few phone calls in his time at the restaurant.

"Great! A friend of mine recommended your restaurant. She said it was the best in town. Melina Arnoni?"

"Sì. Signorina Arnoni is a favorite of ours," His voice is warmer now. "I'm pleased she told you about us."

"Me too, and I'd like to surprise her." I put on my best, pretty-please-can-you-help-me voice. "Can you tell me when she'll be dining at your restaurant next? Please?"

And he does.

Someone pounds on the bathroom door just as I'm hanging up the phone.

"Hurry up in there. The rest of us want to clean up before dinner," Lotus hollers through the wood.

"What if I had been on the phone with the restaurant?" I call. "You could have ruined it."

"You weren't," he fires back. "I was listening to make sure."

"Great," I say with a laugh. "We're back to the eavesdropping."

"What can I say?" Lotus chuckles through the door. "Now get out of the bathroom. I stink."

"He does," Julep puts in.

"Hey," Lotus says with mock affront.

"Is everyone out there waiting for me to be done?" I ask, making sure my towel is fastened securely around my chest, even though none of them can see me.

"Yes," Starling says with laughter in his voice.

My hands tighten around the rolled top of my towel. "You're all a bunch of creepers. Go away so I can finish up. I'll be out in a minute."

A chorus of answers in the affirmative comes through the door, and my body relaxes. Don't they have something better to do besides hover around the hallway waiting for their turns in the bathroom?

But I dress and gather my toiletries quickly, all the same.

All three of them are still lingering outside when I open the bathroom door. "Seriously?" I ask. "Can't a girl get some privacy around here?"

"No," Lotus says. "Unlike in the Tower, here we only have one bathroom, and you've been in there for a half hour." He taps his watch face, holding it up so I can see. Sure enough, he's timing me.

I roll my eyes, faking annoyance. "Please. You've taken much longer showers."

Lotus sweeps a hand over himself, quirking an eyebrow. "It takes effort to look this good."

"Fine, get in there."

As Lotus passes me, I pretend to take a whiff, then fan my hand in front of my nose. "Wow, you do smell. Pee yew!"

"You think that's bad, huh?" He laughs, lunging for me to try to put me in a choke hold so I get an even closer encounter with his armpit.

I squeal and dodge, skittering past Julep and Starling, who side-step to let me pass. They're not about to interfere.

Lotus gives up the chase. "Thought so," he taunts me, and saunters into the bathroom, toiletry bag in one hand, closing the door firmly behind him.

Julep stifles a giggle with one hand as she and Starling turn to face me.

"You talked to the restaurant?" Starling asks, eyes prompting me to fill him in on the details.

"I did. We're on, tomorrow night at 18:00." I look him over. "And dress nice. I like my dates to look sharp." My smile is sly as Starling, without skipping a beat, responds.

"You know I will." He winks at me, and I have to work to keep my first impulse, to look at him with googly eyes, in check so Julep won't see it. I bet Starling will look nice dressed up, though. I've never seen him in anything fancier than the slacks and button-up shirt he was wearing today. My thoughts are starting to get away from me, so I pull our rules to the front of my mind. Rule number two: no touching unless we're working. Why did we make that rule again? The reasons are fuzzy in my head.

I'm saved by my watch.

Royal
We can decide what movie to see after dinner.
Everyone, be ready to vote.
We're down to three choices.

The messages sober me right up. We have three days to case Arnoni's house to get a feel for it before we go in to get Clarity during the family's annual Ferragosto celebration. If we don't succeed in getting my sister out during that party, we'll have to mount an all-out assault on the house, and my instincts tell me that that line of attack would be much, much messier. It's time to get this done, so we can all go home.

Chapter 25

An agent from the U.S. consulate arrives the next morning to take custody of Aunt Megan. Royal decided she wasn't of any more use to us, and thought it better she become someone else's charge while our team finalizes our rescue plans over the next two and a half days.

Royal himself frees the traitor from her inner room and marches her down the stairs in handcuffs before handing her over to the man in black who is standing just inside Rosa's front door.

"I'll make sure she gets back to the United States for prosecution," the agent says, nodding to Royal.

"Thank you," my dad responds, handing the man my aunt's purse and her few belongings. "It'll be a relief to see her go."

The woman frowns at this, shooting a sad glance toward me.

I look away, not wanting her to see my disappointment. I am saddened that I didn't get to talk to her more, but under the circumstances there wasn't a lot I could do.

"Goodbye, Megan," Royal says.

Aunt Megan looks up at him with a steely expression.

"Goodbye, Royal." She says his name with a sneer, before looking at me one more time. Her tone is gentler when she says, "Goodbye, Loveday."

A pang runs through me at her calling me by my codename instead of the name my mother gave me, a name I haven't used or heard in years and that feels less like me now than Loveday, even though it's at the core of my being. I clench my jaw.

All I allow myself to say is, "Bye." Maybe someday there will be time for more, but there definitely isn't right now. Starling and I have a date with Melina Arnoni and Lando Baldinotti in a few hours. They just don't know it yet.

Julep finishes the last touches on my makeup—a killer smokey eye and red lip combo—which she says is perfect for a night out. "You're going to knock them dead," she says as she sits back to check her work.

I'm sitting on the bed facing her with one leg slung over the side of the mattress and the other tucked under me. "I'd better," I say, my eyes on the carpet. "This is our last shot to ingratiate ourselves to Melina and her boyfriend before the celebration, and I'm tired of this mission. It's taking forever. I just want to get my sister and go home."

"I totally understand," Julep says, reaching out to squeeze my calf. "I can't imagine what you must be feeling, being separated from Clarity for so long."

I nod, my eyes lifting to meet hers. "I'm never letting her out of my sight again after this. I'll be as clingy as she is." The memory of Clarity's constant presence, her even nature, calms my nerves. "She's bound to get sick of me." But the moment I say the words, I know they aren't true. Clarity and I are each other's person. I can't imagine ever getting sick of her, and I know she feels the same way about me. Unlike the sisters in the movies, we almost never fight. In fact, the only time I can remember her being mad at me was when I didn't tell her I was dating Vale, for various reasons. Other than that, we've always been best friends.

My thoughts begin to trail, until Julep gives my shoulder a shake. "Loveday?" she asks, her head tilted to one side, her eyes unmoving from mine. "Where'd you go just now?"

I uncurl my leg and place both feet on the floor. "Nowhere. Sorry."

Julep gives a light smile. "We're so close to getting Clarity back. You can do this, you just have to stay focused."

I nod and lean forward, pushing myself to stand. "Thanks. You're right." Squaring my shoulders, I cross to the closet where the two fancy dresses I bought on our shopping trip are hung, airing out. I run my finger down one, a creamy backless halter with a slit up one side, before turning to the other dress. To be honest, this dress terrifies me. It's so not something I would ever wear outside of the job. I eye the rose-gold sequined long-sleeve dress with a feathered mini skirt. "Isn't this a bit flashy?" I ask, turning to Julep.

"Nope," Julep laughs. "You're going to an upscale restaurant, and then clubbing, remember? You have to dress the part."

I bite my lip. "I've never worn anything this... loud."

Julep's brassy laugh fills the room. "Girl, I know, but it's the role you're playing. Tonight you're a bubbly, flirty woman who's supposed to be having a blast with her hot boyfriend. Embrace it."

I titter. "Clarity would love seeing me in this."

"She will," Julep says with a reassuring smile. "Now get dressed." She stands, already wearing the slinky black dress she chose for our evening out, and strides out of the room, shutting the door quietly behind her.

I strap on a thigh holster and stow my tranquilizer gun, my handgun, and two extra cartridges inside. My karambit knives go in as well. I shouldn't need to use them, but you never know.

For the second time in a handful of days, I find myself walking down the staircase in Rosa's house, about to make a grand entrance. And it has got to stop. "Is everyone down there?" I call over the bannister.

"Yup," Lotus calls.

"Well, go away. I hate this whole making an entrance thing. It's so not my style."

"Says the girl who bursts into rooms on a regular basis," he retorts.

At that, Royal chuckles. He actually chuckles.

"It's not funny," I say, suppressing a laugh. "It's not my fault I often have important information to share."

"You have to admit, you do come barging in quite often," Royal says, his voice full of mirth. The rat.

I stop on the stairs, peeking over the solid, stuccoed railing. Sure enough, Royal, Rosa, Lotus, Starling, Calisto, and Julep are all sitting in a haphazard circle, having pulled many of the wicker furniture pieces in the room closer to the coffee table so they could play a card game. "Seriously? You all have nothing better to do than sit around waiting for me to come down?"

"We already ate Rosa's delicious dinner," Royal says, shrugging. "And Lotus and Julep can't leave until the two of you do."

"Stop stalling," Lotus says, looking up at me. "We're

waiting." He waves for me to continue down the stairs.

"Next time you're dressed up, I'm making you do this."

"Naw," he says with a roll of his eyes, "I always look this good."

A laugh escapes from Julep.

"Oh, go milk a goat or something," I retort.

"He already did," Rosa says, smiling wide. "Lotus is a good helper." She reaches down to where he's sitting cross-legged on the floor, and pats him on the head.

"Thanks, Rosa," he smiles, then turns to me with eyebrows raised. "Did you hear that? Rosa says I'm a good helper."

"What a good little boy you are," I say, the teasing thick in my voice.

"No need to get nasty," Julep chides.

"Would it help if I come up?" Starling stands, cocking his head to gaze up at me.

I take him in, standing there looking handsome in his tweedy gray suit and cerulean blue tie. With a sigh, I reply, "No, thanks. I'm a big girl." At ease in the heels I'm wearing, I conquer the remaining stairs and float into the room. If only Clarity could see me now.

"Nice," Lotus says, clapping. "Points to Julep."

Julep smiles bashfully and looks away, twirling a braid around one of her fingers.

"You look nice, like a flapper," Royal says, face somber. He, at least, hasn't forgotten why I'm trussed up like this.

"A sexy flapper," Starling says in such a way that makes it sound like he's joking, but the way his eyes avoid mine makes me wonder if he is.

I shoot a look at him that I'm hoping says, "Cut it out!" But it's too late.

Royal swivels to look at Starling from his vantage point on the couch, eyes piercing and lips pressed into a grim line. He opens his mouth to speak, but I jump in between them, patting Royal on the shoulder. "Dad, he was kidding! There's nothing to worry about. We're professionals, remember?"

The older man looks up at me, his sandy brown hair, graying at the temples, is ruffled. He lifts his palm, offering me an earbud.

I take one and pop it into my ear. "Thanks." I squeeze his shoulder in a bid to reassure him.

Outside the house, a car horn honks.

Relieved, I lean down and give Royal an awkward hug. "We'll be back in a few hours, with a way into the Arnoni house." I pull away and meet his eyes. "You can count on us."

He studies me for a moment, then lifts his chin. "Be safe," is all he says.

"We'll be just out of sight if you need anything," Julep says, standing beside Lotus.

The sight of them standing side by side, dressed for an evening out, catches my eye. They look good together, her in her black slip dress, and him in camel-colored slacks and a turquoise button up, loose enough to conceal the holster at his waist.

I shake it off, and return my gaze to Royal. "Don't wait up."

"Remember, no drinking," he says, handing Starling an earbud as well.

"No, sir," Starling says.

Earlier in the day, when we'd discussed the no-drinking thing, Rosa had objected. According to her, practically all of the young people in the area of the city we're going to tonight will be drinking, and we'll stand out if we don't follow suit. So,

Royal looked up non-alcoholic drinks we can order without raising suspicion. Rosa, who hovered over his shoulder at his laptop, agreed that it would work since they look like cocktails.

My partner for the evening holds the front door open for me, and we step into the pleasant evening air. It's just after 18:00, and the sun is beginning to sink below the horizon, its glow ebbing away at last.

I step off the porch toward Vico's car, walking purposefully in my stilettos.

Starling jogs to pass me and opens the car door, gesturing for me to slide into the back seat.

"Thank you," I say, bending to get into the car as gracefully as I can, but not managing it the way Clarity does.

Once I'm tucked inside, Starling closes the door and moves around the car to climb in on the other side.

"Buona sera, amici," Vico greets us.

"Buona sera," I respond.

"Very good," Vico says, smiling. "Are we ready?"

I glance toward the house, where Julep and Lotus are emerging from the front door, each carrying a small bag of equipment. They climb into Rosa's old Volkswagen, Lotus in the driver's seat, and the engine ignites.

"We are now." I pat the side of Vico's seat, signalling for him to drive on.

He drives us into the twilight, nearing the lights of Palermo. It's almost the time most Italians start to eat dinner, Rosa told us before we left, so we aren't surprised to see pedestrians walking along the city streets, heading to one restaurant or another.

I cast a furtive glance toward Starling, and catch him looking at me. I give him a small smile before turning to focus on the sights outside my window.

On a street corner, a crowd of Italians are standing around an open restaurant, chatting away. Their arms are slung around each other as they stand on the sidewalk in the warm evening air. Laughter breaks out among them, making several toss their heads back in glee.

A sigh escapes me, and the ache in my chest grows. When will I be able to go out somewhere with my family and friends again, and enjoy their company without looking over my shoulder? I chew on the inside of my lip, thoughts of Beppe Arnoni at the forefront of my mind. Royal is right; we'll have to make sure he's arrested and put behind bars for quite some time, or he'll definitely come looking for Clarity again. And to that end, Calisto assures us that the police department here in Palermo is taking the abduction seriously, despite their reticence to go to the house and question Arnoni themselves.

"Hey." Starling's voice breaks into my thoughts, and I turn to look at him.

"You ready?" he asks.

"Ready?" I echo, not sure what he's getting at.

"We're here," he says, gesturing for me to look out the window.

I lean over to look, and he's right. We've stopped in front of a small but beautiful white stucco home right on the beach, in what Vico referred to as the Mondello area of town. The building is lined with large windows, below which sit window boxes bursting with colorful flowers. Bright pink bougainvillea winds up the chimney at one end of the building.

"Shall we?" Starling asks, his hand on the door handle.

"Give me a second." I close my eyes to focus myself, calming my thoughts and running through our plan. With a deep breath, I open my eyes. "Let's do this." Opening the car, I climb out. Placing a hand on the window well of Vico's open window, I lean down to speak to him. "Thanks for the ride. I'm not sure how long we'll be."

"Don't worry," Vico says, smiling. "I have the food Rosa packed, remember? And if I get bored, I'll take a nap."

I grin. "Thanks. You're the best."

"Sì," he says in return, lowering his chin modestly.

Starling comes up beside me and takes my hand, weaving his fingers into mine. Then he leans down and whispers in my ear, "You look beautiful tonight."

"Thanks." My voice is tight, knowing that Lotus, Julep, and Royal can hear every word we're saying through our earbuds. "Let's go." Tonight is our last chance to ingratiate ourselves with Melina Arnoni and get access to the house. If we don't pull this off, I'm not sure what I'll do.

Chapter 26

We walk through the cool sand, me taking careful steps to avoid getting the gritty stuff inside my shoes, and up the stone steps to the front door of the restaurant. A nicely dressed man in a white, button-up shirt, black slacks and a black bowtie opens the door for us, welcoming us to the restaurant in Italian.

"Grazie," we respond as we step past him into the dimly lit interior.

In front of us, a smiling man stands behind a dark wooden podium, waiting to help us. "You have reservations?" he asks, and Starling steps forward to give him our names.

"Right this way," the host says, gesturing for a waiter at his back to lead us to our table.

The inside of the restaurant is dark. The only light source is candelabras overhead that cast warm, flickering light on the occupants of the small tables. The low hum of voices murmuring around us in different languages is soothing. It's not loud and overpowering like it would be in a restaurant back home.

The waiter takes us out onto the small patio at the rear of the house, and I gasp at the view. Below us, there's a narrow strip of sand that spans the fifteen feet between the restaurant's foundation and the ocean's rippling waves. The water is dark, almost as black as the sky above, and the moon's rays shine down, lighting a glimmering path over the water.

The waiter seats us at one end of the patio, right against the wrought iron railing.

We each order a glass of water, and the waiter bustles away.

I look past Starling to study the patio. There are only three other tables out here, all of which are set for two. All are empty. Melina and her boyfriend are not here yet. We'll have to wait for them to arrive, then find an excuse to make contact. With any luck, they'll invite us for a drink or an evening stroll after dinner.

"I wish you guys could see this," I whisper.

"We're right outside the restaurant," Julep says. "It's gorgeous out here tonight."

"Yeah, it is," Lotus intones.

"Did you remember to pack snacks this time?" I ask. "I'm not saving any of my dinner for you." My London accent sounds funny to my own ears, but Starling gives me an encouraging thumbs up.

"Yes, I remembered," Lotus says. There's a rustling on the other end of the line.

"My gosh. What didn't you bring?" It's Julep, surprise in her voice.

"Um…" Lotus says, and they both start laughing.

I turn my eyes to Starling. "I think they're set," I whisper.

"Sounds that way," he says, giving an amused smile. He looks out over the water and the shadows play on his face, catching under the definition of his chin.

"Enjoy some fresh bread, baked this afternoon," the waiter says, stepping forward to place a basket of crusty focaccia bread and a small bowl of butter on the table.

"Grazie," we both say, and the waiter retreats with a nod.

I take a large piece of bread, load it up with creamy butter, and dive in. "This is the best bread I've ever tasted," I say after the first bite.

"Is it?" Starling asks, taking a bite of his own. A groan escapes him and he nods in agreement. "Mmm."

"You two are making me hungry," Lotus says. The sound of wrappers crackling comes over the earbud. Then Lotus starts making exaggerated eating noises of his own.

"Gross," I whisper, but can't help laughing.

"Keep it down, Lotus," Royal says. "This isn't a competition to see who is most enjoying their food."

"That's what you think."

I can almost hear Royal rolling his eyes through our comms, which draws another laugh from me.

"Is it always like this?" Starling asks, amusement shining in his dark eyes.

"Yes." I pick up my menu. "Shall we decide what to order?"

Twenty minutes later, Melina Arnoni and her boyfriend, Lando Baldinotti still haven't shown up. I peer past Starling at their empty table, then turn slightly to scan the inside of the restaurant. There's no sign of them.

"Do you think their plans have changed?" Starling asks in a low voice.

"I hope not." I sit in my seat, making sure my skirt isn't riding up. "Why did you join the military?" I ask Starling after a quick bite of food.

"I wanted to see the world," he says easily. "It may sound a bit naive, but I had grand ideas that being in the armed forces would provide opportunities for that. Besides, I was bored at home, alone."

I nod. From what he's said in the past, I know that his mom passed when he was young, and his dad wasn't around a lot. "If you want to travel, you've ended up in the right place. In the past year, we've been to England, Malaysia, Italy, and Russia. Not bad."

He grins. "That sounds quite good."

"It has been, for the most part." My face darkens at the not-so-great memories that beckon my attention.

"What?" he asks. "What's wrong?"

I look up at him, trying to decide what to say. "It's come at a price," I whisper finally.

Starling leans across the table toward me, and speaks low. "You're thinking about your teammate? The one who died in Malaysia?"

I clench my jaw, waiting for the jolt of pain to cut through me, but it doesn't. Instead, a dull ache needles at my chest. I nod. "Yes, Vale."

Starling doesn't respond beyond a small smile, and quiet settles around us. I'm surprised that Lotus doesn't interject. Perhaps he too is waiting to hear what I will say.

"Julep told me the two of you were close," Starling prompts.

My hand is steady as I take a sip from my glass. "Very close." Somehow, it's soothing to admit this to Starling, a person who isn't so invested in everything that has happened to our team over the past year, because he wasn't there.

Starling doesn't push past that. Instead, he asks a different question. "And you're close to Clarity? Your adopted sister, correct?"

I pause. Clarity is actually my half sister, and Royal's

daughter, but not even she knows it. It's one of the reasons I'm so desperate to get her back, to be able to tell her what I found out. She'll burst when she hears the truth. Though from happiness or from anger at Royal for not telling her sooner, I can't be sure. "We're close, yes."

"That must be nice."

I cock an eyebrow at Starling, not sure what he's getting at.

"To have siblings you're close to, I mean. I'm an only child," he says by way of explanation. "And my dad was gone pretty much all of the time."

"You've said that, but what does he do? Why is he always gone?"

Starling leans back at this, fidgeting in his chair. He's clearly uncomfortable with the question.

"You don't have to answer that," I say. "Sorry for asking."

Starling shakes his head, and pushes his sleeves up his wrists. "No, it's fine. It's just that my dad... He's rather famous, and I got a lot of flack for it at the academy."

Over the comms, Royal sighs, and I can practically hear him saying, "No more personal details."

The corners of my mouth droop. My inclination is to push for more, but knowing Royal's thoughts on the matter, I resist. "I'm sorry. That must be hard. Want any more bread?"

Starling's eyes widen at this abrupt change of conversation.

I can hear Lotus snuffling in quiet laughter over the comms.

I open my mouth to explain, but I'm interrupted.

The waiter moves into my line of sight, ushering Melina Arnoni and a much older man, whom I'm assuming is her boyfriend, to their seats two tables away from us.

"I hope they have lobster on the menu," I say in a hushed voice.

"Copy that," Royal says. "Stay on them."

"Me too," Starling says in acknowledgement. He reaches over the table and takes my hand, encasing it in his larger one.

"Show time," I whisper, squeezing his hand, and am surprised when Starling doesn't smile in return.

Two tables over, the waiter addresses our quarry, speaking low so Starling and I can't hear.

"It's much easier eavesdropping on Americans," I whisper.

"That is true," Royal says.

Finished speaking, the waiter hustles away from Melina's table, leaving the two whispering and smiling to each other.

"How do you want to do this?" Lotus asks.

"Hold on a second," I say, watching as Melina stands, leans over to kiss her boyfriend on the cheek, and walks into the restaurant.

"I think she's going to the bathroom. I'm going to follow her." I'm out of my chair and walking after her, careful not to make too much noise with my high heels. The last thing I want is for her to turn around and catch me tracing her steps.

She winds through the restaurant with casual familiarity and steps into a dark hallway.

"She's going into the bathroom," I whisper. "I'm going in."

"Be careful," Starling says through the earbud.

I step into the dark hallway, but wait a beat before opening the dark wood-paneled door to the ladies' room.

Inside, the entire room is lined with travertine tile that shines under the globe lights lining the mirror. I scan the room, noting that there are three bathroom stalls, only the middle of which is occupied. Melina must be inside.

I stand at the mirror, washing and drying my hands in a methodical manner, waiting for Melina to emerge from the stall. Once I'm done with my hands, I pretend to fuss with my hair, adjusting small strands here and there.

Finally, the bathroom stall opens and Melina steps out, her eyes on the tile at her feet. She walks up to the sink and begins to wash her hands, her eyes glancing up to me before lowering to her hands. Then she does a double take, her gaze flying up to my face again, and she smiles. "We've met, right? You're Mia? You were at my olive oil shop the day before last?"

I feign surprise. "Oh, hello! What a surprise, meeting you here."

Melina grins. "You took my advice! I'm thrilled. You'll love the food here."

"We do!"

She grins brighter at this, then turns to focus on her reflection in the mirror. She fluffs her silky, light brown hair and straightens her dress.

I make a show of eyeing her Dolce and Gabbana purse. "Your purse is gorgeous! Where did you get it?"

"Oh, they have two shops right here in Palermo."

"Really?"

"Yes." She's almost done in the mirror, and she still doesn't seem interested in me. I'm losing her.

"Can I ask you a question?" I try.

Melina's eyes turn to me, expectant.

"Leo and I are wondering where the best place is to go for drinks and dancing, after dinner? Can you give me any tips?"

The woman nods in the mirror. "Yes. There are several great clubs along the street here in Mondello. I'm sure you'll find a good place if you walk a block or two from the restaurant. It was nice to see you." And with that, she leaves the bathroom.

"Did you get all that?" I say.

"You'll have to try again," Royal says.

"Don't I know it." I leave the bathroom and hurry to our table, where Starling is waiting.

He gives me a wide smile. "Have I told you how beautiful you look tonight?"

I smile at the compliment, assuming it's part of our cover, but then I see the serious look in his eyes. He's not joking, not at all. My eyes fall to my lap, not sure what to say. The line between reality and our covers is blurring more each minute. Lifting my gaze to his, I decide to go for it. "You look great, too."

He bites his lip, pleased.

"You're sure laying it on thick," Lotus says in our earbuds.

"I'm sure they're only doing it because the situation warrants it," Julep inserts in a confident voice. "They're professionals."

"Right," Lotus says. "They're not flirting at all." He snickers.

"For your information, we are not flirting!" I whisper roughly, glancing over Starling's shoulder to where Melina and Lando are sitting to make sure they aren't paying attention to us.

"Stop interrupting, Lotus," Royal says in a flat voice.

Starling nudges my foot under the table with his. It's reassuring.

I paste a smile on my face and take another few bites of my food.

The rapid mumble of a hushed argument reaches our ears. Starling perks up in his seat, and I surreptitiously glance over his shoulder at the other table. Melina is sitting facing away from me, but the jerky way she's moving her hands as she speaks, coupled with the grim line of her boyfriend's mouth, makes it clear that they're having a heated discussion.

"Can you hear anything?" I mouth to Starling.

"No," he mouths. Stretching his arms, he leans back in his chair, trying to hear the angry couple. After a moment, he lowers his hands, resting them on the edge of the table.

I raise my eyebrows at him, but he gives a slight shake of his head.

I lower my face, but keep my eyes glued on Melina and Lando.

The man wipes his mouth with his white cloth napkin, then whispers something, his face twisted in frustration. The salt and pepper grizzle on his chin makes him look even older than his approximately forty years.

"Fine!" Melina says, loud enough for us to hear it. She throws her napkin down on the table, pushes back, and stands in a huff. Spinning on her high heels, she stalks toward where Starling and I are sitting, still trying to get control of the angry expression she's wearing. She stops in front of our table with her hands on her hips, and peers down at us. "You said you wanted to know the best places to go drinking and dancing?"

Anger permeates her words as she looks at us, barely containing the scowl that's attempting to take over her features.

I stare up at her, not sure how to respond. Is she angry at us for some reason? If that's the case, it's better not to say anything so as not to give her any more ammunition. I remain silent.

After a beat, she shakes her head. Taking a deep breath, she lowers her arms. "I'm sorry. Let me try again. Would you like to go out with me? We'll find someplace to party?"

I glance at Starling, who nods, his brown eyes wide in surprise.

Smiling, my gaze glides to Melina. "We'd love to."

"Great!" the tall woman exclaims. "Let's go." She pulls her purse strap up onto her shoulder and spins to walk away.

Starling and I glance at each other with shocked expressions, but scramble out of our seats after her.

Melina weaves through the restaurant expertly, stopping only for a moment at the host's station to tell them to put our dinner on her bill, before pushing outside into the warm, starry night.

Quiet footsteps sound behind us. I'm assuming it's Melina's bodyguard.

I glance over my shoulder, a look of confusion on my face. "Um, we're being followed?" I say to Melina. "What do we do?"

Her nose crinkles as she looks at me, then over my shoulder. "Oh!" Her eyes widen in recognition. "That's my bodyguard. Ignore him."

My voice is shaky as I respond. "Okay."

She smiles, her voice teasing. "Unless you're here to kidnap me, he won't bother you."

Then she's off down the street. Melina's tall and takes great strides in her heels, so I practically have to jog in my heels to keep up. Lucky for me, I have to do the same thing when I go anywhere with Clarity, so I'm well practiced in hustling while wearing stilettos.

The sounds of music and laughter grow louder as we walk along the beach, passing restaurants, cafes, and bars packed with revelers. Finally, Melina halts in front of a club called Coniglio Bianco. Judging from the neon sign over the door, the name means "white rabbit." There's a large man guarding the entrance, and a line of people waiting to be granted entry.

Melina walks straight up to him and starts crooning something in Italian.

The man clearly likes what he hears, because a sly smile plays on his lips. He nods, and she gestures for us to follow her as the bouncer steps aside and lets us into the dark interior of the bar. The bar level, where we're standing, is packed with people ordering from the barman and standing around in clumps drinking colorful cocktails from fancy shaped glasses. Below, there's a dance area that opens out onto the sandy beach. A scrolled wrought iron fence surrounds the area so no would-be party crashers can sneak in that way. The only exit gate in the fence is guarded by a man similar in stature to the one Melina charmed to get us in the door.

"Here we are," Melina says, turning to us with a smile. "It's new, but I've heard their cocktails are delicious. I'll get us some."

"No! No," Starling says. "You were gracious enough to help us get inside, let us buy you a drink."

Melina grins at this. "You've got a deal."

Starling strides over to the bar, where I know he'll order non-alcoholic drinks for the two of us, and something with more kick for Melina.

Melina grips the wrought iron railing with both hands and looks down at the people crowded onto the dance floor.

I lean closer to her, studying her face. "Can I ask… Are you all right?"

Melina casts a quick glance at me before focusing on a group of people who are doing a wild dance move with their arms. "I'm fine."

"It's just that, back at the restaurant, it looked like you and your boyfriend were having a pretty heated argument."

Melina bites her lip, then focuses on me. "Lando is much older than I am. I'm sure you noticed."

I acknowledge this with a nod.

"He's very busy with his work, and often is too tired to go out with me. Honestly, I think he'd rather stay home every night and relax with a glass of wine, but I want to go out. It's a fight we have often." Her shoulders rise in a slow shrug. "He was supposed to come with me tonight, but he said he was too tired."

I frown. "I'm sorry. That sounds hard."

She nods, refocusing her eyes on the dance floor below.

Starling sidles up beside me just then, holding out a bright pink drink for Melina. "This one's a Cranberry Foot Fetish."

Melina takes the glass from him, and giggles. She takes a long drink, and her eyebrows rise in appreciation. "Mmm, that is good."

"Good." Starling hands me a deep orange drink, and keeps a cerulean blue one for himself. "Yours is a St. Clemens, and mine is a Toxic Dump."

"Thanks," I say, laughing. We sip our drinks in silence for a few minutes.

Melina takes the final draft of hers, sets it down on the pub-height table to our left, and turns to us. "Ready to dance?" she asks, gesturing toward the dance floor with one hand.

"You girls go ahead. I'll wait here," Starling says. "Guard the drinks."

"Oh no you won't," I fire back. "Come dance with me, sweetie, please?" I grab his hand and pull him toward the stairs, down which Melina is already traipsing.

Through my earbud, I can just hear Lotus mimicking my words. "Please, sweetie," he says, then breaks out into laughter.

"You're such a child," Julep says, but there's laughter in her voice as well.

Starling shakes his head. "No, really. It'll be better if I stay here."

"Not a chance," I grin, pulling his hand again.

Starling puts his drink down on the table, and I yank him down the stairs. "I'm not a very good dancer," he calls to my back, but I don't stop.

We push through the crowd to the outer edge of the dance floor, where Melina is already moving to the rhythm of the music, eyes closed.

To our left, the DJ is at her table, bobbing her head as she works.

Holding my hand up over my eyes, I scan the dance floor, doing a perimeter check. There are cameras on the ceiling, one pointed inward toward the dance floor, and one pointed outward toward the swath of sand within the bar's perimeter fence. I catch Starling's sleeve and give a slight tug. He responds by leaning down so I can whisper in his ear. "It's too dark in here to get decent photos of us, if those are real cameras, but keep your face low, just in case."

He nods, standing stiffly on the dance floor beside me. Someone bumps into him from behind, pushing him toward me. "Shall we?" he asks, holding out his hand.

"Yes!" I take his proffered hand, and we dance along with Melina, moving to the beats of the loud music.

I stifle a giggle at Starling's cheesy dance moves, covering my mouth with my free hand.

He catches me laughing and pulls me closer to him, craning his neck to whisper in my ear. "Are you laughing at me, Mia?" His breath tickles my neck.

I grin up at him. "Only a little."

"Well, then," he says, wrapping a strong arm around me and dipping me low.

A great laugh gurgles up inside me and bursts out as he lifts me up. Our eyes catch and a wave of electricity flows between us.

I break the look and move away, my pulse rapid. The feathers covering my skirt float in the air as I spin, softly brushing my skin.

Beside me, Melina smiles. "You too are so cute," she shouts over the music, swatting at me with her hand.

"Thank you," I shout.

"Are you doing anything on the fifteenth?" she asks, leaning down so I can hear her over the bump of the music.

"Isn't that the date of that celebration, Ferragosto or something?" I ask, feigning uncertainty.

"Yes!" Melina says, dancing to the rhythm of the pulsing music. "My grandfather is having a party at his house. You both should come."

"Yes!" Lotus crows over my earbud.

Royal and Julep hiss at him to quiet down.

"We'd love to," I say to Melina, giving her a wide smile. "Thank you."

Melina beams at this. "Excellent. Lando can't make it, so it'll be nice to have some friends along."

"We're honored."

"Oh!" She squeals. "Let me take you shopping tomorrow for something to wear. I need to stop at my Nonna's house first, but it'll only take a minute."

"Really? Shopping sounds brilliant."

Melina grins at me, and I reach out and give her arm a squeeze.

"Are you thirsty? I'll get us some drinks!"

Before we can stop her, Melina hurries through the crowd and up the stairs.

"Well," I say, "the good news is my plan worked."

"Yeah, it did," Julep says.

"The bad news is, I think Starling and I are about to get a little tipsy."

Julep laughs at this. "Drink slowly, and make the one drink last. You'll be fine."

"Whatever you say."

Then I throw myself into the music, dancing with everything I have, relishing in the triumph I feel at finally having an invite to enter the Arnoni house that no one will question. Melina doesn't know it, but she's just given us the opportunity we were looking for—the chance to case the Arnoni house, and rescue Clarity from right under his nose.

Chapter 27

Starling and I climb out of Vico's car and amble up the drive to Rosa's house. My body and mind are still buzzing from the cocktail Melina bought me, so I'm practically floating.

I bobble over the pebbly ground, and Starling catches my elbow to steady me. "Was that your first adult drink?" he asks.

"What tipped you off?" I ask, tottering along beside him.

The lamp post that illuminates the driveway is still on, bathing the gravel drive in warm yellow light. It catches on the sequins of my dress, making it sparkle. "Pretty," I say, too loud.

Starling laughs. "You're getting a bit silly, aren't you?" He steps onto the porch and turns to offer me a hand up.

I take it, giggling, and he pulls me up onto the concrete. It's not until I'm standing facing him that I realize the porch light isn't on. I'm alone with Starling in the concealing dark. "What time is it?" I whisper.

He looks down at his watch. "Almost four."

"That explains why there aren't any lights on."

"It does."

Slowly, the boy standing in front of me takes his earbud out of his ear, turning it off and pocketing it. His hand brushes my arm, and I giggle, positive it was inadvertent. But then it happens again, and he doesn't pull away. Instead, his fingers curve around my bicep, his touch feather-light.

My eyes fly up and lock on his, and I'm transfixed. Without breaking our gaze, I reach up and remove my own ear bud, deactivating it and dropping it into the small black clutch I'm carrying.

I study my companion, from his ruffled hair, messy from dancing, to the loosened collar of his shirt, the blue sleeves rolled up to pointed elbows, his shiny black leather shoes, standing less than a foot away from my own cream-colored heels. When my eyes rise to meet his again, I'm struck by just how handsome he is as he stands there, relaxed, gazing down at me.

Starling's eyes lower to my lips for just a moment before rising again, and something like a spark ignites in the general vicinity of my chest.

"Starling," I begin to say, but he interrupts, his hand putting just a touch of pressure on my arm.

"You were wonderful tonight," he breathes.

My skin heats under his fingers, sending tendrils of warmth up my arm. "Thank you, but it wasn't all me."

His eyes are heavy as they lift to mine. "You don't have to be modest. You're brilliant at this. I've been watching you."

My cheeks flush. I open my mouth to respond, but no words come out.

He shuffles his feet, inching closer to me.

My heart is beating quicker now, and the spark glows brighter. "Starling, we…" But the words are lost as he takes another step toward me, and raises his free hand to rest it lightly on my other arm. Warmth rises from there as well, traveling to my heart and igniting the spark, making it start to flame.

Starling's hands slide up to my shoulders, and he reaches up to twist a strand of my chestnut brown, bobbed wig around his finger.

I shiver under the touch of his warm hands, and move closer to him almost without thinking about it. The sequins of my dress brush against his shirt. The spicy scent of his cologne fills my awareness, and I inhale deeply. "We're breaking one of our rules..." I try again, but it's no use. Whatever is happening between us at this moment, I'm powerless to stop. Or, more truthfully, I don't want to.

His voice is low as he says, "I've been wanting to do this for weeks."

"Really? It's been more recent for me."

A low laugh rumbles in his chest.

My heart is in my throat as he leans down, inclining his face toward mine in an agonizingly slow motion.

I tilt my face up to meet him and my eyes slide closed.

His nose brushes against mine, and his breath is warm on my lips.

We're almost there...

A car horn honks, bringing our momentum to a screeching halt.

Starling pulls his hands from my face in a hurry.

I swivel away from him and am blinded by the bright white headlights of Rosa's car.

I can't see them, but I know Lotus and Julep are in that car. I gulp in an attempt to force my throbbing heart down into my chest where it belongs, but it's stuck in my throat.

I've just been busted kissing a teammate. Again.

Chapter 28

Lotus gets out of the car, slamming the door behind him. "Whatcha doin'?" he asks, his white teeth shining in the dark. He saunters over to us, eyeing Starling and me where we're standing stiffly a few feet apart, and tilts his head. "Because it looked to me like you were... Standing closer than you are now." He wags his finger between us. "Are you two hooking up?"

Starling, bless him, remains stoic. "We're not." He shakes his head in a slow, deliberate movement, peeking at me out of the corner of his eye. "Definitely not."

"Good," Julep says, coming to stand beside Lotus. "Because the last thing this team needs is distractions. I don't have to remind you what happened last time, do I?" She eyes me with a pointed expression.

My jaw drops, and I raise a finger to argue.

Julep holds up her hand to silence me. "Later," she says, voice firm.

My hackles rise. "No, we're going to do this now," I retort. "You can't tell me what to do and then turn around and do the opposite."

Julep's eyebrows rise, and she crosses her arms over her

black slip dress, which is wrinkled from having been sitting in a car for the past six hours. "I don't know what you're talking about."

I scoff, grimacing at her. "Don't lie to me. I've noticed how close you and Lotus are getting. Taking long walks, just the two of you. Buying each other presents..." I stare at Julep's wrist, which is encircled by a narrow silver bangle that appeared there after Lotus and Starling went into town early yesterday morning.

Julep shifts, enfolding her hand around her forearm to hide the offending article. "That's not what it looks like."

Lotus's eyes widen at this, and he whips around to look at Julep. "It's not?" He looks dejected, his shoulders sagging.

Julep sighs loudly. "Let's all calm down. We can talk about this in the morning, once everyone's got some sleep. And once the two of you are sober." She indicates Starling and me with a pointed finger.

"I'm plenty sober," I say, voice hard, but a hiccup escapes me, negating my words.

Julep cocks an eyebrow at me as if to say, "See?"

"Fine. Tomorrow, then." I push past Starling into the house, too embarrassed to meet his eyes.

Behind me, Julep asks, "Can you help me bring in the gear?"

Assuming she's talking to Lotus, I don't bother looking back.

Breakfast is a silent, tense affair. At the table, Lotus sits as far away from Julep as possible, and refuses to look at her. For her part, she's sullen and tense, picking at her breakfast with a pinched expression.

Starling, in a brazen move against Julep's warning, takes the chair right next to me. He tries to catch my eye, but I shift my weight so I'm angled away from him.

Clearly, he doesn't want to let it go, because he nudges my knee with his own.

I ignore it, instead glancing toward the office to make sure Royal isn't witnessing our odd behavior.

If Royal was at the table, he'd be able to tell in an instant that something is wrong. He'd call a team meeting and stare us down until we all confessed to our intra-team coupling. I can only imagine the horror that conversation would hold. Fortunately, Royal is already in the office off the kitchen, working on the extraction plan we'll use to retrieve Clarity from the Arnoni house on the night of the Ferragosto celebration. We're going with a simple bump-and-grab. Divert attention, then take what we want.

I'm absently chewing on my bread and butter when Starling once again presses his knee against mine. A whirl of emotion blows around inside my chest like a tornado in a trailer park, upending my insides and turning my stomach. "I have to go," I blurt, pushing away from the table and shooting out the back door. I have a few hours before I'm meeting Melina in town, and stomping down my emotions on a good hard run is the only thing that sounds remotely appealing this morning.

At 11:00, I'm standing outside a nice hotel in the heart of Palermo, waiting for Melina to arrive. We planned to meet here, in front of the place where I'm supposedly staying, then do a little shopping for outfits for the party tomorrow night. It's five minutes 'til our arranged meeting time, and Melina isn't here yet. My eyes scan the street, looking for signs of her. From what I know of her based on studying her behavior over the past week, she tends to run right on time, or a few minutes early. Each minute that ticks by makes me more anxious. She can't have decided to visit her grandmother before meeting me, could she?

I curse under my breath, and roll my ankles in my espadrilles. My feet are still sore from dancing in high heels last night, so even the lower, more sensible platforms I'm wearing are tiring my ankles more quickly than normal.

"She hasn't already gone to the Arnoni house, has she?" I whisper.

"No," Royal says through the earbud. "We've got eyes on the house, and she's not there."

I reach up, pretending to adjust my sunglasses. "If you're sure."

The morning sun is warm on my skin, making me glad I chose to wear Clarity's floral sundress again today. Rosa was kind enough to hem it up for me last night, so it no longer drags on the ground.

A car horn chirps as it makes its way up the street, and Melina pulls to the curb in her smart, navy blue Fiat. An unmarked black sedan pulls in behind her, the driver a grim-faced man with dark sunglasses.

Melina rolls down the window and smiles at me. "Hop in!"

I do, arranging my skirt so it doesn't catch in the door. I've barely got my seatbelt on when Melina puts her foot on the gas and the car shoots forward again.

"Sorry I'm late. My Nonna called asking me if I could stop by work and pick up one of our new infused olive oils for her to try." She reaches into the back seat and hands me a large bottle of lemon and roasted garlic-infused olive oil. "You don't mind, do you?"

Smiling wide, I say, "Not at all."

"Thanks." She drives through town, a few kilometers per hour over the speed limit, and navigates up the winding hill that leads to Beppe Arnoni's house.

I can't help but admire the tree-lined drive leading to the gate. The landscaping they've done around the house is breathtaking.

Melina pulls up to the gate and pauses, pressing a button on her steering wheel. The gate sweeps open and she proceeds inside.

Although my adrenaline is pumping at finally being inside the Arnoni compound, I remain composed and relaxed in the passenger seat.

The car pulls up to the large, white-stucco house, to the front door, which is flanked with large, bright red bougainvillea bushes, and stops. "Here we are," Melina says, turning to me.

"Your grandparents have a beautiful home," I say, feigning admiration.

"It's even better inside. Want to come in?"

"Oh no, I don't want to impose…" I trail off.

"Not at all. Come on. My nonna is used to hosting people in her home." Her comment catches my attention, making me suck in a quick breath. Could she possibly know about Clarity? Surely not! So far, Melina hasn't struck me as the dishonest, conniving sort, and I'm not usually wrong. But I don't have time to question her.

Melina grabs her purse, along with two large bottles of olive oil, and gets out of the car.

Knowing that my team has eyes on me, I follow suit, walking behind Melina up to the front door. She knocks once, rapping her knuckles on the beatiful, carved wooden door, and waits, arm weighed down by the green glass bottle in her hands.

The front door creaks open and a large man wearing a black t-shirt and jeans appears, face blank.

"Morning, Carlo," Melina greets him with a flat voice. "I'm here to see Nonna."

"Sì, come in," Carlo says, face blank as I pass.

The door closes behind us with a thud, and I'm inside the house.

Carlo moves past us, walking under the wide staircase to the second floor and up the hall.

I gape and gawk at everything, mouth open in a small "o" shape, feigning amazement at the beautiful furnishings inside the home. Really, I'm scanning for security cameras. There's one facing the front door, and there are small sensors over all of the other exterior doors, and each of the windows. There must be a security hub somewhere in the house with monitors that show the video feeds, and indicate when a door or window has been opened.

Melina leads me into a spacious room furnished with a large, driftwood coffee table and two white, comfy-looking sofas. Multicolored poufs are situated in various spots around the room, to be used as footrests or makeshift additional seating.

"Wait here, will you?" Melina asks me, gesturing with her shoulder. "I'm going to take these up to show Nonna." Her heels clack as she traipses across the floor and up the stairs.

I nod in agreement and turn toward the large oil painting on the wall. It's a beach scene, depicting the colorful homes that sit along the shore here in Palermo, with the sun sparkling off the water, and a small fishing boat off in the distance. Slowly, I turn in a full circle, pretending to admire the rest of the house.

The wide, marble staircase leads upstairs to a landing, but I can't see much more. Craning my neck, I peer down the hall. There's no sign of Carlo, or anyone else. I inch across the floor, careful not to make any noise with my shoes, and set my foot on the first step. Pausing, I listen for coming feet and hear none. It's now or never.

I hustle up the stairs and find myself in a loft. To one side, there's a sitting area with two comfy chairs, and behind them a bookshelf with colorful volumes, framed photos, and knick knacks. On the other side, the hall opens, lined with closed doors. One door at the end of the hall catches my attention. There's a small black box on the wall next to the lock: a security panel. That has to be where they're holding Clarity.

I strain my ears, willing myself to hear something that indicates my sister is here, but nothing comes.

The mumble of voices carries down the hall, alerting me to Melina's approach.

I sprint down the stairs and settle myself down on one of the couches, the blood in my veins pulsing at an elevated rate. "Want me to pick up some fresh bread on the way home?" I whisper.

"Sounds delicious," Royal responds. "How many loaves?"

"Four."

"Is the baker right- or left-handed?"

"Right."

"Copy. Good work, Loveday."

Melina appears at the top of the stairs, smiling. "Ready?" she asks as she makes her way down.

I stand and smooth my skirt. "Yes."

"Then off we go." She hooks her arm through mine and propels me out the front door.

"Where are we going shopping?" I ask once we're in the car.

"Don't worry. I know just the place."

I'm hunched on the couch, trying to focus on Royal's words, but the covert looks Starling sent my way near the beginning of the meeting fried my focus. This is why I should not get involved with other members of my team, even if they are smart, attractive, and deadly capable in the field.

"Does everyone understand their part in tomorrow's events?" Royal asks, standing in the center of the living room with his fingers steepled together.

The rest of us respond in the affirmative, with a chorus of nods and "yes, sirs."

"Good." He looks down at his watch. "Then lets all get some sleep. It's late."

I stand and give my dad a good night salute, hoping he didn't notice my inattention.

He chuckles at this. "Good night, Loveday."

I guess I'm in the clear.

I troop up the stairs with Julep on my heels. It's been eighteen hours since our argument, and the anger I felt toward her is starting to ebb away. I should probably talk to her tonight, and make sure we're squared away before tomorrow. We can't go into our rescue operation with anything less than one hundred percent communication.

Julep follows me into our room and sifts through her suitcase, looking for her toiletries.

I swipe my toothbrush and paste out of my bag and pop down to the bathroom to wash up before bed.

Starling beats me there, but takes a step back. "Go ahead," he says, gesturing with one hand.

"Thanks."

He gives me a half smile, and I stride into the bathroom.

Starling hovers for a moment, then presses into the small room, closing the door behind him. "Can we talk?" he asks, voice low.

"Why are you whispering?" I ask, not matching his whisper. "No one is listening," I say with a smirk. I'm hoping my cavalier attitude will cut off whatever DTR chat he's got planned.

It doesn't.

"I want to know," he says, leaning closer to me, still whispering, "what we're doing."

Next move: play dumb. "We're rescuing Clarity." I pull my eyes away from his face and focus on putting toothpaste on my toothbrush.

He grunts. "You know what I mean." His finger pokes my side, sending me rearing back and fighting to keep an errant giggle in my throat.

Our eyes lock, and I sigh. I can't wiggle out of this, whatever it is. And I don't want to. I bite the inside of my cheek, trying to decide what to say.

Starling's head tilts, and his eyes fall to my mouth. He takes a step toward me, his intent clear.

"Wait," I say, holding up a hand. "This is getting confusing. I can't tell where our cover ends and we begin."

A corner of his mouth lifts, and he closes the gap between us. "Then let me make myself clear." He lowers his face to within inches of mine. "I like you, and not just as a super spy, as an intelligent, kick-ass, beautiful woman."

My heart leaps, thinking he's going to kiss me. My eyes slide closed.

Nothing happens.

The sink turns on.

I crack my eyes open to find Starling grinning, his frothy toothbrush in his mouth.

"What was that?" I ask, incredulous.

"'Always leave them wanting more,' my father always says."

"You, you… Funny. Very funny." I step up beside him and brush my teeth, laughing at what just happened. I feel lighter, less worried about whatever is going on between the two of us. We can figure it out later.

"Night," I toss at him as I retreat up the hall to the room I'm sharing with Julep.

When I enter, Julep stands and makes for the door, but I stop her. "Starling is in there right now. Can we talk?"

Her mouth tightens at this, and she gives me a curt nod. "You're right." She sinks onto her bed, her toiletry case gripped in her hand.

I sink onto my bed opposite her, chewing my lip. Where to start?

"I'm only trying to keep you safe," Julep blurts, raising her eyes to meet mine.

"I know."

"I don't want you to get attached to Starling, and then get hurt if something happens."

I mull on this for a beat, my eyes rising to the ceiling where the small fan bobbles on its mount. "Here's the thing. I don't know what's going on with Starling and me. Nothing has happened."

"Yet," Julep adds.

A smile rises to my mouth. "Yet," I agree. "But it's not like with Vale. Don't get me wrong, I loved Vale. I thought he was it for me. But…"

Julep tilts her head, waiting for me to continue. "But?"

I sigh loudly. "I never wanted Vale in the field. I wasn't completely confident in his abilities, and I was worried about him. When he died, I blamed myself for asking him to do more than he was capable of. That's why I stopped asking anyone for help. I didn't want anyone else getting hurt." My lips fall into a frown. "Maybe if I had been more insistent, Royal wouldn't have put him in the field." I lower my gaze to my lap, where my hands are wringing.

Julep shakes her head. "Oh, honey, you can't blame yourself for that. Royal thought Vale was ready for field work, and he was. Vale did an amazing job that night."

I pull my eyes up to hers. "He did, didn't he?"

She smiles. "He did. The problem was, we didn't have all the information. We didn't know we weren't dealing with simple car thieves. And, further, this business can get messy. People get hurt. Sometimes they don't make it." Her brown eyes meet mine, and my mind moves to her former partner, Sean. He, too, was killed in the line of duty.

My mouth cracks into a tentative smile. "That's kind of what I like about Starling. The guy is a natural spy. When I'm in the field with him, I trust him completely. I know he'll have my back, and he has the skills for it. He feels more like an equal than Vale did. Does that make sense?"

Julep nods. "Complete sense." She crosses her legs. "Just, take it slow, okay? Don't get into something unless you're sure it's what you want. You have to consider how it'll affect your work, and the rest of your team."

I nod. "Of course. You won't tell Royal, will you?"

"What would I say? Hey, Royal, is it cool if Loveday and Starling hook up? Because they're adorable."

"Hey."

"Sorry," she laughs. "You two are pretty cute together. He makes you look like a little, muscled pixie."

I cross my arms playfully. "What's wrong with a buff pixie?"

Julep shakes her head, her braids swaying from side to side. "Nothing at all."

I lean forward, eyeing her. "What about you and Lotus?"

A smile plays on her lips. "He's very persistent."

I laugh outright at this. "Yeah, he is. You should have seen him trying to convince Royal to let him learn to fly a plane. He wore that sucker down."

Julep titters. "I can see that."

"So, have you…"

"No! We're not even close to that yet. We're… getting to know each other."

"But there's jewelry involved," I point at her wrist, where she's still wearing the silver bangle.

She holds up her wrist. "I was just as surprised as you were. The only thing I've ever given him is—"

"The shot glass."

Her eyes fly to mine. "You noticed?"

I clear my throat. "I, uh, may have overheard you talking."

Her head falls back in a laugh. "Oh boy."

"Yeah."

"So, what do we do now?" she asks, folding her arms.

"Proceed with caution. And don't tell Royal."

Our quiet laughter mingles, and relief fills me. It's nice to have Julep on my side again, and all our cards on the table.

Chapter 29

Music wafts down the hill from the Arnoni house as I navigate Vico's car up the winding drive. The car crests the rise, and the large, white edifice comes into view. Twinkle lights glimmer from the trees along the line of the front fence, making the property look as if it's glowing in the twilight.

Expensive cars line the road, making the street incredibly narrow. My eyes scan for opening car doors, thankful that Vico's car is slight.

In front of the gates, two large men stand at the ready, wearing black suits with black shirts.

As we draw closer, I realize that one of them is Carlo.

"Buonasera, Carlo," I say, pulling the car to a stop a few feet from the gate.

"Buonasera, Mia," he says, his voice gruff.

"Good memory," I say, giving him a sweet smile.

"Step out of the car," is the only response I get.

For a split second, I wonder if we've been made. I glance in the rearview mirror. There's no one behind us, so I could throw the car into reverse and back down the street... But it would leave us exposed to gunfire if Carlo and his pal pull the firearms they've got stowed under their suit jackets.

"I'll park your car," Carlo says, stopping my escape route formulation in its tracks.

Beside me, Starling unbuckles his seatbelt, and I do the same. We step out of the car, and I hold the keys out to Carlo, who takes them. He turns to his companion and gives a slight nod.

The other man presses a small button on a fob in his hand, and the gate glides open to admit us.

"Grazie." I smile at Carlo, stepping over the gate track and onto the paved driveway.

Starling slides his hand down my arm and intertwines our fingers. His touch sends a shiver through me. A confident smile breaks out on Starling's face. He must have noticed my reaction to his touch. Leaning down, he whispers in my ear, "Don't get carried away, now." Amusement shines in his eyes.

"Shut up," I whisper, pulling him up the drive toward the house. All of the windows are lit from within, beckoning us forward.

Once we're out of earshot of Carlo and his gate buddy, I whisper. "We're approaching the house."

"We see you," Royal says. "Lotus, are you in position?"

"Yes, sir. We're ready, whenever Loveday gives the signal."

I hold the smile on my face, not reacting to their words. Between our two pairs, I'm beginning to think that Starling and I have the easier job.

The large, wooden door opens as we approach, and a smiling woman in a simple black dress welcomes us inside. "Beppe and Alba Arnoni welcome you to their home. Please enjoy the music, and help yourself to the food and drinks provided."

"Grazie," Starling and I say, stepping past her into the house.

I lean into Starling, feigning delight. "Isn't it beautiful?"

"It is," he responds, leading me through the living area toward the formal dining room. All of the furniture has been cleared out of the house to make room for the guests. Everyone is dressed to the nines in designer gowns, perfectly tailored suits, shiny shoes, and sparkling jewelry and cufflinks.

I glance at Starling, grateful that Melina advised me to have him pop into town to rent a designer suit for the occasion. And, I have to admit, he looks devastating in it. Plus, he surprised me with a rose gold tie that matches my dress, which is adorable.

The walls are lined with detailed oil paintings of Italian landscapes, each piece lit from above by a dainty LED light. We step toward one, admiring it, and then turn to scan the room. There's a guard, dressed in a suit matching the one Carlo wore, standing at the foot of the stairs, preventing guests from passing. The upstairs is off-limits to the partygoers. It's a good thing we anticipated this and made accommodations in our plan.

I don't see Melina anywhere, so I step off the wall and lead Starling further into the house.

A waiter approaches us offering tall, fluted champagne glasses, which we accept with a quick "Grazie." I raise the glass to my lips, pretend to take a sip, and lower it. Seeing me, Starling does the same. We have to keep our heads clear

"There you are!" Melina rushes up to us as we enter the spacious dining room. She gives me a quick hug. "I'm so glad you could come. Have you been outside yet?"

When we shake our heads, she takes my hand and pulls me along behind her. We weave through the party guests and step outside through a pair of white French doors flung open wide. "Isn't it gorgeous?" She breathes, stopping on the edge of the patio.

"Wow," I say.

The entire backyard is strung with a canopy of twinkle lights, bathing the yard's occupants in their flattering golden beams.

To one side of the yard, a piano quartet is playing. They've wheeled a shiny black grand piano out onto the terrace for the night's festivities. Dancing couples dot the patio near the musicians. I watch them, their movements graceful and rigorous.

Starling's hand tightens on mine, but I don't dare look at him.

"Go ahead," Melina says. "Dance, if you want to." She grins at us, practically pushing us onto the patio.

Starling smiles down at me. "Shall we?"

His warm smile makes me melt, just a little, and I flash a wide smile at him. His eyes light as he leads me onto the dance floor, and before I can quite gather myself, we're waltzing. I'm not much of a classical dancer, but following Starling is a breeze.

"I thought you said you weren't a good dancer," I ask, gazing up at him. "Liar."

He winks at me. "I like to keep you on your toes."

I laugh into his shoulder, and his arm tightens around my waist, pulling me closer. Sighing, I rest my cheek against his chest, allowing him to guide me around the dance floor.

"Loveday," Starling whispers, and I look up at him with bated breath.

But he doesn't say anything. Instead, his brown eyes linger on mine before falling to my bright red lips.

In response, I incline my face up toward his, asking him to kiss me. I tell myself it's part of our cover, that it's natural for a boyfriend and girlfriend to kiss while having a romantic dance at a fancy party. But I'm kind of a liar. The truth is I'm dying for him to kiss me, and I have been since I surprised him with that kiss in Rosa's living room. And this time, Royal isn't hovering over us, keeping me from enjoying it.

My eyes close just as Starling's lips graze mine.

Feedback from a microphone screeches through the yard, making me recoil from the boy whose arms are wrapped around me. My heart is pounding as I survey the scene.

The quartet's violin player is smiling sheepishly as he adjusts the microphone. "Mi scusi," he says, taking up his instrument. Glancing at his fellow musicians, he waits for the pianists signal. Together, they begin playing again.

"Close one," Starling says, and a laugh rumbles in his chest.

"I don't find it funny," I say, looking away from him. It *was* close, but it's probably good we got interrupted. Who am I kidding? Royal will never let us be a couple while we're on his team. I need to stop this. A pang cuts through my chest. I need to, but I don't want to.

I search the crowd for Melina. She's standing on the patio where we left her, sipping her champagne and staring off into the night. "Come on," I say, and lead Starling off the dance floor to rejoin her.

"This is lovely," I say, smiling. "I'm so glad you invited us."

"Me too," Melina says, glancing over the crowd. "I'd be bored if you weren't here. Most of my Nonno and Nonna's guests are old enough to be my parents. Speaking of…" She trails off, scanning the crowd. "There they are! Let me introduce you. Follow me." Melina takes off through the crowd, leaving Starling and I to trail after. We follow across the yard to a wood gazebo, also strung with twinkle lights. There's a handsome couple standing inside the structure, glasses in hand, watching the proceedings with gentle smiles. They beam at Melina as she approaches.

From our briefing with Calisto, I know they are Nestore and Catia, Beppe's son and daughter-in-law. Clarity's uncle and aunt. I wonder if they know their long-lost niece is locked in a bedroom upstairs?

"Mamma e Papa, I'd like you to meet my friends," Melina says, greeting her parents each with a kiss on the cheek. "This is Leo and Mia. They're visiting from London."

We smile and shake hands awkwardly, clutching our champagne flutes in our free hands.

"It was so nice of Melina to invite us," Starling says. "We're glad to have met her."

Mr. and Mrs. Arnoni smile in response.

Mr. Arnoni's eyes slide past us, and he grins. "Melina, look." He points, and we turn to follow his gaze.

Melina's eyes widen at the sight, and she lets out a happy squeal. "Lando!" She scurries down the gazebo steps and across the yard to where Lando is standing at the microphone, smiling at the crowd. He gestures to the pianist, and the music stops.

Guests from inside the house are streaming into the yard to see what's happening. Expectant energy surges through the crowd. All eyes are focused on Lando and Melina.

I catch Starling's eye, and he gives me a slight nod. Now is our chance. We may not even need Lotus and Julep to create a diversion for us after all.

We weave expertly through the crowd without drawing attention.

Lando has started to speak in Italian, and the partygoers are hanging on his words.

I step inside with Starling at my back. The house is deserted. Even the catering staff have snuck out onto the patio. My heels click as I cross the marble floor, so I lean down and take them off. If this is our shot, I can't afford to make any noise.

We walk through the eerie stillness of the house.

I stop at the corner, and take a slow breath. I have to see if there's still a man guarding the stairs without letting him see me. Slowly, I inch my head around the corner just enough to see the foot of the stairs, and my eyes practically pop out.

The staircase is empty.

I can't believe our luck.

"We've got an opportunity," I whisper, "and we're taking it. We don't need a ride."

"Are you sure?" Royal asks.

"Yeah, we're ready to go," Lotus chimes in.

"Negative," I say. "Hold your position. If we succeed, we'll be out of the house with Clarity in three minutes. Be ready to neutralize the guards at the front gate."

"Roger," Lotus says. "We're moving into position now."

With silent steps, we move to the bottom of the staircase. I start to reach under my skirt for my tranquilizer gun, but change my mind. If we're caught going up the stairs, we won't be able to talk our way out of it with guns in our hands.

Starling slips his hand down the inside of my arm and laces his fingers between mine. Together, we creep up the stairs.

Lando's voice emanates into the house through the open windows. I can't understand his words, but it sounds like he's working up to something.

"Hurry," I whisper to Starling. "We don't have much time."

We reach the landing, and it's deserted. I break into a run, streaking down the hall to the room with a black electronic panel by the door. I stop in front of it, studying the device. The red light in the upper right corner indicates that it's locked. My fingers run along the outside rim of the pad until I find what I'm looking for. I reach into the holster I've got strapped to my thigh, and out comes a tiny electronic USB device. I plug it into the open slot on the pad, and wait.

In the span of a second, the red light turns green and a click sounds in the doorframe.

"We're in," I whisper, gripping the door handle with white fingers. The knob turns without a sound, and I push open the door.

The room that greets me is, in fact, a bedroom. There's a twin bed, its sheets and blanket wadded into a ball, along one wall. A half-eaten plate of food sits on the small desk, abandoned. Above the desk, a small window looks out to the dark sky. A pair of shiny black heels has been discarded on the floor.

Clarity's shoes.

"Where is she?" Starling asks, peering into the room over my shoulder.

On the wall opposite the bed, there's a small closet with slatted wooden doors, pulled shut. She must be in there, hiding. My heart starts pounding in anticipation of seeing my sister again.

I look up at him, holding a finger to my lips, and point toward the closet.

He nods, gesturing for me to go ahead. "I'll keep a lookout," he whispers, remaining where he is in the doorway, and leaning back to scan the hall.

I slink across the floor, grip the closet door knobs in steady hands, and pull them open.

It's empty.

My shoulders sag. "She's not here," I say, my heart hammering into my ribcage. "The cat is not in the house."

Chapter 30

The weight of my words threatens to drag me down.

"What do you mean?" Royal asks. "She's not there?"

"She's not here." My voice cracks, and I hang my head.

A slight breeze catches a strand of my wig and brushes it across my face.

Wait.

How is there a breeze in here?

I spin to face the window, my heart pounding. That's when I notice, it's not shut all the way. There's a gap along the bottom of the window, as if it's been opened recently.

I'm across the room in a second, peering out the window. It opens onto the roof, facing the back of the house. Down below, twinkle lights shine on the patio.

Lando is kneeling on the concrete ground, holding out a small ring box to Melina, who is bright pink and grinning like a fool.

I bring my focus to the window, and scan its frame. The paint is chipped in the top corner, catching my eye. My gaze falls to the floor behind the desk, and I spot it: the security sensor. It's been smashed to bits by the wooden desk leg.

The corner of my mouth pulls up in a smile. I know what

happened.

"We have to move," I say, crossing the room to Starling. "We have to get downstairs."

"Okay."

I pull the closet doors closed without making a sound, and wipe them clean with the hem of my dress. My eyes travel over the room, making sure I didn't touch anything else.

I hurry out of the room and close the door, wiping the door knob clean.

Beside me, Starling has a handkerchief out and is wiping down the security pad. At my look of pleased surprise, he grins. We're in sync just now, he and I.

Loud, happy voices trickle up the stairs. The partygoers have come inside the house. Crap. We have to get downstairs without being spotted. Pressing my back against the wall, I advance toward the staircase, with Starling following.

Footsteps at the foot of the stairs reach my ears, and we freeze. Eyes wide, I point in that direction.

Starling follows my gesture with his eyes, seeming to understand my meaning. He tiptoes around me, craning to see down the stairs without being spotted. When he looks at me, I know: the guard is in position at the foot of the stairs, effectively trapping us up here in the exact place we can't afford to be caught. If anyone comes up here to check on Clarity and finds her missing, they're going to think we were involved, even though, in an unexpected twist, we weren't.

I gulp. I have to think of something, fast.

My eyes fall to the security pad. We could unlock the door and climb out the window, as Clarity did, but Melina would miss us. What if she mentioned our absence to one of her family members? Would they grow suspicious of the two Londoners who vanished from the party? Probably.

My mind runs through our options, not liking any of them. "We may need that diversion after all," I breathe.

"We're ready. Give us the signal," Royal responds.

At the foot of the stairs, a pleasant voice speaks in Italian, followed by a lower, rougher voice. I'm guessing it's the guard.

And then someone starts climbing the stairs.

My heart drops into my expensive high heels.

We're caught. Our careers as spies are over, and so, potentially, are our lives. My eyes land on Starling, who despite having a wide-eyed expression, appears to be calm and collected.

"What do you want to do?" he mouths. How is he not losing his cool?

I take a deep breath. All I have to do is remember my training.

Find a defensible position, and wait.

Once the guard makes it up the stairs, tranquilize him and get the hell out before anyone notices. That's assuming there isn't another man waiting for him at the bottom of the stairs.

Hold on.

I look up at Starling. "Do you trust me?" I mouth.

"Yes. Why?" he responds.

But I don't wait long enough to answer.

Instead, I fling myself into his arms, wrap my legs around his waist, and land my lips on his. In an instant, his arms are around me, one under my butt to support my weight, and the other across my back. His fingers play at the base of my neck, caressing my skin, pulling me in deeper.

My mind wants to abandon itself to the current flowing through me as I'm kissing Starling, but I can't. I push the desire down and focus on the footsteps coming up the stairs.

We have to sell this. It's the only way we're getting out of here unharmed. But I can't ignore the flush of pleasure that's building in my chest.

I tighten my legs around Starling's waist and wrap both arms around his neck. My fingers dig into his hair, something I've been aching to do for days.

Breaking our kiss, I plant a trail of light caresses along his jawline and move to the base of his neck, just inside his shirt collar.

He groans in response, his arms tightening around me.

"What is going on in there?" Lotus says through my earbud. "All I can hear is kissing noises... Oh." The line falls silent.

Behind me, someone clears his throat.

I look up, eyes wide in feigned surprise, to find Carlo watching us, a doggish smile playing about his lips. He shoots an attaboy look at Starling, who gives a roguish shrug in return. Carlo's eyes fall to me, and I place one hand on my hot cheek, putting on an embarrassed expression.

"I'll ask you to come downstairs," Carlo says, the amusement clear in his voice.

Starling nods. "Sorry about that." Taking my hand, he helps me down the steps.

I could swear I hear a chuckle as Carlo follows us.

Once we reach the bottom of the stairs, Starling turns to Carlo. "Can you point me to the restroom?"

Carlo does, pointing down the hall, an amused smile still in place.

Starling thanks him, taking my hand, and leads me down the hall in the direction Carlo indicated.

We step into the darkened bathroom and close the door, locking it behind us.

Starling flips on the light and surveys himself in the mirror.

A smile creeps up to my lips at the sight of the bright red lipstick along his jaw.

His eyes catch mine in the mirror, and he winks at me. He wets a paper towel under the faucet and starts wiping at his fawn brown skin, hoping to get the telltale signs of a makeout session off before we return to the party.

I take my lipstick out of my purse and touch it up. "That was close," I dare say.

My companion chuckles, still wiping at the skin at the base of his neck. "It was."

"Do you still need a diversion?" Royal asks. "Or are you safe?"

Starling and I glance at each other, and the tension breaks. We both bust up laughing, not able to stifle the sounds as they erupt from our throats.

"Uh oh," Lotus groans. "They've cracked."

I take several deep breaths to get my giggles under control. "We haven't cracked. We're safe." My face grows serious again. "But Clarity isn't here. We need to get out of here and go find her, before Arnoni's men realize she's gone. Lotus, can you and Julep do a perimeter sweep? See if she's still here somewhere?"

"Consider it done," Julep says, "but if it were me, I'd put as much distance between myself and this place as I could."

"I agree," Royal says. "Leave the party as soon as you can."

"Yes, sir," Starling says, finishing up with the paper towel. He turns to me. "How do I look?"

Reaching up, I straighten his collar. "Perfectly respectable."

"Excellent." He holds out his hand. "Shall we?"

"Let's."

We make our way down the hall, moving between small

231

groups of people, all of whom are chattering excitedly in Italian.

We're almost to the front door when a voice from behind us calls, "There you are!"

We spin around to find Melina careening toward us through the crowd, dragging Lando along behind her. "Isn't it exciting?" she grins, holding up her hand so we can see the giant sparkler of a diamond she's wearing.

"Wow!" I say. "What a gorgeous ring."

"I know!" Melina exclaims, shooting a wide smile at her new fiance. "I was so surprised. Lando said he wasn't going to be able to make it!"

"I wanted it to be a surprise," the man says, smiling a close-lipped smile.

"Oh, tesoro," she says, going up on tippy toes to claim a kiss.

The happy couple devolves into a murmur of whispered endearments, leaving Starling and I standing awkwardly in front of them.

"I think we're going to excuse ourselves," Starling ventures finally. "It's late."

"Mmhm," is the only reply we get from Melina, who's too busy rubbing noses with Lando to spare us any attention.

"Thanks so much for inviting us," I say. "Congratulations!" I feel kind of bad for disappearing on her, even though Royal has drilled into me that as agents, we're supposed to develop assets when we can, and leave them behind without a trace once we're finished. And I've done that. If Melina goes looking for me at the hotel, the staff there will deny any knowledge of me, since I never set foot in there. It's too bad, because under different circumstances, she and I could have been friends.

Taking my hand, Starling leads me through the house to the front door, which is no longer manned by the woman in the simple black dress.

We step out into the cool night air, closing the door behind us.

Walking in a casual manner, we reach the gate, where Carlo has resumed his post. "Here are your keys," he says, smirking at us.

"Grazie," Starling says, and we stroll down the drive to where our car is parked fifty yards away, under an olive tree.

"Have you checked the perimeter?" I ask once we're out of Carlo's hearing.

"Yes, and there's no sign of her," Julep says.

"She has to be somewhere," I say.

"We'll find her," Royal says. "Let's all meet at Rosa's and we'll form a plan."

"We'll have to do it fast. It won't take long for them to notice she's missing, even with the excitement from Melina's engagement." And once they do, Arnoni will stop at nothing to find her. Right now, our head start is our only advantage.

Chapter 31

As I drive down the hill, my eyes scan the road, looking for any sign of my sister. But there are none. I have to remind myself that she has received the same training that I have, and if she wants to move without being detected, she's capable of it. In fact, considering the amount of times she's snuck up on someone without them hearing her, she's probably the best on my team.

"Where do you think she's gone?" Starling asks, looking over at me.

"I don't know." I bite my lip, careful to keep my eyes on the road.

We reach the bottom of the hill, and a car's headlights come on. It's Lotus and Julep in Rosa's car. They make a U-turn and follow us toward Palermo.

Ahead of us, the moon looms over the ocean, creating a silvery path over the water. I roll down my window. The music from the party fades as we leave it farther behind, and is replaced by the gentle sound of the waves buffeting the shore. Breathing in the salty night air, my hands grip the steering wheel. A flicker of a conversation I had with Clarity the first time we were here alights at the forefront of my mind.

"I think I know where she is," I say into the dark. My pulse quickens. If I'm right, this mission is almost over.

"Where?" Royal asks over the earbuds.

"Lotus, follow me," I say, putting my foot down on the gas pedal and making the car lurch forward. I drive as quickly as I dare along the dark roads toward the beach, thankful for all of the training I've received in handling vehicles at high speeds. It's late, but there are still quite a few pedestrians strolling along the town's cobbled streets, gathered outside of restaurants and bars, laughing and talking in contented voices.

I maneuver the car through the town, my eyes scanning for a specific spot.

Behind our car, a loud pop sounds.

Starling whips around, his gun at the ready.

"It's just us," Lotus says over the comms. "We've got a flat tire. We'll catch up to you."

"Put on the spare and come to Rosa's," Royal says.

"Yes, sir," Julep answers.

I return my focus to the road, driving a mile further until I see the overlook I have in mind. I pull to a stop on a crest over the beach. Hopping out of the car, I take off my high heels, and toss them into the seat. Slamming the driver door behind me, I run along the low stone wall, looking for the break that leads down to the ocean. The sand digs between my toes, providing traction on the slick stones.

There it is!

My feet slow as I reach the opening, and I swerve through, my toes gripping the sandy floor. I step off the path onto the beach and stop, scanning the coastline. It's the beach Clarity and I never got to visit, the last time we were here in Palermo. She's here; I can sense her presence.

"Is she here?" Starling asks, coming up beside me.

Glancing down, I notice he's removed his shoes and socks and is standing barefoot on the sand.

"I think so," I say, scanning the deserted stretch of beach.

To my right, a mound of stone rises out of the sand, creating a platform for the waves to pummel as they march inland at high tide.

To my left, a pier juts out into the water, raised off the sand by wide wooden pylons that continue into the water. Orange lights shine off the pier, shrouding its underside in darkness.

Squinting my eyes, I walk slowly toward the pier, digging my toes into the cool, dry sand. As I near it, there's a hint of movement under the wooden structure that makes me stop where I'm standing. For a second, I'm sure my eyes are playing tricks on me in the dark, but then I see it again. There's definitely something, or someone, under the pier.

I take my tranquilizer gun out of the holster strapped to my thigh and motion for Starling to do the same.

Then, we advance toward the pier, weapons at the ready.

"Clarity?" I call in a loud whisper as I draw closer. I don't want anyone to hear me, but it's a risk I have to take.

The night is silent, and then I hear it.

"Loveday?" Her voice is quiet, timid, but it's there.

"It's me," I say, louder this time, drawing into the darkness under the edge of the pier.

She's on me before my eyes have a chance to adjust, throwing her long arms around my waist and toppling us to the sand. "I knew you'd come," she says into my neck.

"I'm here," I say, arms gripping my sister tightly. "And I'm never letting you out of my sight again."

"Right back at you," she says, relief flooding her voice.

"Let's get you to Rosa's."

Starling is standing above us, grinning in the light of the moon. "Do you need a hand?"

Clarity takes his hand and he hoists her off the sand like she's a lightweight paper doll. She works at brushing herself off.

"It's good to see you," he tells her.

Clarity beams at him in response, her smile reaching her eyes.

Then Starling leans down to offer me his hand. I take it, pulling to a stand. His hand lingers on mine for a moment before I drop the contact and turn to Clarity. "Let's go. Everyone is dying to see you."

"Put her on," Royal says into my ear.

"Will do." I take out my earbud and hand it to my sister, who places it gingerly into her ear.

"Dad?" she whispers, then quiets. Her eyes well up and silent, happy tears slide down her cheeks.

I take her hand, and she follows me to the car. We have to get to Rosa's so Clarity can give her statement to Calisto, and fast. The sooner he can get to the station and start the process to arrest Beppe Arnoni, the safer we'll be.

"Let's get out of the open," I say, stepping aside so Clarity can slide into the backseat of Vico's car.

I haven't heard from Lotus and Julep, so I'm hoping Arnoni doesn't know Clarity's missing yet. I'd like to keep it that way.

Chapter 32

Rosa's house is aglow with light when we pull up the drive. Rosa's car isn't anywhere in sight, so Lotus and Julep must not be back yet. I throw our car into park, shut off the engine, and the three of us hustle into the house.

Royal wraps his arms around Clarity as soon as we're in the door.

Starling steps aside to give them room, turning to lock the front door.

My dad raises his face to look at me, and opens one arm for me to join the hug.

I do, wrapping one arm around Clarity and the other around our dad's waist.

Clarity squeezes us tight, whispering into Royal's shoulder. "I'm so glad you found me." A sob escapes her.

"Did they hurt you?" Royal asks, his voice tight.

I suck in a breath, waiting for my sister's answer.

"No," she breathes. "They didn't. I think he was hoping I'd decide to stay, and join their family. He said a person with my skills could be useful to him." She shudders, pressing closer to Royal.

I look up at Royal and wait until his eyes meet mine. "Can I tell her?"

Clarity pulls back enough to look down at me. "Tell me what?"

Royal gives a slight nod. "Go ahead."

"Should I step out?" Starling asks. "To give you a minute?"

Royal looks at him over my head. "Please do." A flicker of a smile crosses his face.

Starling brushes past us and climbs up the stairs.

Once he's gone, I pull out of the group hug, my hand resting on Clarity's arm.

Clarity, still shivering, watches me. "Way to build suspense," she says in a wry tone.

A relieved laugh escapes me. "I found something interesting before I left D.C., about your parents."

My sister's eyes go wide at this. "Are they, are they still alive?"

My eyes cut to Royal, then to Clarity's hopeful expression. "Well, one of them is: your dad."

"He is?"

"He's standing right behind you."

Clarity's brow furrows, and she turns to look at Royal. "My adopted dad, you mean."

I shake my head. "No. Royal is your biological father. Your blood."

Clarity stills, as if she's been frozen in place by these words.

I try again. "Giada Arnoni was your mom, but Carmine wasn't your biological dad. Royal is."

A slow smile breaks out on her face, and she throws herself into Royal's arms. "You have no idea how happy it makes me to hear that!" She cries, burying her face in his shoulder again.

"I'm glad," is all he says, but if I didn't know any better I'd swear there were tears in his eyes. He wipes the back of one hand across his face, holding her tight.

A quiet knock sounds on the front door.

I swivel around to look, which is silly because the door is solid wood with no way to see through.

"That'll be Calisto," Royal says. "I told him we'd recovered you and asked him to come take your statement. Can you talk to him?"

Clarity nods, a solemn expression on her face.

Starling comes running down the stairs, his footfalls loud on each wooden step. "Don't open the door!" he yells.

I spin around to look at him, but catch sight of Royal instead. The look on his face makes the hairs on the back of my neck stand up. "What is it?" I ask.

Royal looks past me to the door, where another knock sounds, harder this time.

"Open up. It's me," Calisto says through the door, his words sounding off.

I take a step away from the door, blocking Clarity. "What's going on?" I whisper.

Starling steps up to stand beside me, his gun gripped in both hands. "Calisto is outside, and guess who's with him?"

Clarity goes still, eyes widening. "Beppe Arnoni?" she asks in a quiet voice.

Starling gives a slow nod. "Calisto works for him. Lotus just sent me a message giving me the heads up. They saw Calisto drive by, followed by three other cars."

"How many guys did they see?"

"They couldn't tell. It was too dark."

240

I turn to the door, retrieving my handgun from the holster at my waist. "So, you're telling me that there are four of us…"

"Five," Rosa says, stepping up beside Royal with an assault rifle in her hands.

I hide my surprise. "Okay, five of us against, say twelve to sixteen of them?"

Starling gives another nod.

"Open up!" Calisto shouts through the door. "We know you're in there."

"Give us the girl and no one will be hurt." This last sentence is Beppe Arnoni. His voice is commanding, as if he's used to getting exactly what he wants.

Well, that's not going to happen tonight.

"No," Royal responds. "We've called for reinforcements. They'll be here in minutes." It's a bluff, but Arnoni doesn't know that. He continues, speaking lower. "Clarity, can you go through the house and make sure all of the doors and windows are locked? Close all of the curtains, and turn off the lights."

She scurries into the kitchen. The light above the dining table goes out.

A moment later she bolts through the living room and up the stairs.

"We have the house surrounded," Calisto calls through the door. "You can't win this fight. It'll be better for everyone if you let us inside."

"Not a chance," I call.

"Have it your way, little girl," Calisto taunts.

I bristle at this, and turn to glance at Royal. "What's our tactical advantage?"

Clarity comes jogging down the stairs. "Everything is locked."

"Good work," Royal says, reassuring her with a faint smile.

The lines around his eyes are deep, giving his face a grim pallor. He glances at our hostess. "Rosa?"

"I'm ready," she says with a determined expression.

Royal looks down at Clarity. "I want you to go through the hall closet, down into the basement, and lock yourself in. They won't be able to get to you in there. And stay put, no matter what happens up here."

"But Dad—"

He grips her shoulder with his free hand. "I'm serious. I need you to stay safe. Leave the rest to us."

"There's a cache of weapons behind the middle cabinet," Rosa puts in, rattling off a passcode.

"How will I know it's safe?" Clarity asks.

"Listen over your earbud, and wait until Loveday or I gives you the all clear."

Clarity bobs her head, more nervous than I've ever seen her. With one more glance at me, she hurries down the hall. The closet door slides open, and then closed.

"What now?" I ask Royal.

"We dig in and wait. They'll have a hard time getting into the house. The walls and doors are all reinforced with steel and the windows are ballistic glass. Go upstairs to my room and get another earbud for yourself. Do it quickly."

I nod and hurry up the stairs, sprinting down the hall, and almost lose my footing when the rug underneath my high heels skids toward the wall. Letting out a grunt, I kick off the shoes and throw myself onto the floor to reach under Royal's bed for the small case of surveillance equipment he always carries when he travels. It's not easy to find in the darkened room, but I manage, turning on an earbud and popping it into my ear. "Can you hear me?" I say, standing in the middle of the bedroom.

"Loud and clear," Royal replies. "Lotus, Julep, what is your status?"

"We've parked down the street and are approaching on foot."

"Be cautious, but see if you can sneak up to the house and count the number of men outside."

"Yes, sir," Julep says. "We'll take care of it."

"If you can pick any of them off without letting them know where you are, do it."

My heart rate increases at this. It's about to get real.

"Will do," Lotus whispers.

Someone outside pounds on the door. "Last chance! Open up, or we start firing."

Beside me, Royal, Rosa, and Starling square their bodies, holding their firearms snug in steady hands.

I reach under my skirt and pull out my handgun, making sure it's loaded, and join the line formed by my teammates. My heart is pounding now, but I hold steady. Situations like this are what I trained for, and I'm not about to back down.

"Loveday, Starling, go to the back door in the kitchen. Rosa and I will take the front door."

"Yes, sir," we say together.

Starling motions for me to go ahead of him, and we stalk into the kitchen. It's eerie and dark with the lights off. I position myself behind the island work station, my head peeking around it to keep both eyes on the door.

Starling crouches down beside me, peering around the other side of the stucco and tile structure.

"By our count, there are fourteen hostiles outside the house," Julep says over the comms. "We'll try to take down a few of them, but they're moving in groups of two or three, so it won't be easy."

243

"Do your best," Royal says. "Once they start shooting, we'll have to engage them."

"Is there anyone we can call for help" Starling asks, "since we're outnumbered?"

"I don't want to risk it," Royal says. "Calisto was supposedly a good cop."

"And we can see how that turned out," I say, my words soaked in sarcasm.

"Right," Starling says. He shifts beside me, and whispers. "You guys sure get into some interesting situations."

A corner of my mouth lifts. "It's true." I glance at him to find he's watching me. His eyes move down to my mouth, and I know he's reliving our kiss from earlier this evening, just as I am. My face heats at the memory of it, but I push the thoughts away. Now is not the time.

The kitchen door makes a thunderous rumble as someone pounds on it from outside. "Let us in," a man says in a gruff voice, "and we won't hurt you. We just want Antonia."

"Not on your life," I yell back.

And that's when it starts.

Gunfire rings out, battering the walls. The windows hold, but the noise is ear-splitting.

My eyes are trained on the door as bullets hail against its outside panel.

Whoever is outside shifts to fire at the window over the kitchen sink, making it quiver under the pressure. Silverware in the sink basin shakes at a high tinny pitch. It's like nails on a chalkboard.

"You take the door. I'll watch the window," I say to Starling, who repositions to clear his line of sight.

"Be careful," he says with a quick look at me.

"Back at you." But I can't tear my eyes away from the window. It's beginning to cloud under the strain caused by the hail of bullets hitting its surface. "How's it going up front?" I yell, hoping Royal can hear me over the roar.

"The windows are holding," he yells.

A cracking sound reaches my ears, sending my heart thudding against my ribcage. Fear shoots through my veins like ice.

"They've brought out bigger guns," Royal yells. "Stay where you are."

Glass shatters at the front of the house, and I resist the urge to spin toward it.

"Hold position," Royal yells, firing his gun. "They've broken the front window."

Sparks that sound like firecracker pops fill the air. It's Rosa's automatic rifle.

A man's cry chills me to the bone, making me freeze in place. "Royal?" I call, afraid of what I might hear in response. Or that I won't get one at all.

"We're fine," he says. "But I want you to retreat to higher ground."

"What about the back door?"

"Is it holding?"

"Yes."

"Then don't worry about it."

"Screw that," I say, jumping to my feet. I cross the room to where the heavy, solid wood dining table is standing. "A little help!"

Like he's reading my mind, Starling moves toward the dining table, lifting it on its side and helping me push it up against the door. It won't keep them out forever, but it's one more layer they have to break through to get inside.

The house trembles under the assault coming from outside.

"Lotus. Status?" I yell, hoping he can hear me.

"We're okay. Four men are down, but they're returning fire now, so we're having to move."

"Be careful!"

"Don't worry about us," Julep says. "Focus on keeping Clarity safe."

"Will do." I beckon with my hand for Starling to follow. "We have to get to a higher position."

"You go first. I'll cover you."

"Agreed." I press against the wall and inch toward the living room. The flash of gunfire catches my eyes, and I blink to clear them. The front window has a gaping hole in the middle, but so far Royal and Rosa have prevented anyone from getting inside by laying down fire whenever one of Arnoni's men shows himself at the window.

Seeing an opening, I bolt around the corner and up the stairs.

Starling follows.

I run up the hall, thankful I tossed the heels.

Rosa's room is at the back of the house, so I'm hoping we have a better chance of getting outside without being seen. I creep up to the window, where the curtain is pulled closed, blocking any view in or out. Using a finger, I lift the curtain an inch out of the way so I can see out. Below us, two men are banging on the kitchen door, trying to get through its wooden surface, but the reinforced steel underneath the mahogany facade seems to be holding.

"You ready?" I ask, meeting Starling's eyes.

"Where you go, I go," he says.

The weight in his voice catches me off guard, and my stomach flips.

"Starling, I…"

"You were about to climb out the window, right?"

I smile. "Yes."

"Then let's go." He holds his gun in a sturdy grip, watching, while I unlock the window.

"Here's hoping it's not stiff," I say, putting a slight amount of pressure on the frame. It slides open without a sound, and I peer out.

The two men have moved off from the door and are shooting at the windows again. From the looks of frustration on their faces, they aren't making much progress.

"Loveday, hurry," Lotus says. "It looks like the guys out front are about to breach the front window."

"Help them!" I return. "Royal and Rosa are down there."

"We're doing our best," Julep says, followed by the sound of a handgun with a silencer being fired.

My breath catches as I look at Starling. "Let's go." As slowly as I can, I put one leg out the window, then the other. I'm completely exposed. But the instant I meet Starling's eyes, I know he'll protect me. And I'll do likewise.

The guys down below must not see me, because I'm able to climb up the dormer over the window and flatten myself into the valley in the tiles.

In a moment, Starling is beside me.

"That was close," he says.

"Let's take the two down there," I say, pointing toward the ground below us, "then turn toward the front. I'll take the one on my left. You take the one on the right."

"On your mark," he says.

"Ready?" I take a deep breath, waiting for the men to make their next move. As I expected, they start shooting again.

"Now!" I lean forward, take aim, and fire a bullet into the heart of my man.

He drops, not moving, onto the grass.

My stomach clenches.

It's my first confirmed kill.

My heart rises into my throat, making it difficult to breath. I gulp it down. There isn't time to think about it now.

Beside him, the other man goes down in a heap.

"Two hostiles down," I say to my team. Then I look at Starling. "Nice shot," I say, trying to lighten my mood.

Starling's mouth is set in a grim line.

"Was that your first?" I ask.

He nods.

"Me too."

A woman's cry sounds through the earbuds.

"Rosa? Julep?" I ask.

"It's Rosa," Royal says. "She's hit, but she's alive."

My heart twists, thinking about the woman who welcomed us into her home. She didn't deserve to have her house shot to hell like this. I reach out and put a hand on Starling's forearm, motioning with my chin toward the roofline.

His eyes follow mine, and he lifts his chin in acknowledgement.

Working as a well-oiled machine, we move our position until we're facing the front of the house, shielded by the roofline.

Gunshots flash between the trees down the drive. That must be where Lotus and Julep are positioned.

Three of Arnoni's men are facing the trees, taking cover behind the cars and firing at my teammates. Two more are crouched near the ground, facing the house. I can't see Arnoni, Calisto, or the last man from where we're positioned. They must be on the front porch, trying to get through the broken front window.

We're outnumbered, but I guarantee that Beppe Arnoni is having a much harder time storming Rosa's house than he anticipated.

"Royal. Status?" I whisper.

"I'm holding position, but I'm almost out of ammo. Whatever you're going to do, do it now."

"Yes, sir," I say. Pushing with my feet, I slide my body upward so I can shoot over the roofline by propping my elbows on the cold clay tiles. "Let's take the men firing toward the trees first."

We signal each other which side we're taking. Line up our shots. And fire!

Two more of Arnoni's men go down, which leaves one man shooting at Julep and Lotus. He's crouched behind a tree stump, looking terrified that the men to either side of him have just been shot. Spinning around, his eyes travel upward toward the roof where Starling and I are hiding.

We duck below the roofline out of sight just as bullets come streaking toward us. My throat is tight and my heart pounds against my ribcage.

It goes quiet, so I chance a peek over the ridge. The man is on the ground, and Lotus and Julep are creeping out of the trees, moving toward the house.

As Lotus moves, I can see that he's favoring his right side. He's injured.

"You're surrounded!" Julep calls toward whoever is left of Arnoni's team. "Put your hands up, or we'll shoot you."

I don't hear a response, but Arnoni and Calisto must have agreed, because Julep and Lotus stride forward. "Toss your weapons onto the grass," Lotus says, "and no sudden moves."

Someone lunges off the porch toward Julep, arms outstretched in an attempt to grab her.

She fires twice in quick succession, making the man's body jolt in the air. It lands on the grass with a dull thud.

Then Julep raises her eyes to the two men remaining on the porch, her expression grim.

Two handguns fly out onto the grass where I can see them, shiny black in the dark grass.

"Get down on the ground," Julep says, voice firm. After a moment, she moves up onto the porch out of sight.

Behind her, Lotus holds his gun steady, eyes focused on whatever is happening under the eaves.

"Arnoni and Calisto are secure," Julep says after a minute. "It's over."

Royal's ragged sigh comes over the comms. "I'll call the consulate. They'll send someone to help us sort this out."

I open my mouth to respond, but am cut off by the sound of police sirens drawing closer. Hopefully they're on our side.

I glance at Starling, whose eyebrows are scrunched together.

"Think they're friendly?" he asks.

"I was wondering the same thing."

"In that case..." He trails off, leaning toward me, inclining his face toward mine.

The clay tiles dig into my elbows, but I don't care. I lean the rest of the distance between us, meeting Starling's lips with my own. His mouth is warm on mine, but only for a moment. Then he breaks contact.

"What was that for?" I whisper, leaning in again.

"Just in case." A smile crosses his features, and I can't help but smile too.

Two police cars come careening up the street, lights flashing and sirens blaring. They pull into the drive, throwing their cars into park, and sliding out of their car doors. "Put down your weapons," one of them shouts.

"Hello, Officer," Julep says, loud and clear. "We're putting down our weapons."

The police officers move forward and kick two guns into the grass, where they join the ones discarded by Arnoni and Calisto.

"Do you mind telling us what's going on here? Where is Rosa?" the other officer asks, his voice rising off the patio. "And why is Officer Calisto restrained?"

"I'll answer that," Royal says. "Rosa is in here, with me. She's been hurt. And Officer Calisto is working with Beppe Arnoni. He's a dirty cop."

"It's true," a woman's voice says. It's Clarity. She's come out of the basement. "I can explain everything."

Two more police cars screech to a halt on the drive, and the police officers pile out.

The first two officers to arrive step off the porch to confer with the newcomers in whispered voices.

From where we're stationed on the roof, Starling and I watch the proceedings, not making a sound. If this goes south, we're the only ones of our team who are in a position to fight back.

But it's not necessary.

"We've been investigating Officer Calisto for quite some time," one of the officers says, moving onto the patio. "If you let me inside, I'll take your statements. My fellow officers will survey the bodies in the yard."

"Yes, sir," Royal answers.

Starling and I wait on the roof until we're sure the police officers who arrived are honest, and then we climb down into Rosa's bedroom.

The sound of animated chatter reaches us as we descend the stairs.

Calisto and Beppe Arnoni are on their knees on the ground, their hands restrained behind them.

Two of the locals are speaking with Royal in low voices. One of them, a woman with dark red hair and a mole beside her mouth, looks up at us as we approach. She takes in our disheveled appearance at a glance, then returns her focus to whatever Royal is saying.

Clarity is standing beside him, ler legs braced to support her weight. Her entire body is trembling.

On the couch, Lotus's shirt is off. A bullet has left a red, angry graze on his side, and blood is trickling down onto the white cushion underneath him.

Julep is bent over him, prepping a bandage for his wound, whispering to him in gentle tones.

Lotus moves to cover the injury with one of his hands, but Julep swats it away.

The way Lotus looks up at her with a knowing smile makes my heart squeeze.

Julep's cheeks round in a smile at his gaze, and she lowers her eyes.

Starling's arm snakes around me, and his warm hand rests on my shoulder.

I look up at him, surprised he'd make such a gesture in front of Royal. But I don't push his hand away. Instead, I lean into it. The pressure of his touch is comforting, making me finally take in a deep breath.

It's over.

"You okay?" he asks in my ear.

I nod, my relief awash in my throat, preventing me from forming words.

The front door opens, and Rosa steps inside, flanked by the other two police officers.

"How does it look out there?" Royal asks, lifting his gaze to meet hers.

She simply purses her lips in response, her face grim. Sinking into a chair, she lays her head back.

My eyes travel down to the wound in her thigh, which she's bandaged with a kitchen towel. When she found the time to do that, I don't know.

I lean against Starling, my legs nearly collapsing under me. But I don't dare close my eyes. I'm still on high alert, my gun gripped in my fingers.

Arnoni and Calisto are being uncharacteristically quiet, and it's unnerving.

But maybe I'm being cynical, because a few minutes later, the officers drag the two men off the floor and push them out the door to their waiting squad cars. They're loaded into one of the police vehicles, and the doors are slammed shut behind them, imprisoning them behind steel and glass.

Two ambulances arrive, signalling their approach with flashing lights, but no sirens. The medics approach the house, and Royal ushers them in, pointing to Lotus and Rosa.

Now that I think about it, it's kind of a miracle that of the seven of us, only two are injured, and not seriously. Still, the paramedics bundle up both of them and lead them to their waiting vehicles.

"I'd like to go with them," Julep says, meeting Royal's eye.

"Go ahead," he says with a sigh. "Keep me informed of any developments."

"Yes, sir." She gives a quick bow of the head before ducking out the door and jogging down the drive to the ambulances. She climbs into the one carrying Lotus, and a small smile finds its way onto my face.

Once the ambulances, police officers, and coroner have gone, Royal sits on the couch next to Clarity. He pats her knee with his tan hand, and looks over at me. "They've assured me they will be prosecuting both Beppe Arnoni and Officer Calisto to the fullest extent of their laws."

"Meaning?" I ask, my voice tired.

"Neither of them will see freedom again for a long, long time."

"That's a relief," I quip.

"Yes, indeed," Starling adds from where he stands, towering over me.

Clarity smothers her face in her hands, and bursts into tears.

Chapter 33

The afternoon sun filters into Rosa's kitchen through the cracked window, casting prisms of rainbow light over the surface of the table's knotty surface. Rosa's beautiful wooden dutch door sags on the hinges, the metal core exposed beneath the splintered wood of the exterior panels.

Rosa herself sits on a bar stool by the stove with her injured leg propped on a milk crate. Her voice emanates in whispered waves as she coaches Julep through cooking a hearty minestrone soup for lunch. Already, there's a chunky loaf of herbed ciabatta bread cooling on a rack on the countertop.

Lotus sits across from me at the table, watching Rosa and Julep work, his eyes rarely leaving them. A trace of a smile plays on his features, but it's replaced by a wince whenever he moves. It's a reminder of the gunshot wound he's hiding beneath a baggy gray T-shirt.

Beside me, Starling is focused on a cryptic crossword puzzle on his phone. Occasionally he polls the room for ideas about the answers to the puzzle's riddles, speaking in hushed tones.

Clarity is still upstairs, asleep, and has been for the past twelve hours. She crashed after our showdown with Arnoni last night, and hasn't made a peep since. I know without having to go upstairs that Royal is hunched in a chair beside her bed, holding a vigil over his daughter as she slumbers.

A creak on the stairs draws my attention, making me sit upright and watch the doorway. Royal moves into view, a tired but relieved look on his face. He catches my eye and smiles.

"How is she?" I ask, pushing my chair away from the table.

Royal motions with one hand for me to keep my seat. "She's coming down. I asked her if she felt up to talking us through what happened, and she seems ready. Let her go at her own pace, all right?" This last question is posed to me.

"Of course. I would never push her."

He nods, pulling out the chair beside me and lowering himself into it. "That minestrone smells delicious, ladies."

"It's going to be amazing," Julep says over her shoulder. "Just you wait."

Rosa clucks her tongue in agreement.

"Hi, guys," Clarity says, having simply appeared in the doorway.

"Clarity," I say, rushing to throw my arms around her. "I'm glad you're awake."

"Thanks," she says, running a pale hand through her shaggy brown waves.

"Come sit," Royal says, gesturing to the chair at the head of the table. "I told everyone to let you talk without interrupting, so whenever you're ready…"

She gives our dad a wan smile and takes the chair he indicated.

I plop down in my seat and scoot in, resting my elbows on the table and propping my chin on my intertwined fingers.

Silence settles over us as Clarity sits, staring at the table in front of her, gathering her thoughts.

Starling shifts in his seat beside me, putting his phone in his pocket and focusing on my sister.

"We know from the security footage that you were almost to the van when Arnoni arrived," I prompt. "And that he tased you to subdue you."

Clarity nods absently at this.

Lotus winces. "What did that feel like? It looked like it hurt."

"It did," Clarity says. "It was strange. My entire body seized. I lost all control of my muscles. I thought I was screaming. Was I screaming?" Her face lifts to look at me.

"No, you weren't. You just went down."

"I was really sore from that. It felt like I'd done a hard core workout."

"What happened then?" Lotus asks.

Royal clears his throat, reminding us not to interrogate Clarity, but she waves him off.

"It's fine," she says. "It's better talking it through with you all, rather than going over it in my head. I feel much less alone."

Royal takes her hand and gives it a squeeze. "You're very brave. I'm proud of you."

Hearing this makes Clarity smile. It's the first time she's looked genuinely peaceful since I found her under the pier yesterday. "Thanks, Dad." She turns to the rest of us. "So then, they dragged me onto a small plane, and we flew…"

Clarity goes through the story of her time in Arnoni's custody in great detail, sitting up straighter and looking lighter, more like herself, the more she talks.

What sticks out most to me is the fact that she makes sure

to emphasize that they didn't hurt her (after the tasing part, of course). "I think he hoped I would bond with him, and maybe choose to stay with his family," she says finally, looking up. "So I played along, and that's when he introduced me to his son, my uncle."

"Nestore," I supply.

"Right. He was shocked to see me. He had no idea I was alive. I guess Beppe never told him that he'd been looking for me, or that he'd... kidnapped me and brought me to Sicily."

"Did you ever meet Melina?" Starling asks.

She shakes her head. "No. I think Uncle Nestore kept her away. He didn't say anything for several days, but I could tell he was angry that Beppe had brought me here against my will. One day, he came to see me, and he told me about the Ferragosto party Beppe was hosting. He said it would be a good time for me to escape, since all of Arnoni's men would be working security for the party."

"So that's how you did it!" I exclaim. "I was wondering about that."

Clarity smiles at me. "Yep. Uncle Nestore said he'd disable the security sensors long enough for me to escape, so I waited until he gave me a signal. Then I smashed the sensor and climbed out the window."

"Wow," Lotus says. "You're such a badass."

Clarity's eyes start to shine. "Thank you."

"Truly, you're amazing," Starling adds. Under the table, he nudges my foot with his own, his toes resting on mine. It's as if he's saying, "You're amazing too, Loveday," without actually using the words.

I lower my face and hide my smile behind my hand.

The warm scent of the soup permeates the kitchen, and Lotus's stomach rumbles loudly.

We all burst out laughing, pushing the tension from the room and replacing it with glee at being all together again.

"It's ready." Rosa smiles from her perch on the bar stool.

Julep turns toward us, grinning. "It's delicious, y'all."

Royal stands, patting Clarity on the shoulder as he passes her. "You ladies have a seat. I'll serve everyone."

They thank him and take seats at the table, Julep next to Lotus and Rosa at the opposite end from Clarity.

Lotus shifts in his seat, wincing, and his hands disappear under the table. From the way Julep's sitting, I'm pretty sure they're holding hands.

My eyes slide to Starling, who gives me a lopsided smile, and widens his legs so our knees are touching. The contact sends a warm flush through me, but I manage to keep a straight face. I don't know what will happen between us, but I'm enjoying the easy rapport we're building.

Royal sets a bowl of the steaming soup in front of Clarity, who smiles up at him gratefully. "Let's eat!" she exclaims. "I'm starving."

And we do.

Chapter 34

My entire team is bone tired as we trudge into the Ivory Tower.

All I want to do is drop my bags in the middle of the den, crash on the couch, and sleep for days, but Royal won't go for that. He's always insisted we put our gear away immediately upon returning to the Tower. "If you don't do it right away, it won't happen for days," he says, and he's probably right.

So I shuffle down the hall into the armory, stow my weapons, and drag my duffle bag down the dormitory hallway to the room I share with my sister. There's a funky smell in the hallway, but I can't place it.

"You're back!" Haru squeals, running out of her bright yellow room and crushing me in a hug. "I'm so happy to see you. It's so boring here all by myself!"

"Thanks," I say, giving her a feeble, one-armed hug in return. "Hey, what's that weird smell?"

Haru's cheeks redden, and her eyes dart away. "Oh, I spilled some soup, and it didn't all come out of the carpet. Sorry about that!"

Her high voice, spotty eye contact, and fidgety movements indicate that she's lying, but I'm too overcome with fatigue to call her on it at the moment. She probably did something silly like break a plate or something while we were gone.

She plops down on Clarity's mattress and chatters away while we unpack.

I'm not sure which clothing items are clean and which are dirty, so I shove every single piece into my laundry hamper.

Clarity does the same, dumping everything out of her bag in one fell swoop. Then she sets about caring for her wigs.

In the hallway, the sounds of my other teammates moving around their rooms reaches my ears. There's no chatter or teasing, just dull, heavy movements. We're all so exhausted we're ready to drop.

"Can I get everyone's attention?"

I blink, rubbing my red eyes with one hand, and peer out into the hall.

Royal is standing at its end, his cell phone clutched in his hand.

"What is it?" I ask, stepping out into the long space and leaning an elbow against the wall.

Royal waits until all of us are in the hallway, standing in a clump halfway along the space, before he speaks. "I just had a call from my contact at the CIA. He had some interesting information to give me about The Chin, and Nexus."

Hearing the name makes me intake a sharp breath, and push to stand up straight. "What about him?"

"Apparently, Nexus didn't only hire The Chin to steal XCom's facial recognition software. He was also behind the car thefts in London."

"What?" I ask, my mouth dropping open.

"Somehow, he knew that Charles had those files, so he hired the thieves to steal them."

My thoughts are sluggish in my head, so I reach up and scratch at my scalp with one hand, hoping the stimulation will spur my tired brain to faster computing speeds. It doesn't.

"So this Nexus person has tried to steal both classified MI6 documents, and has software that allows him to hack into the facial recognition software used by governments and financial institutions around the world?" Starling asks.

"Yes."

My forehead scrunches up in confusion. "Okay, I get why he would want the facial recognition software, but why the files on agent and civilian casualties?"

Royal shakes his head. "The CIA doesn't know, but they're going to try to find out."

"What can we do?" Julep asks, arms crossed over her chest.

Lotus shifts beside her, holding his arm away from his injured side.

"For now? Get some rest. My contact will let us know when they need us."

That's good enough for me. I step into my room, climb the ladder to my raised bed, and plop down on the mattress. I should probably shower first, but right now I simply don't care.

So what if Nexus was behind both of the biggest jobs my team has been assigned in the past year? For now, all that matters is that my entire team is safe in the Ivory Tower, where no one can get to us. And with Beppe Arnoni behind bars, there is no outstanding threat to any one of us.

We're well protected... And I intend to keep it that way.

Acknowledgements

I can't believe that I've written three books in my first series. I'm having so much writing about Loveday and the rest of the Ivory Tower Spies crew. But writing a book wouldn't be this fun if I didn't have the support of my husband, Adam, and our two beautiful daughters.

I also have to thank my proofreader extraordinaire, Christina Kobel, who makes my work look spiffy and clean.

And lastly, I'd like to thank my writer friends, whose daily encouragement keeps me going on the days when all I want to do is take a nap.

About the Author

Emily lives in sunny Southern California with her husband and daughters. She started writing in elementary school and continued writing in college, where she earned a degree in creative writing. She often gets ideas for stories from the lives of her friends and family. When she's not writing, she enjoys cuddling with her two dachshunds Nestlé and Kiefer, crocheting, watching television, and enjoying the sunshine with her daughters and their flock of backyard chickens.

To learn more about Emily, visit her website: www.emilykazmierski.com

Keep reading for a sneak peek at book four of the Ivory Tower Spies series, *Spy Got Your Tongue.*

Chapter 1

The dawn sky is streaked with orange over the indigo hills. A hush falls over my team as we skim the clouds, with Lotus at the wheel of our small aircraft. The hum of the engine is the only break in the silence of the early spring morning.

Behind the pilot's seat, Julep sits awkwardly in her gear, talking to Clarity in a low voice.

I can't make out her words. My curiosity is peaked, but I don't have time to investigate. We're almost to the jump site.

A shiny black boot noses against my black tennis shoe, bidding for my attention.

I look up into Starling's eyes and smile.

He gives me a confident, easy smile in return. "You ready for this?"

"I was born ready."

"Except for the part where you're supposed to land without ending up black and blue."

I bite my lip, trying not to laugh.

Starling's been teasing me about my uniformly ungraceful parachute landings since he first saw me jump a month ago. Really, he's not wrong. I've done over a hundred jumps and I still end up flat on my back, or my face, in the dirt.

In contrast, Starling glides smoothly to earth each and every time, a product of his years of military training. It's disgusting. And super hot.

"Remember what we practiced," he continues. "You can do this." Hidden between us, his hand finds mine, and his thumb caresses my skin. My heart speeds up.

It's been six weeks since we got home from Sicily, and his touch still sends a shiver through me. We haven't talked about what we're doing, sneaking kisses in the spare moments we're not with the other members of our team, but I don't care. There's a sense of contentment between us that I never felt with Vale.

"We're here," Lotus calls back. "You guys ready?"

I stand, checking in with each of my teammates. Once I confirm the all clear, I make my way to the front of the plane. "We're ready," I tell Lotus, reaching up to grip a handle on the plane's ceiling. "Open the door, will you?"

"Roger that." With a grin, he reaches up and presses a button on the plane's console.

At my back, the side door of the plane slides open, revealing the shiny green fields below us, illuminated by streaks of golden morning sun.

The hair on the back of my neck whips in the wind, the icy cold of it raising goosebumps along my skin. My pulse quickens with excitement as the time to jump nears.

"You're up," I call, pointing to Starling.

He marches to the plane door and sits, resting his feet on the sill outside the open hatch. "See you on the other side." He gives me a playful salute before flinging himself out of the plane. His body moves into a practiced, perfect formation for the freefall portion of the jump.

"Clarity," I say to my sister, meeting her large, brown eyes under perfectly arched eyebrows. "Are you ready?"

She bites her lip, and nods.

Truthfully, parachuting has never been her favorite part of our job, so she avoids it whenever she can. Still, Royal insists we all brush up from time to time, which is why we're an hour north of the city on this beautiful spring morning, taking turns nosediving out of our airplane.

If Clarity is afraid, she doesn't show it. Her facial expression and movements are sure as she moves to stand beside me in front of the open hatch. "I'll see you on the ground," she says, putting a hand on my shoulder. Then she too sits on the sill before launching herself out of the plane.

Julep comes up beside me. "I'll bring up the rear," she says, patting my bicep with one hand. "You can do this. I know it."

"Thanks." I tip an imaginary hat to her before following in the footsteps of my teammates.

Breathing in the crisp morning air, I count down from five, and shove myself away from the safety of the plane.

The freezing air pummels my face and body, but I'm ready for it. I move into the proper form and begin counting the seconds. We're doing a twenty second freefall this morning, and keeping count is crucial.

The screen on my watch blinks brightly as I descend, keeping track of my altitude and speed.

Bright light fans out around me as the sun rises, blinding me for a second.

But I don't let it distract me from counting down. I've only got seconds to go before I deploy my chute.

Five

Four

Three

Two

I pull the cord and my chute springs out of my pack, billowing above me and jerking me upward by my pelvis. The cords of my harness cut into my skin in a familiar pinch, and my momentum slows. My equipment is functioning just as it should.

Gripping the toggles, I steer toward the designated landing zone.

Below me, I catch a glimpse of Starling landing smoothly on the ground, without even having to run out his remaining momentum.

I shake my head. Sometimes that guy is so good it's maddening. It's obvious why Royal recruited him to join our team of spies, based out of the Ivory Tower in Washington, D.C.

Thankfully, after my quick work in Sicily, I've been reinstated to the team. No more concierge work for me. And Summer has been sworn to secrecy by the higher-ups in the CIA. I'm not sure what exactly they told her, since I'm not allowed to contact her anymore, but it must have been a great story.

Clarity hits the ground running, burning off the last of her speed as her parachute floats to the ground behind her.

Starling is at her side in a moment, helping her unclip her gear and clearing the path for me to land.

I visualize the movements Starling and I talked about, getting ready for my own landing. I'm determined. Today is going to be the day I stick this landing, instead of eating a mouthful of dirt.

My body tenses as I approach the ground, but I will it to relax.

I slow my speed and level out, preparing to run once I hit the dirt.

The slick, grassy plain is hurtling toward me, stretched out all around in an expanse of green.

Ready, steady, run!

I hit the ground running and burst forward, propelled by the wind.

Adrenaline surges through me, and I let out a cheer. "I did it!" Flinging my arms in the air, I turn to my teammates. "Did you see that?" I can't help it; I'm beaming.

Clarity runs over to me and throws her arms around me. "You nailed it!" she says, smiling. "Wait until we tell Dad."

Starling saunters up behind her, smiling at me over her head. "You were brilliant," he says.

The moment is broken by a shout from above. "Incoming!"

We swivel to look upward, and not a second to soon.

We jump out of the way as Julep skims over our heads and lands, skimming along the ground like she was taught. Her body is positioned just like a baseball player sliding into second as she glides through the grass.

Standing up, she brushes herself off. Her eyes are shining as she walks over to us. "What a rush."

"I'm coming in for a landing," Lotus says over our earbuds.

"See you in a few," I respond, turning back to get my chute. "Let's roll and go," I say.

"Yes, ma'am," Starling says with a chuckle. He's teasing me.

I roll my eyes, secretly loving it.

It takes us a couple minutes to roll up our chutes and tuck them under our arms. We'll check them over once we get back to the Tower.

"Let's get home," I say, slinging my arm around my sister's waist and pulling her close.

She grins down at me and puts an arm around my shoulder. "Ready when you are."

And we tromp across the grass, ready to start yet another unpredictable day.

"Think anyone will shoot at us today?" I quip.

At my side, Clarity's body tenses. "I hope not," she says.

Concern needles at me. I open my mouth to respond, but Julep beats me to it.

"Don't worry, we're ready for it," she says, winking at us over her shoulder.

But Clarity doesn't relax as we walk, making me more sure than ever that something is wrong with my sister. I just don't know what.

Printed in Great Britain
by Amazon